A MISSING MADONNA

Cicely van Straten

DISCERN
PRODUCTS

Published by Discern Products
724 Parkdale Ave.
Ottawa, Ontario, Canada K1Y 1J6
info@discernproducts.com
www.discernproducts.com

Illustrations and cover design by Marleen Visser

ISBN 978-1-988422-14-5

Disclaimer:
Kubiri Hill and all characters in this book are fictional, except for
Paulo and Fesito who were our gardeners on a hill overlooking
Lake Victoria Nyanza.

Contents

Prologue

If you follow the little red-earth road up Kubiri Hill, not far from Kampala, where tyre tracks blend with cattle prints, you will hear the bleating of goats, the dull clunk of goat bells and the song of heat in shrilling cicadas. Tall forest trees loom beyond the bush beside the little red road as it climbs steeply, curls into a bend and emerges on the top of the hill. Here it becomes an avenue of nandi flame trees and flamboyants leading through short green grass. The bleating of goats fades and another sound flows on the breeze over the crown of the hill. It is music, strange and yet familiar. At the end of the avenue, beyond the green lace and vermilion of flamboyants, a very large woman beckons you.

She is an African woman, twice life-size, and she stands smiling towards Lake Victoria Nyanza that stretches blue and silver to the horizon. Her long robes flow back in a breeze from the lake, her left arm cradles a child. Her right arm gestures welcome to all who walk up the little red road. They call her The Welcoming Mother, and her face is the face of Grace Makubiye. She has deep, smile-wrinkled eyes, a wide nose and a generous but determined mouth. It is entirely suitable that you meet Grace Makubiye glorified as you enter the precincts of St Mary's School on Kubiri Hill, for it was her passion and tenacity that led to its founding.

The little red road circles The Welcoming Mother. Behind her, steps lead up into a school quadrangle. There is a fountain in the middle of it, surrounded by lawns and trees. Deep verandahs run along the school buildings on all sides of the quad. Pause a moment at the top of the steps and look right to where an L-shaped, double-storied boarders' block rises in cream stucco with red tiles. Beyond it, a low, tin-roofed brick building embraces the far corner of the quad. To the left of that, a wide path descends to distant lawns, blazing purple bougainvilleas and the dark mango trees brought by Arab slavers to Uganda in the nineteenth century. To the left of the path rise the imposing two storeys of the senior school: the domestic science rooms, mathematics, history, geography and language classrooms, the science laboratory and other breeding grounds of academic excellence, not to mention the all-important accounting, typing, sewing and art rooms dear to the heart of Grace Makubiye.

Be patient now, and walk slowly, for we are entering African time. Turn left into a gravel path and skirt the house where the nuns of the senior school live. And now, set a little way ahead to the right, you see a chapel built of chunks of the mottled, ferrous stone that strews the hills of Buganda. The chapel's tin roof is very old, its walls are freckled with moss, but the music that is pouring from its open doors is new. It is a French mass-setting sung in English by pure, shrill voices and accompanied by *amadindas*, the hardwood xylophones of Buganda. This river of sound streams away over lawns and a congregation of every colour sways like water weeds in its current. Women in full-sailed *basutis* – purple, green and orange, young men in suits, older men in white *kanzus* and the children squatting at their feet, all catch the stream of music from the chapel. They claim and amplify it, repeating again and again the phrases they love, and lingering over long-drawn 'Ameeens'.

Follow the gravel path that leads to the western end of the chapel, walk up three steps to the first chapel door and peer inside. Above the heads of girls in blue, choristers in white and the flashing hammers of *amadinda* players, you will see the ebony fingers of a celestial puppeteer, Sister Agnes, who bestrides the worlds of Western and African music, weaving together strands of disparate sound into a flow of rejoicing that enters your feet through the trembling ground, rises through your body and flows into the quivering air.

Beyond Agnes's hands you'll see the bald dome of Père Sulpice, on loan for mass from the Dominicans, as he raises his arms before the altar and looks up at a large wooden crucifix on the wall above. The cross beams droop slightly, like tired wings, but the arms of Christ have broken free from them and are lifted, with his upturned face, to the Father just out of sight in a dazzle of light from the high windows. It is a crucifix that embraces past and future in the seamless present of African time.

In old wooden stalls to the left of the chancel sit the grey-habited sisters of St Mary's, Mother Julienne, their Superior, sits near the altar in the front row, very small, very upright, her dark eyes glinting as she watches Sister Agnes. In the back stall, second furthest from the end, a tall nun is wiping strands of grey hair from her sweating forehead. She is Sister Frances, who fashioned the statue of The Welcoming Mother and supervised the creation of the tall crucifix by her gifted pupil, Benedicta Kivengere. Her mind is straying from the mass and her thoughtful grey eyes have wandered to the back of the chapel. In an arched recess between the two open doors stands a Madonna with her child in African olive wood. The Madonna is looking over her child with an expression of tender heartache, a sad foreknowing. Benedicta had made the Madonna while her own mother was dying of *Slim* and her infant with her. Three years later the Madonna was Benedicta herself as she cradled her dying sister in her arms.

Frances's brow furrows. She still marvels at Benedicta's gift for embodying the suffering of thousands in an object of immutable beauty. She glances at the crucifix. Where had that come from? All the crucifixes she had ever seen were of the nailed and suffering saviour with the drooping head. And then this! She smiles wryly, remembering how her own merciless finger had pointed to imperfections still to be sanded and polished till Benedicta had laid her head on her arms over the wood and wept. Her tears and sweat had seeped into the saviour till at last they had raised him beyond the altar. Will there be another letter from her this week, and will it be happier than her last? She must get down to answering that last letter tonight.

1. Excellence of the Best

Frances started as the congregation suddenly rose. She got to her feet, glanced at the board with the hymn numbers on it and rummaged through her hymnbook for the recessional. Père Sulpice, Frère Joseph-Marie and Mother Julienne were processing down the aisle followed by the choir. Père Sulpice's bald head bobbed shining down the steps and he raised his hands to bless the congregation of valley people from around Kubiri Hill who were devoted in attendance but could not all cram into the chapel. The nuns left their stalls and followed the white-robed choir. Frances's eyes followed the horny yellow heels of Sister Perpetua treading stern, measured steps. At the door Perpetua paused, her glasses flashing in the sunlight. Out over the lake, pearl and purple thunderheads were massing.

'Shouldn't be surprised if we have a storm this afternoon.' She glanced over at the science labs. 'I'd better shut the windows.'

To the north of Kubiri Hill, a rumble of thunder rose from Namirembe Cathedral where enormous drums were summoning the faithful. The school, chirruping starlings released, followed the junior-school sisters to the main dining room to drink orange juice and eat biscuits. The senior-school nuns made their way to the refectory in the nuns' house.

Frances stood alone on the chapel steps. A breeze off the lake licked at the sweat on her forehead and her eyes wandered to the distance. Only Turner could have done justice to the massing of cloud against such light and wind-chased reflections over water. Well, a storm would be welcome, provided Gabriel didn't get stuck on her way back from Acholi, though Mother would suffer, as always. Forerunners of storm, heavy-bellied leviathans, came dragging shadows over roofs and walls, over the trees and lawns. Then they were gone and bougainvillea and yellow coreopsis blazed again. She went to the refectory where there would be coffee and Consolata's lemon cake, on account of Père Sulpice and Frère Joseph-Marie.

They were in the senior nuns' sitting room, drinking coffee after lunch when thunder rumbled beyond tossing trees. Sister Consolata, 'Culinary Science' and the source of the excellent lunch they had just eaten, whose head was slumped over her comfortable bosom, opened her eyes and yawned. Sister Felicitas, 'Typing and Book-Keeping', dropped her knitting and scurried out to the verandah to bring in cushions. Annunciata, Consolata's second in command, plump and benevolent, rolled after her to help. Theodora, 'Mathematics', got up and slammed windows as the first whiplash of lightning sizzled over the lawns, illumining the room with a green glow. As usual the first strike extinguished the electric lights. Sister Mattea, 'English Language and Literature', her sea-grey eyes glowing, stalked out to the verandah, closing the door behind her, to enjoy the storm. Sister Theresa, 'Needlework, Dressmaking and Weaving', folded the embroidery on her lap with trembling hands and hunched over. Mother Julienne patted the chair next to her. 'Come and sit with me.' Theresa stumbled over and collapsed beside her while Mother laid a small, arthritic hand on her arm. She lifted the rosary at Theresa's waist and placed it in her hands. Theresa gripped the wooden beads and the sweat of her fear dripped over them. So it always was with Theresa. A storm cracked open her memories. As a small child, she had been trapped in a hut struck by lightning. By the time her screaming mother had dragged her toddler and infant from under falling, flaming thatch and had gone back for Theresa, she had been severely burned. Her father had run with her through the rain to the mission. She had been wrapped in a wet sheet, bundled into a car and driven in an endless lurching nightmare to Mengo Hospital in Kampala. There she had stayed for months, small and alone. Operations had been performed, skin grafts planted and slowly a left hand was formed out of a burnt claw. It was when she was learning to use her new left hand that Sister Eveline had come to her, three afternoons a week. Slowly she had coaxed fumbling fingers through *makeka* work, many, many squares knitted and sewn into a blanket. And then – oh the wonder! – Sister Eveline created a dazzling flower on a square of cotton. From that moment all joy was centred in the wide, warm lap of Sister Eveline. Here a needle winked in the sun as it pierced white cotton, trailing a brilliant tail then winked again as it emerged, dragging silk to form a glistening petal, the flare of a bird's wing. The day came when her own trembling fingers tugged the shining silk, keeping the edges of the stitches precisely where Sister Eveline had drawn an orange, a flower, a leaf. Sister Eveline never scolded when her left hand dropped the cloth. She only waited and said that if Nagadya kept trying she would get it right. And in the end she did, and Sister Eveline showered praise. When at last it was time to return home, she had wept and clung.

'You're going home, Nagadya, back to your máma. All these things you're taking – she will be so pleased!' Sister Eveline bent and lifted the embroidered cloths in her little brown cardboard suitcase.

But the tears spilled faster, 'You are my máma!'

'Come now, Nagadya. Your máma is waiting at home. She is pleased you are well. Remember the letter, dear.' Sister Eveline extracted from Nagadya's pocket the much-folded paper. But her máma had left her long ago, her face was faded, not close like Sister Eveline's. Sister Eveline closed the cardboard suitcase and tapped it, 'Your máma will be very proud of your sewing.'

Nagadya wiped her cheeks to no avail. 'Sister, you will forget me!' She buried her face in the folds of grey habit.

'No, no, no, I shall not forget you!' Sister Eveline fumbled in a pocket for a handkerchief to wipe Nagadya's nose. Skeins of red and blue embroidery silk fell from the handkerchief. She picked them up and opened the suitcase. 'There. I am giving you these, as extra. Now, give me your máma's letter, Nagadya.' She took it and copied the address of the little school where Nagadya's father was a teacher. 'I will write to you and you will write to me. Always, see? And I shall send you drawings for embroidery. You shall prick out the pictures onto cloth your máma gives you – remember how I showed you? When the silk is finished write and tell me and I shall send more. Understand? Nagadya?'

The waiting taxi hooted and passengers called and thumped the doors. Sister Eveline closed the suitcase and handed her up into the taxi. Nagadya's eyes streamed and her nose streamed but she held the suitcase very tight into her stomach because all her life and Sister Eveline were inside it.

When, hours later, the taxi stopped and hooted at their *shamba* next to Dáda's school, she had felt strange, standing where the path came through the peanut beds from the house. It was a different house; the *mabati* roof made her blink. 'No more thatch,' Dáda had said in the letter. Everything smelt different, sounded different. Then Máma came running out.

'Jesu-Máma Méri, *webali, webali, webali*! My child is home!'

When she had opened the suitcase on the table Máma and *Sengawe* had called everyone to look. They were waving the cloths, patting, smoothing, praising. So, in the end, the ugliness hadn't mattered quite so much – the hair that never grew on the left side of her head, the scars like melted plastic down her arm and leg. As she grew older she had realized slowly, painfully, that she would never be plump and pretty like the other girls. But she had learned to make beauty with her fingers, see it reflected in others' eyes.

She earned money embroidering collars, mats, handkerchiefs and teaching sewing at the school. She sent money to Sister Eveline in Kampala for more silks and fine lawn. She could do something no one else could. Which was why, when she left school, she went back to Kampala with only a slightly bigger brown cardboard suitcase, to St Mary's Convent at Kubiri to ask for Sister Eveline because she wished to become a Sister Eveline. Which was how Nagadya Namusoge became Sister Theresa who taught weaving, sewing and exquisite embroidery, long after Sister Eveline passed away. Mother's hand tightened over her arm, 'Not much longer now, I'm sure.' Theresa emerged from her memories, clutched her beads, pulled her disordered mind into place and said firmly, 'We shall have to make tea with the primus again, Mother.'

Again, lightning blazed into the gloom and Frances saw

Mother Julienne illumined, her beautiful aquiline face smiling. She relished a good storm but it played havoc with her rheumatism. 'Mother, can I get you some aspirin?'

Just then a door slammed beyond the refectory and a swirl of damp air flung the sitting room door against the wall. There was a sound of wet sandals slopping up the passage and a figure in muddy slacks and sodden blouse burst in. The dark brown curls plastered to her head were enlivened by a red hibiscus over her left ear. 'Well, me dears, here I am, and glad to be. Mother of all cloudbursts hit us downhill.'

'My dear child – Dieu merci! I was wondering.' Mother Julienne reached to feel for a plump face she could barely see.

Consolata rose ponderously, 'I put aside lunch for you.'

'Take off those wet clothes first,' said Felicitas.

'Just a minute, I've brought you something.' Gabriel hurried out and came back with a thin puppy in her arms.

'At least it's not three new orphans.'

'Covered in fleas, I'll bet.'

'I've powdered her, but I think I've still got a few meself.'

'The Irish always have fleas.'

'Sure an' that's because the blood's so sweet. There, you have her. Fleas don't suck sour Sassenach blood.' Gabriel deposited the wilted puppy in Perpetua's sparse lap.

'Gabriel, please go and take those clothes off!' Felicitas shook a knitting needle at her.

Gabriel was turning to leave when Consolata entered with a bowl of peanut soup. Gabriel sat and ate it while the puppy raised a quivering nose. She ate half the soup, then blew on it, and placed the bowl on the floor. The pup slithered from Perpetua's lap and ate with trembling intensity, her belly slack between staring ribs.

'That's right, now we'll all get worms.' Perpetua sniffed.

However, her long hand stroked the knobbed spine and a bald tail wagged tentatively. Consolata brought in a plate of stuffed peppers, mashed potato and gravy of which Gabriel wolfed half and deposited the rest in the empty soup bowl.

Consolata clucked, 'you give my food to the dog!'

Gabriel gave her an angelic smile. 'She's starving, Consolata. And I've always had a weight problem.'

'It is not true anymore. You must eat properly. I think they starve you in the camps.'

'How was it this time, ma fille?' Mother's brown eyes held Gabriel's.

'Well … good and bad. But not so good really.' She turned and stroked the puppy, which began to scratch under her left foreleg.

'Now you've eaten, Gabriel, go and change into dry clothes. It is time …' Mother Julienne paused while thunder rolled over them. 'Time for our afternoon rest. Gabriel, come to my sitting room when you are dressed. Felicitas, Theresa, help me, please.' Felicitas rolled up the pink jersey on her knees and bustled over to Mother Julienne's right elbow while Theresa took her left. They raised her to her feet and supported her as she moved with fragile dignity to her private sitting room. Felicitas plumped the cushions in the old armchair and they lowered her into it and covered her legs with a light rug.

She sank back gratefully. 'I wouldn't say no to those aspirin now, Felicitas.' And while Felicitas rummaged in the medicine cupboard in the tiny cell next door, Mother Julienne squeezed Theresa's hand. 'The worst is over, ma brave. I recommend a light novel this afternoon and the sound of rain on the roof is very good for sleep.'

Mother laid her head back and closed her eyes but she knew when Gabriel came in and patted the chair next to her, 'God be thanked you're back,' she murmured. 'Father Andrew had a call from the Jesuits in Masindi two days ago. They said you'd been caught in some firing on a school, but you were not injured. The Lord's Army, I suppose?'

'Who else? It's lucky books survive gunfire. We got nearly five hundred textbooks through. Morale's going up now. I think they feel less forgotten.'

'And?' Mother Julienne's eyes searched her face. 'Is there something else you want to tell me? What about the shooting?' Suddenly Gabriel slumped to her knees and buried her face in Mother Julienne's lap. 'Oh Mother, two fathers and meself. We took some textbooks to a little bush school north of the camp. One of the few still going. It had been half wrecked a couple of weeks back and part of the roof was on the ground. It saved our lives. We were just coming out of a class when shots were fired from some trees beyond the *shambas*. The teacher fair tore my arm off and flung me down under the *mabati* and the fathers too. We heard shots hit the windows, then the *mabati*. And the fathers were praying but all I could say was "Shit, Lord, shit!"'

'I am sure the Lord agreed.'

'Yes Mother,' Gabriel choked and was silent a moment.

'But when it was over and we got out, there were three children lying next to us! Right next to us! We never even knew they were there! Mother, we saved ourselves and they died right there! Oh God! Oh God!' The erstwhile headmistress of a Dublin school wept on Mother Julienne's knees until, at last, peace seeped into her heaving shoulders from the blue-veined hands that rested on them.

Not for the first time, Mother felt a twinge of concern at having allowed the young Irish nun to join them. When the Jesuits had put out a call for teachers for the thousands of people in refugee and internally-displaced people's camps across the globe, many of whom spent almost all their lives in these places, Sister Gabriel had been fired to come to Uganda. In Acholi, north of Buganda, thousands had fled to camps to escape the brutality of Joseph Kony's Lord's Resistance Army. Gabriel had worked in camps north of Gulu for three years before being felled by dysentery and brought to Mengo Hospital in Kampala. Her recovery had taken months and she had grown bored with enforced inactivity. She had offered herself as a temporary junior teacher at St Mary's. Old Sister Claudine was delighted to have a replacement and Gabriel had stayed. But after much pleading, Mother had allowed her to visit 'her' camp children during school holidays and the occasional long weekend when new text books had arrived. She had fallen in love with Africa's children and had no wish to return to Ireland. However, her excursions to Acholi sometimes brought emotional repercussions that Mother had to help her bear. Once, she had forbidden a return, but the face of the young woman, staring disconsolate over the quiet gardens, her uncharacteristic silence, had worn her down and she had let her go again. On the proviso that she kept her experiences private between them and did not allow anger or heartache to infect the children or staff of St Mary's.

She extracted a handkerchief from her pocket as Gabriel rose and sniffed. She took the handkerchief and gave a watery smile.

'Alors, to bed with you and do not rise before supper, or I shall demand of you a thousand Hail Marys on your knees on the gravel path to the chapel. Understood?'

'Understood, Mother.' The penitent, whose contrition was only ever temporary, departed gratefully to her bedroom.

***

By the time afternoon tea was over, the last of the storm had rumbled away northwards and Frances went outside. The world had been rinsed cool under a pale golden sky. The rays of the setting sun were casting long shadows from the mango trees and lighting the school walls. She looked fondly at the old buildings that had survived so many changes and upheavals. The school on Kubiri Hill had been founded by an Anglican mission in the nineteen-twenties to serve the area between Kampala and the lake. A couple of old photographs on the refectory wall showed its staff, faces half-shadowed by Bombay Bowlers standing next to pupils, stiff, straight and solemn in front of simple brick classrooms with tin roofs and deep verandahs. To the left stood a stone chapel of earlier date, the same simple chapel they used today with a tin roof that ticked as the day heated and cooled, where rain spiders sheltered, geckos stalked and swallows nested.

A new era had dawned when, in post-uhuru euphoria, the school had been expanded into a vocational school for senior boys. Under a dynamic headmaster, two-storied buildings rose, equipped with elementary science labs and wood- and metalwork-rooms. A school hall, library and sick bay were added and accommodation for boarders with kitchen and dining room. The school had grown and prospered until the wrath of General Amin fell on it. The headmaster was an Anglican and, when Amin had had Archbishop Janani Luwum murdered, the headmaster, voluble in support of his Archbishop, had disappeared one night for a destination unknown.

The school was ransacked by soldiers and closed. Empty and derelict it stood alone on the hill top, a haunt of bats, snakes, weeds and goats. It was mourned by many but no one dared approach its desolation.

Until Mrs Grace Makubiye rose up. Grace was a proud

product of Loreto and her battle cry was 'education for our women and girls!' Sixty percent of Uganda's Christians, she reminded all who would listen, were Roman Catholic. Dominican St Paul's served only boys. St Paul's was big. Loreto was small. Too, too small for all the girls who needed a good Catholic education! Grace had grown up in a valley below the abandoned school. Although she now lived with her prosperous husband in a large house on Nakasero Hill in Kampala, she regularly visited her mother in her valley homestead. Before driving back to Kampala she always walked up Kubiri Hill to gaze at facilities that cried out to be filled again. With girls. With many, many bright girls like her own daughters. Four of them needing that excellent Catholic Education that had equipped her to assume an eminent position in a Kampala business. Nobody, nobody, nobody could teach like the Sisters. These government teachers! Where was their dedication? They went home after school with a bit of marking. But the Sisters – they were with the children all day, all night. They imprinted, yes, they imprinted dedication.

So Grace Makubiye rose up. She marshalled other capable and determined mothers, grandmothers and aunts. They had gathered, drunk tea together and prayed. They had marched and sung those invigorating hymns that go with marching. They besieged the Archbishop until he telephoned Loreto in Nairobi, the Loreto of all Loretos. The sad reply came that Loreto was over-extended, the number of novices from overseas was declining. African novices were increasing but were not yet fully trained. In troubled silence, the marchers retreated to drink tea and pray.

Then a phone call came from Loreto in Nairobi. Mother Superior had driven out to a small Catholic school near Limuru and conferred with the superior there. The school was run by French nuns who had fled the Congo in nineteen-sixty. When the train had disgorged them, shaken and disorientated, in Nairobi Station, together with hundreds of other refugees clutching bags of hastily-gathered clothes and dazed children, the French sisters had found refuge at a local mission. Here they had recovered their wits and nerves and mourned their little school. Here, on a wide verandah with an African view, they drank tea and prayed. When the mother house in France enquired as to their welfare and expected date of return, they drank more tea and prayed earnestly. Finally Mother Julienne wrote back to France on behalf of all ten sisters. Could they wait in Kenya until the Congo troubles blew over and then return to their school? Mère Bernadine replied that Père Benet SJ, who had stayed on in the Congo, advised against their return. More trouble was expected. The mutinying army was unpredictable. Large areas were fast descending into chaos. They could travel by train to Mombasa and embark for France when they were rested.

The sisters looked at one another in dismay. Leave the wide-eyed, eager children of Africa and return to teach near Paris where education was regarded with cynicism by the rebellious young? France was a foreign country to them now. Fatally, they had fallen in love with their new life. Julienne retired to her room, bowed her head a long while in resignation and obedience and wrote that, if Mother Bernadine decreed their withdrawal, so be it. But, Julienne looked out of a window over hills green with little *shambas* where children herded goats, and added a final sentence: the fathers who ran the guest house they were staying in, had mentioned only yesterday how they wished a school could be established just outside Nairobi for a needy and fast-expanding population beyond easy reach of the Nairobi schools. She sealed the airmail letter, bowed her head again, not in obedient resignation, and prayed.

A correspondence ensued between Mother Bernadine and

her recalcitrant nuns in Africa. Points were argued to and fro and several high-level advisors dragged into the debate. Mother Julienne and her sisters were asked to examine their motives in depth. They examined them, became convinced of their rightness, drank tea together and prayed hard. Six months later, the mother house in France granted permission.

Father Fogarty drove them innocently through the Limuru district and slowed down as they passed a dilapidated school, standing empty, abandoned for a larger and better building five miles away. Mother Julienne ordered him to stop the car and she marched over to peer through a smashed window pane. She called her sisters to her. They stalked the premises and pronounced it perfect. Within four years the little order of St Marie Claire accommodated two hundred girls and was gaining a name for excellence. Over time, Loreto's mother superior pronounced their academic results as being on a par with Loreto's and sent her A-level girls to Mother Julienne 'pour la conversation française'.

When Loreto's mother told Mother Julienne that women in Uganda were crying out for a school near Kampala, Mother Julienne did not reject the idea out of hand. She remembered Uganda with affection, having enjoyed two brief holidays there. She had never forgotten how, when they'd made that desperate drive to Bwera, just over the border, and their petrol had run out, local people had welcomed them kindly, given them bread and tea, and walked several miles to fetch petrol. They were only ten out of thousands streaming over the border, making their way to the railhead at Kasese for trains to Kampala and Nairobi. Yes, she would willingly discuss the matter with the mother house in France.

Grace Makubiye and her women gathered weekly, drank tea and prayed, prompting angelic intervention in distant France.

Three months later permission was granted. Mother Julienne phoned Grace Makubiye to say that at the end of year she would come up to Kampala to investigate the premises on Kubiri hill.

On a sweltering December day, she was driven up to Kubiri, bracing herself to face dereliction. What she found was a hundred women standing on steps lined by beds of blazing orange cannas, mauve salvia and yellow coreopsis. A hundred women swaying, singing in welcome. Grace Makubiye hopped nimbly down the steps and clasped her hands. In her penetrating eyes Mother Julienne saw the will of heaven writ in capitals. As Grace and her women led her through classrooms and passages, she saw that walls and floors had been cleaned. Some windows upstairs still boasted glass. Here and there rows of desks, not yet purloined for firewood, stood dusted and polished. Murmuring women trod behind her. 'We thank God, Mother, we thank God. It is Mother Méri who is looking after.' Grace, staunch beside her as they peered into broken wash basins and lavatory bowls full of green slime, declared, 'We stand firm with you, Mother. We shall stand firm on this!' Frances smiled, remembering Mother's description of her first arrival. When she herself had left Limuru to come to Kubiri she had met Grace Makubiye before she passed away; a force of nature never to be forgotten. It was from a photograph of her face that she had modelled the head of The Welcoming Mother in the school driveway.

Mother Julienne had returned to Limuru to begin calculations. Only two sisters at St Marie Claire could be replaced from France before January. The Limuru convent would thrive under the able guidance of Sister Jacqueline as superior. She, Sister Maria and sister Léonie would start in Uganda alone. They acquired a concentrated course in Luganda and sat up late at night. They visited Kampala again in April to watch Grace

Makubiye harassing workmen at the school. Basins and toilets had been sourced from business connections at knock-down prices and were being installed under her all-seeing eyes and pointing finger. Reassured, they went back to Limuru and returned in June to interview local teachers for their school. Phone calls flew between Kampala and Limuru. Letters fluttered between Limuru and France. Calculations were re- and re-calculated. Mother Julienne laboured, begged, cajoled, wrote, phoned, sweated, drank tea and wondered sometimes whether they had been lured into the undertaking by some source other than divine. However, January found them on the summit of Kubiri Hill. The school opened its newly-painted doors to fifty girls. A hundred women were singing as they opened.

Only one thing grieved them that first year – the silent groups of women and girls who gathered under the mango trees round the lawns to watch the fifty privileged with longing eyes. In the second year, thanks to more funds from France and wealthy co-conspirators of the Makubiyes, they took in a hundred pupils. The next year a hundred and fifty were embraced, and a couple of years later they housed two hundred and twenty girls, a hundred of them boarders.

At the beginning of every year, Grace Makubiye presided over the first school assembly. She gave voluble thanks to the staff and to Mother, encouragement and exhortation to the pupils and every year she raised her forefinger towards the ceiling: 'You must excel, pupils of St Mary's School. This is a place for those who will excel. Excellence of the best is what we expect. Not only in the academic line. Yes, we will bring forward future doctors from this school. We will bring forward social workers and teachers. There will be some who go on to Makerere. But we will bring forward women for business. Yes, it is business that will move us on! The businesses of Kampala are waiting for secretaries, for accountants, for typists. The restaurants and hotels are waiting for skilled caterers! The fashion shops are waiting for young women who can sew and design. Fabric designs of Africa – we need them! It is these things that underpin the economy of Uganda. Without a strong economy, without production we are nothing!'

Then followed a full minute of silence while the finger pointed to the ceiling and Grace's eyes travelled the rows of upturned faces with intent. 'I am pointing to the future here, pupils of St Mary's. It is the future. We shall make it here, a future of excellence!' Slowly the pointing hand fell to the table in front of her. The girls rose, solemn and inspired, a future of excellence gleaming in their eyes, and sang a final hymn.

Six years later St Mary's reputation had spread. Sisters from France and a small sister house in England, together with several who had completed novitiates at Limuru had swelled the ranks of teaching staff. Their O- and A-level results became known. Sleek Mercedes-Benzes began driving up the little red-earth road, disgorging hopeful parents. Their daughters were bright and deserving and their fees (graded by the school according to income) would be welcome? Wouldn't they?

Mother found herself in a quandary. The school could expand no further. She remembered the eager faces of those first stalwart women from the hills and valleys around Kubiri. Their courage and persistence had brought the school into being. Was it right that the élite of Kampala should take places their daughters and granddaughters needed?

Mother and Grace Makubiye summoned a meeting of staff and founders. It was decided, once and for all, that St Mary's, founded by local women, would serve Catholic families within a twenty-mile radius of Kubiri Hill, some of them boarders from far-flung homesteads with poor roads. Yes, pupils of excellence from distant counties such as Toro, Ankole and Bugisu were permitted, if they were the top scholars in Catholic primary schools. But, for the rest, the girls were to be their own girls.

The meeting was all but over when Grace had held up a list of fee-paying parents and suddenly announced, 'Twenty! We have thirty pupils who are subsidised because they deserve. We can manage two hundred and forty pupils – I shall get support. We can get more beds – I have the contacts in business. We can permit twenty girls from wealthy Catholic families. These people can afford. I know them,' she began writing a new list.

'They have requested. We shall allow it. They must give with greater generosity. They must support!' She had handed the list to Mother, 'These are the right ones. It is not just ambition there. The girls are good girls, not like some of these *Wabenzi* children,' she clucked and shook her head.

Mother had put in a plea for several daughters of diplomats from francophone countries and Grace had granted admission, provided – here the forefinger rose – provided they did not subvert the use of English in an English-medium school. Several heads had bowed in shame, remembering francophone lapses under stress. However, a couple of weeks later, Grace had admitted to Mother, over a cup of tea, that, thanks to her unusually fluent French, her daughter Gladys had landed a plum job in imports and exports. Within a month of the meeting the decision had percolated through Kampala's élite and only approved *Wabenzi* approached The Welcoming Mother.

Frances smiled to herself again and walked over the lawns to stare over the lake through the dangling sausage fruits of a kigelia tree. How heavenly, this great stillness after storm when the only sound was the soft drip of water from leaves. Suddenly a robin chat burst into song. A small brave silhouette pulsated against the golden sky, sparkling in spontaneous joy. What more heartfelt vespers than ... The ten-to-six bell for chapel rang out clear over the hill and she hurried back to the school. As she came up the verandah steps Felicitas waved from the door. 'Ah, there you are! Mother wants you.'

Mother was still in her armchair, 'Frances, I am in too much pain to attend chapel tonight. There is nothing I dislike more than to spread pain around. Would you be so kind as to read the service here with me – in French – a concession to malaise?'

'A pleasure.'

'Oh, and would you ask Agnes to end, this evening, with the Cantique de Jean Racine?'

'Certainement.' She ran across into the chapel where Agnes sat, hands poised over the piano. Agnes looked at her over her spectacles, nodded and then brought her hands down into the first evening hymn.

'How many aspirin, Mother?'

'Three please – and a half, but don't tell.'

Frances watched the little lumps go down the thin throat and found the prayer book. She waited till Mother had made herself comfortable and began to read while Mother intoned the responses. At times she caught her breath and grimaced as the fire in her feet spread and echoed in knees, hips and hands. Sometimes she groaned and laid her head back in silence till ready to go on. And Frances, sitting alone with her in the quiet room, with the music from the chapel floating into the gardens, smiled, remembering how she, one of Mother's 'A-level girls', had sat beside her in a Limuru convent long ago, 'pour la conversation française'.

Vespers was an informal affair with guitars and choruses for the homesick but at last, out of a brief silence, rose the first notes of the Cantique. Agnes's deep contralto intoned the men's lines initiating the canon and slowly the high voices of the choir rose pleading into the night. The old woman's face relaxed and her head fell back into the chair. 'Ah, grace à Dieu! La musique c'est la prière. Verbe égal au Tres Haut ...' She quavered the first lines and then lapsed into silence as the melody soared and sank at last into peace.

'Mother, I don't mean to be curious, but it looks as if Gabriel's been crying. Did something happen at the camp? Would it help if I knew?'

Briefly Mother told her. 'Yes, she has wept and that is good. Mais elle se tormente. It is only natural ...' There was a brisk knock on the door. Felicitas, who slept in the next room and watched over Mother, bustled in to help her to bed and Frances leaned to brush a kiss on her forehead. 'Bonne nuit,' she murmured, knowing full well the night would be pain- racked. Why should the pain of the good be so increased in old age? She went upstairs past Agnes who was still humming the Cantique. 'Thank you. It helped. Carry on.' Agnes grinned, pushed her slipping spectacles up her round nose and her rich humming rose like a happy bee in the stairwell.

Frances opened her cupboard and took Benedicta's letter out of a shoebox. She had read it several times and must reply. She sat at her table and unfolded it. 'Here it is wet and very cold. But the darkness is the worst. Everyone is kind. In the coffee room they try to make friends. But, Sister, I am lonely. This is not to complain, but to tell you because you asked me. They ask me about Uganda, what it is like. I tell them, but I know they do not understand. When I talk about the lake, now that I know what a lake is here in England, I see that when I tell them about our lake they see in their minds the small, cold lakes of England, not our big warm, shining lake that stretches away to the sky. When I talk about a storm they don't see the clouds towering up purple and white and gold. They see low, grey clouds and cold rain. Our forest at home is not like the forest here. Here it is bare and cold. Our forest is warm and smells – how can I describe it? It smells of hot life. They ask me these things and then laugh and say yes, they know hot places too. But they mean Italy or Turkey or Greece. Those are the places they know. So in their minds my words have no meaning. Fire! The gas fire in my room smells bitter, but at home our fires smell of sweet wood and grass.

'You ask about the lessons in casting. We have been five times to the foundry and made some small things. They are nice, yes. But I feel this metal is not in me. I will learn how to manage it, but I do not think I will work in bronze. It is cold, like here. It is fired clay and wood I wish to work in. Warm things. You are right when you say the impressionist palette is best for Uganda. I go often to look at that hot, light colour in the gallery. I am making sketches for wood sculptures but the woods here are not the same as at home. Please, Sister, if you can, collect some good pieces of *majarati* and red ivory for me. Perhaps Brother Sebastien will give it? I will be grateful. Please don't forget to write to me this week ...'

Frances sighed and leaned her forehead on her hands. Had she done right to persuade Benedicta to do a postgraduate year in England? Well, it was Sunday evening and she must reply ... and encourage. She yawned and smiled. Sunday evening. The reading and rereading of the precious weekly letter from the distant farm. All the years of boarding school in Nairobi and the homesickness that bit suddenly in the emptiness of Sunday afternoon and evening. All the years and the letters. Her father's accounts of cattle, rain – no rain or too little rain – crops, defaulting tractors, maize-shellers and coffee-mulchers. Her mother's descriptions of flowerbeds and vegetable garden, of sick farm children, of cats, dogs, horses, calves and piglets and, with her artist's eye, a sunset or the blooms of a *kirikiti*. And homesickness surged and was comforted in the same moment. She took her pen and paper and began as she had begun so many letters to her own two boys at boarding school. When she had written her part she would shove the unfinished letter under Doug's nose and he'd put down his glass of whisky and smile as he supplied the scores of cricket and tennis matches, the misdeeds of tractors, maize-shellers and pyrethrum driers and how the Guernsey bull had sent him and the vet flying when they'd applied coal tar to the abscess on his stomach ...

'My dear Benedicta, talking of storms, we had a terrific one this afternoon and guess who arrived in the middle of it – Gabriel with a new puppy, horribly skinny and rather mangy. The puppy has already discovered that Sister Consolata is indeed the mother of all consolation. She knew it from sniffing Sister Consolata's shoes and the hem of her habit, because she followed her straight to the kitchen after lunch and spends her time there, when she's not staggering after Gabriel. Yes, I do think wood is your calling. But I hope the experience of bronze may come in useful, if you ever get a commission. Just as well to know what you can and can't do. However, there's no one in Uganda who can do sophisticated foundry work. Don't worry about it and enjoy the other things. The Madonna presides, as always, at the back of the chapel and every time I look at her, I remember you. As always the offerings lie round her – flowers and sometimes a sacrificed sweet or biscuit. By next day the sweet or biscuit has disappeared. I suspect Fesito takes them as his dues for dusting and polishing her. I watch him sometimes and am glad our old leper has enough of his hands left – and some sensation too, I gather – to feel the exquisite texture you have given that wood.'

'Oh, something that will amuse you. Sister Theodora has been on the rampage again, the old dragon. She spied some O-level girls hiding behind the lantana bushes near the school hall and pounced. Four were boarders and one was a rather naughty day-girl. She'd brought a copy of *Hot Chilli* to school and they were perusing it. She was reading one of those dreadful sex descriptions aloud to the others when Theodora got to them. She hauled them all off to Mother Julienne and made her read the article in question. I wasn't in on the scene, of course, but one of the girls is an art pupil. She was sniffling all through the art lesson and afterwards I got out of her what had happened. She said Sister Theodora had ranted and raved but that Mother was very calm. She had merely torn the paper in half and thrown it in her waste-paper basket and told them not to waste their time on silly filth. But Theodora went on and on about it and when they'd left Mother's sitting room, she threatened them all with writing to their parents about their dirty minds and said she would get them all expelled because they sullied the purity of the school. So they're all pretty scared. We know that Theodora cannot do anything of the sort. But the girls don't. What Theodora forgets is that girls can read *Hot Chilli* any time they wish during school holidays, so what it had to do with the purity of the school I don't know. Of course, if any of our boarders fell pregnant or got infected during term time, there would be hell to pay. But we cannot control their lives outside of school. We all remember poor Sala and I think the grief over her fate was lesson enough to the girls. So, the old dragon who humiliated you by calling you a dirty slut because you came to lunch with clay under your fingernails and sent you out to scrub and then withheld your pudding – not to mention always scolding you for having wood dust in your hair – is still going strong!

'You have survived Sister Theodora and you will surely survive an English winter. Remember you're always welcome with Mrs Soames in Oxford when life gets you down. They expect you for the Christmas holidays. God bless you and keep warm.' She put away her pen, folded and enclosed the letter.

The scent of frangipani was wafting through the window, the scent of memories invading her heart. She got up, opened the door to the upstairs verandah and went out. The tall frangipani tree raised arms mottled by moonlight and exhaled ripe peach and coconut. She laid her hand on the smooth skin of a branch and felt the sudden stickiness of milk from a wound where the storm had snapped off a leaf. Yes, the stickiness of wounds and memories of wounds. Her brave words to Benedicta ... and behind them, misgiving. Benedicta, her daughter, now and for always. The fifteen-year-old clinging to her in tears after her mother's death: 'You are my mother now, Sister. It is only you ...'

She had not wept much when her father had died, for by then they knew what he had done. That handsome, charming man who had taken one lonely trip too many to Toro county as a rep for his firm. And then the secrecy, the denial that had brought death in its wake for his wife and unborn child. And three years later the little sister who was raped by a teenage lout who had *Slim*, again unacknowledged. And Benedicta had blamed herself, though God alone knew what she could have done about it, herself a boarder at school and her sister in the care of an aunt fifteen miles away. 'You are my mother now, Sister. It is only you.' Frances sighed ... the life of so many women here – mothers of the motherless. In spite of proud government announcements and hard-working NGOs in the main towns, the handful of Kampala doctors knew the truth. The greater population was deeply rural and *Slim* was barely acknowledged, shrouded in furtive secrecy. In the rustic communities, far from hospitals, it was women who were banding together to deal with the dying and who looked after those that were left.

The great silence shrouded them still. Yes, Theodora's fears were understandable. Her campaign for 'purity', her watchdog harassment of the slightest evidence of teenage prurience. The tragedy of Sala was not forgotten, a scandal that had rocked the school to its foundations. Sala who soon after term began, had rushed from the breakfast table every morning to vomit and had passed under the knowledgeable eye of Sister Monique in the san. When her pregnancy was disclosed, her parents had been told. When Sala refused to reveal the father of her child, her parents had accused the school of negligence in the care of their daughter and threatened a court case. Mother had had to call in Dr Keribye to testify that Sala had fallen pregnant during the school holidays. Whereupon her parents had turned on her in rage until she had named her father's younger brother, residing in their home and contributing generously to the family income, as the child's father. He denied paternity, claimed to have seen Sala sneaking away into the bush with a male acquaintance and incriminated her as a liar. She had been found a few days later, hidden deep under a bush near the homestead, her dead body in a welter of blood with a foetus beside it and a long thin stick. Mother gathered a shocked and silent school in a memorial service in the chapel, a service that was not attended by Sala's parents. And Mother commemorated an exemplary pupil, always willing to help others, gentle, kind, a loving and loyal friend. Mrs Busia, the social worker from Rubaga Cathedral, who had counselled Sala, sat at the back of the chapel shaking her head and blowing her nose, overwhelmed by a sense of failure.

Oh, dear child, poor, poor child ... Frances ran her hand up and down the frangipani branch. Only a few generations back her seducer would have paid a heavy fine to her parents and clan and taken her to give birth among his own people who would have raised the child as their own. Adultery would have been another matter, of course. An adulterer was killed or had an eye gouged out. He had offended the woman's husband's ancestral spirits and exposed him to risk in travel or war.

And Sala. Could they ever know how much her despair had been caused by shame inculcated by the Christian religion with its heavy emphasis on sexual guilt? Had she despaired of her future: a school career ended too soon, a future as a shamed drudge her only hope, though Mother Julienne had made it quite clear that, once delivered of her baby, she was welcome to resume her schooling? Even a trembling and agitated Mrs Busia could not tell them, for the child had become silent, enclosed in a chill hopelessness. How had she felt, branded as a liar by her seducer? By parents who valued money and saving face above their daughter's well-being? Perhaps all these things ... perhaps, most of all, distrust and vituperation in her time of need. Sweet and submissive she had always been, too sweet, too submissive for her own good.

Since then, Theodora's reign of fear had intensified. Fear was a deterrent, certainly. But it also prevented any confiding of troubles. To any girl with a grudge against another, it could provoke tale-bearing or insinuation. To the rebellious teenager, who angled for peer admiration through daring and defiance, the day-girl who escaped the constant supervision of boarders, it led to showing off by importing the illicit *Hot Chilli*. The rag advertised sexual prowess in highly lubricious articles. Had nothing of *Slim* penetrated the minds of certain sex-obsessed journalists of Kampala, apart from the rampant and exotic condom ads that made anything and everything 'safe'?

And the child caught between two worlds ... a world of Christian beliefs that shamed an older world of pride in the gift of sex, within strict parameters, of course. She died by her own hand, a terrible sin in the eyes of the Catholic. Yet she had died by the hands of many, suffered the death of the scapegoat. Frances gripped the balcony wall, took a deep breath and looked for a long time over the moonlit gardens. Then she shook herself, raised her left hand to her lips and sent a kiss into the night, to Ted at Naivasha, another to Jim in western Uganda and a third towards a grave under a thorn tree on a very distant hillside, and went in to bed.

2. Who Has Taken Our Mother?

Early on Monday morning Frances stepped out into the gardens with secateurs and a basket to glean fruit and flowers for the first art lesson. She was sniffing cream-and-egg-yolk frangipani when an aged ford rumbled under the flamboyants, swerved round The Welcoming Mother and shuddered to a halt. She waved and Mark Trevors hooted. He opened the car door, unbent his lanky height, fished a pile of weekend marking from the back seat, waved to her, slammed the car door and tramped up the steps to the quadrangle. How like her younger son he was! Perpetua had been lucky in her request for an expat volunteer to help with science tuition. Mark had taken the school to his heart, and they him. In the quad, girlish titters greeted the appearance of the only male member of staff. She glanced at her watch. Only five minutes till chapel!

Quickly she rummaged fallen pomegranates and hurried over to hibiscus bushes. She paused before the scintillation of vermilion, scarlet and cherry in the early sunshine and reached for a flower. A small chameleon lurched indignantly from behind it. She lifted it gently onto her finger and the prickle of its claws sent a shiver of pleasure down her spine. The tail coiled tight at her fingertip and a crinkled eyelid swivelled to her face, its centre a drop of liquid misgiving. 'I wish we could draw you. But if I took you into class at least three girls would shriek and rush out, poor little scapegoat.' She lifted him to a branch concealed deep in the foliage, lest he be seen and have his head bashed in with stick or stone. With slow lurching steps he swung from her finger, grasped a twig and disappeared into green gloom. 'Oh heavens, the bell!' She snipped three blooms, picked up her basket and ran through the quad to the art room.

The sisters were already following the school into the chapel. She was last again and there was pollen down her front. She flapped at it but the pollen stuck and smudged. Calming her breath, she stood up straight, walked into the chapel and down to the nuns' stalls opposite the choir. Mattea, Theresa and Theodora swung their legs aside to let her pass to her seat. She fumbled for her hymnbook and looked expectantly at Agnes and the choir. Agnes's hands were raised but the choir was staring at her, Frances. Guiltily she glanced at the school. Every eye in the chapel held her in a puzzled stare. Yes, she was late again and yellow with pollen. Agnes sent her a grieved glance, tapped the music stand and launched into the morning hymn. Perpetua beside her was hardly bothering to sing. She was staring at the back of the chapel. Frances followed her eyes to the recess in the wall between the doors and a cricket ball hit her in the solar plexus. The recess was empty. Benedicta's Madonna and Child

32

were gone. Only flowers, notes and sweets lay there, an offering to emptiness.

What had happened? She'd given no orders to have her removed. Who had taken her away? Why? The singing faded and the school sat for the lesson. Was it some sort of joke?

She ran her eyes over the middle school. Too old to be in awe and too young to be responsible, they were pranksters. Could they have removed her? But why would they? They laid their prayers and offerings at her feet as everyone else did. Besides, six large girls together could hardly carry her. No one had ever touched her without permission. The Madonna and her Child were the centre of rituals throughout the year. She was carried by Daudi, Paulo, Fesito and Wiriamu round the school grounds at Easter, on St Mary's Day and St Cecilia's Day when the whole valley congregation gathered to celebrate with them. She was the focal point of the Christmas pageant in the chapel, she was placed before the altar and presided over the Holy Family at Christmas Mass. Girls and staff, mothers and grandmothers from the valleys came to pray beside her for sick and dying children, which was why Mother never allowed the chapel doors to be locked. When Benedicta had finally completed her, after two years of labour, Mother had found her the perfect embodiment of suffering love, entirely appropriate for the mothers of a country invaded by *Slim*. 'And,' she had murmured, sliding her hand over the shining wood, 'she will be a reminder that we are mothers to all. My girls must know that motherhood is not limited to blood family, but to every living thing, especially those who suffer, who are lost. Julian said: Christ is our mother. The Mother will not be locked away. I know Daudi suspects thieves everywhere. Well,' she had given her French shrug, 'maybe that is true in Buganda. Mais çela, je le refuse. The chapel remains open.'

At last the blue-clad girls were filing down the chapel steps into the quad, all attempts at clotting round the chapel to discuss the disappearance of Our Lady being foiled by Perpetua and Theodora.

Mattea's brows arched up her forehead, 'Frances, what's happened to the Madonna?'

'I haven't a clue!'

'I thought perhaps you'd removed her for a clean-up – or something.'

'I haven't touched her. Nothing needs doing.'

'She was with us last night.' Agnes stood swinging her rosary.

'The door's never locked, of course ...'

'Naturally.'

'But who, then? And why?'

'She weighs a ton, sure.' Gabriel was also lingering, keeping a sharp eye on her class across the quad. 'Why would anyone steal her? None of the congregation knows how valuable she is – do they?'

Perpetua glanced at her watch. 'We can't keep classes waiting. I'll send Mark to ask Daudi if he knows anything. Has anyone a free period now?'

No one had a free period. Perpetua turned on her heels.

'I'll spare Mark for half an hour later to help search.'

Darting glances of commiseration at Frances, the sisters walked in silence to their classrooms. Frances went down to the art room and as she climbed the steps, Namkya, the class prefect, rose and came forward, straight-backed and dignified.

'Sister Frances.' She gave the little African bob that always moved her. 'I wish to tell you, on behalf of the class, that we are worried about Our Lady. It is thieves. We are too sorry, Sister.'

'Thank you, Namkya. Thank you, girls. I don't know what to

think. Have you seen … anyone who doesn't belong here? Did you hear anything in the night?'

Rows of heads shook in solemn denial.

'Well then, let's get on.'

Numbly she arranged blooms in sunlight. 'Now, I want good, clear drawing first, girls. No colour until that is done. Has everyone got a 4B and a rubber?'

'Yes, Sister.' It was a mere whisper.

Dark eyes gazed, heads rose and dipped as she passed between the rows of tables to the soft swish of pencil on paper.

'Letitia, remember what I said about placing. Not in the middle – one third and two thirds.' Letitia applied a rubber with vigour and creased her sheet of paper, which Frances replaced.

When composition and drawing were complete, Frances and Namkya gave out paints, water and brushes. As luxurious absorption settled on the class, she went over to a table under a window to put the finishing touches to diagrams and posters she was making for the science exhibition. Perpetua, aided and abetted by Mark, had hit on the idea of holding a science exhibition in the convent grounds for local primary schools, to awaken interest in science as a worthy subject at high school. They had painstakingly concocted what looked like a living Heath Robinson museum but was, she was told, a series of demonstrations of physical forces harnessed for the benefit of humankind in the forms of pulleys, cogs, water-lifting devices, pumps and other precarious mechanisms. Under Mark's guidance she had been detailed to execute eye-catching posters. Perpetua had written above each poster 'Science helps us' in bold letters. Once more she patrolled the class to survey expanding masses of colour. She nodded, pointed here and there, praised or exhorted, all the time feeling strangely removed, as if hovering several feet above the floor. A bell rang. 'Name your paintings, girls, and leave them to dry on the back table.'

She was bent over the posters again, waiting for the next class to arrive, when knuckles pounded the door. 'Sister Frances!' Daudi, the school janitor, indispensable handyman and manager of all things mechanical, tall, broad and formidable, loomed in the doorway with Mark behind him.

'Sister, we have searched down the road, very far. There is nothing – no tyre marks.'

'Only mine from this morning,' Mark interposed.

'It's strange. The Madonna's heavy. It would take a couple of men to get her far. I assume the chapel was unlocked?' Mark lifted an eyebrow.

'It is never locked,' Daudi growled resentfully. 'Mother Superior does not wish it.'

'What time do the lights go out in the quad?'

'Eleven o'clock but Moses and Samuel have torches. I asked them, did they see anybody last night. They heard sounds in the bush, garage side and went there. They went far, after that noise but they found nobody,' Daudi added.

Frances shook her head. 'Probably a decoy. Meanwhile, the chapel was unwatched and the Madonna stolen. It's an old, old trick.'

'So sometime between eleven and about four or five this morning, I guess … someone lifted her. Someone who knows how things are, here. Someone local?' A dam of girls was forming behind them and the men retreated. 'We'll go on searching, Sister,' Mark called as the dam broke and streamed past them.

Frances arranged flowers and pomegranates as the girls took their places. In a daze she supervised composition and careful drawing and the application of colour until a bell rang for morning break. She sat down limply. Somehow running the gamut of concern and conjecture in the staffroom was too much. She wanted to be alone, to try and think. She stared stupidly at the wilting flowers till a soft knock startled her. Ignatia entered with a cup of tea. 'Sister Perpetua said I should bring it.'

'Oh, how kind. Thank you.' She smiled weakly up at the tall A-level pupil, Perpetua's shining star. She'd modelled a head of her last year, a heart-shaped face on a long neck, an elegant carving of some long-ago queen in Toro, where she came from. Ignatia put the teacup on the table and stood wringing her hands at her waist. 'Sister Frances, Our Lady, that way she looks – it is that way we feel, it's that feeling … to be a doctor, you see, Sister? She will come back to us?'

Frances felt a sudden lump in her throat. Her hand was hovering over the longed-for tea but she rose and grasped Ignatia's hands. 'Bless you, girl. Of course, we'll do our best to find her.'

'Thank you, Sister.' Ignatia slipped out and Frances drank her tea. Then she went up to the chapel and sat down in a choir stall. She had wondered sometimes, looking at the sorrowing Mater Dei, why they loved her so, these children and the valley congregation. She herself, in her younger days, had gladly toppled the red, white, blue and gold Madonnas that adorned Catholic Convents and instead had moulded cheerful terracotta mothers, red as African soil, with wide laps, generous lips and arms spread to balance a laughing child. But that had been long ago. It was Benedicta's Madonna that spoke to her people now.

Suddenly Daudi appeared at the door. He did not seem surprised to see her and he stood and glared at the blank recess, as if by being angry enough he could force Our Lady to reappear. 'This is a bad thing, Sister Frances, a very bad thing. I am afraid.'

'What of, Daudi?'

'It could be that kind of thief that means bad things.'

'What bad things?'

'Sister, you remember they stole St Paul from the Brothers. It was two years ago, you remember?'

'Yes, of course. But Brother Sebastien recovered St Paul.' Daudi cleared his throat, 'It was a shameful thing, Sister. It was defilement.'

Frances felt a prickle in the back of her neck, 'How do you mean, defilement, Daudi?'

'It was a bad man, in the valley that way.' Daudi pointed, African style, with his chin towards Masenge. 'He stole to make magic. He said he had captured the power of Saint Paul. Now he could do things with it to get rich. He told people he could give them Saint Paul's power for love charms, to cause their enemies disease, to cure *Slim*. He made much money, but he died very badly.'

'How?'

'Sores on his body, coughing blood, shitting blood.'

'That sounds like *Slim* with tubercular complications and enteric, poor wretch.'

'People said the saint killed him for stealing his power.'

'Daudi! You don't believe that, do you?'

A white smile broke his scowl, 'No. I do not believe it because I have had good teaching. But there are people over there who will say, "Mary, Mother of Jesus is very big in Heaven. Surely she has power. If we pay to come and touch, we will get better." They will do anything, Sister.'

'I know. *Slim* does that to people. It's not only people here, Daudi, not so very long ago, we Europeans used the bones of saints as fetishes, believing that to touch, to pray beside the bones brought the saint's power to heal, to grant their wishes. People paid a lot of money for bones and bits of cloth or wood. But the wood is only wood. It's just a picture to help us to remember, by looking.'

'You say it nicely, Sister, you say it nicely. You know it, I know it. But there are people down there … they do not know it. If one of them has stolen Our Lady … maybe I must start a story to remind them what happened to that thief?'

'Daudi, no! But have you any idea who could have done it?'

He shook his head, 'It is time to ask in the *shambas*.'

A bell rang. Daudi departed to his workshop and Frances to her classroom. When the last art class was over, she hurried out to put up the posters for the science exhibition. Perpetua and her helpers had ranged the exhibits on the wide lawns to the left of the little red road that led to The Welcoming Mother. Frances was fixing the posters to easel-blackboards when two buses arrived and disgorged long crocodiles of children who were herded first to the posters to spell out their message and were then seated on the grass before the array of mechanical devices where Mark, Perpetua, Ignatia, Nambi and Kamya stood ready to demonstrate. Very soon, at Mark's prompting, the buzz of demure conversation became clamorous with offers to help operate the contraptions. Small groups were allowed to approach, to touch and manipulate.

Later, when Frances returned after tea, a reverent crowd seated in the last rays of afternoon sunshine was watching Ignatia light one end of a fuse. A flame crept along a string to a tiny box which exploded with thrilling éclat. Teachers clapped and awed children broke into requests for more. Perpetua delivered a pep talk on the wonders that would open to them at secondary school if they studied science. As they were shepherded back into their buses a chant was rising of 'Si-yence! Si-yence! Si-yence helps us! Si-yence … Si-yence!' that merged into the roar of revving engines. Mark, Perpetua and their helpers began the arduous task of removing the exhibition to the laboratory. Otherwise not one cog or pulley would be left by morning. Frances retrieved the posters and took them to the safety of the art room.

News of the exhibition had got around. On the third and final day, a large contingent of uninvited guests emerged from the bush at the edges of the school grounds to watch and wonder. Again the exhibition soared to its climax as the chemical display was inducted with Perpetua's solemn words:

'You have all heard the explosions at the quarry when they blast the rock apart so they can crush it and make cement for big buildings, haven't you?' Nods and murmurs of apprehension.

'Well, explosions are made with chemicals. Explosions are dangerous and people must be far when the explosives ignite. So the men who make the explosions use a fuse. Ignatia and Mark are going to show you how a fuse works. Ignatia lights one end of a long string and then she runs away.'

Ignatia lit the fuse with a flourish and removed herself at a dignified walk. Mark put down the small box with a little explosive in it and stepped back. In wide-eyed silence the crowd watched the flame creep along the string until it reached the box which blew apart with a crackling bang. 'So! You see what can be done with simple chemicals! Today we made a small explosion using only ammonium nitrate and zinc. Two chemicals found in every school laboratory!' Open-mouthed onlookers pressed forward from under the mango trees.

'Hooray for zinc and ammonium nitrate!' cried an irrepressible teacher.

'Hooray for zinc and ammonium nitrate!' chorused the masses.

One last time, children went singing homeward, all bound in

common dedication to a future in science.

Perpetua sank onto a chair and accepted a glass of orangeade from Frances. 'Whew! Well, that's that. I think it worked. What do you think, Frances?'

'It was splendid. If that doesn't boost the scientific population of Buganda nothing will.'

'Couldn't have done it without Mark.' Perpetua thankfully gulped her juice and then rose. 'Girls, Ignatia, well done all of you. Now before it gets dark, let's get all this inside.'

Frances, taking down posters, found herself surrounded by a group of youths offering help. When they had helped her remove posters they converged on Ignatia whom they had been following with covetous eyes. She condescended to let them carry equipment back to the laboratory. When Frances joined them a little later, the youths were still clustering round Ignatia asking questions and peering into the storeroom. Something in their faces made her suddenly uneasy. The eldest, a tall boy of about seventeen, had a queer glitter in his eyes. There was no overt attempt to flirt but there was concupiscence ... 'You don't stand a chance with our Ignatia, young man,' she murmured. 'Don't even think of it.'

'Thank you, friends!' she bore down on them and ushered them firmly from the storeroom where they had been peering at shelves and mouthing the names on boxes. 'Thank you for your help. We're closing now. It's time to go home.' She gripped the tall youth by the arm, steered him outside and watched him and his four followers walk reluctantly, with sly backward glances, past the mango trees and downhill. 'Well,' she muttered, 'the lure of science is powerful .... science or Ignatia?'

As she walked back to the refectory with Mark and Perpetua she found herself wondering for the hundredth time where the Mater Dei reposed that night.

41

'Thanks for the help, Frances. The posters were a definite hit.' Perpetua smiled.

'A pleasure. It was nice to have something positive to do, instead of racking my brains over the Madonna.'

'Yes, yes, of course. Oh dear,' Perpetua said softly, 'I wonder where on earth she is.'

3. The Real Things

Frances, presiding at the head of a lunch table in the main dining room, doled bread-and-butter pudding into the last pudding bowl and sat back to eat. There was silence as spoons clinked on china. Then Kika, on her left, paused with her spoon above her bowl, straightened up and cleared her throat. The pupil seated next to a sister had to cultivate the art of conversation.

'Sister Frances ...'

'Yes, Kika?'

'Sister Frances.' Kika glanced round for help but none was forthcoming; the pudding was all-absorbing. She caught sight of a face at Felicitas's table and took courage. 'Did you know that Dolosi's father has received gifts?'

'So she's to be married soon?'

'Yes, Sister Frances. At the end of the year, if she passes.'

'Of course she'll pass. Sister Consolata and Sister Theresa have never had a failure. She sews very well, I hear.' Frances glanced over to where Dolosi sat, plump and smugly pretty. She was a popular daygirl, living in a *shamba* across the valley from the school and was known for her gifts of lady's-finger bananas to the nuns and sweets for friends. She herself had received gifts when art marks had fallen. She was never quite sure whether they were gifts of propitiation or bribes.

'She told me,' Kika half whispered, 'that Sister Felicitas has spoken about the sewing machine.'

'That's a good sign.' Thanks to Consolata's culinary discipline and Theresa's ability to adapt any pattern to fit any shape or size known to the human family, their pupils usually passed with distinction and assumed profitable positions in their community. And Felicitas, with her book-keeping and accounting contacts in town, made sure that each school-leaver was equipped to set up in business. A second-hand sewing machine in good order, an array of cooking pots and a guide to nutrition in Luganda accompanied them into the world. A little burst of laughter came from Felicitas's table. Frances turned and caught her eye. Felicitas winked at her, her round, wrinkled face split in some wry crack. Frances always thought of her as a small cockney sun. She exuded a sort of efficient joy. Thoroughly efficient considering the pass rate of the typing and book-keeping girls. She was also the favoured protégée of St Anthony. When things got lost one found Felicitas and all else was found.

'They say,' said Nalubale on her right, after a prod with a foot under the table from Kika, 'they say that Dolosi's er … what do you call it, Sister?'

'Boyfriend,' supplied Kika.

'No, it's another word, Sister — the man you're going to marry.'

'Fiancé?'

'Yes, that's the word. Fiancé. They say Dolosi's fiancé has a car!'

'Goodness!'

'She's going to be a rich wife,' Kika stirred enviously.

Just then Consolata at the head table rose to her majestic height and the school rose with her, said grace and filed out to the rest hour. The boarders went to the dormitories and day scholars reposed on cushions along the verandahs and under the trees in the quad. Drowsy heat spread a blanket of somnolence over the school. Frances had glimpsed Gabriel's darkened eyes over lunch and went in search of her.

She found her in Mother Julienne's garden with the puppy on her lap and an empty tin plate at her feet. The puppy, stomach distended, was asleep. Gabriel was bent over her, gently stroking her from nose to tail. She looked up as Frances came through the arch in the wall and closed the door behind her. 'Hi there, Frances. Any news of the Madonna yet?'

Frances sat down beside her. 'Not a cheep. Not for lack of trying. Daudi's made enquiries in the valley and sent Paulo down too. Nobody seems to have a clue.'

'Sure, I've always thought she was too good for this earth. No tyre tracks, no footprints – she's taken off, ascended.'

'Ridiculous girl.'

'Maybe over the weekend we could look a bit further. I'd happily drive you.'

'The thing is, I don't know where to start. Anyway, you need a weekend doing nothing. You look whacked ever since you got back. Has the gut trouble dried up? I couldn't help noticing.' She smiled wryly. She and Gabriel shared a toilet.

'Yes, pretty well. Dr Pilkington gave me something for it. I always seem to get it in the camps. Not serious this time.'

'Who's Dr Pilkington?'

'He's just joined the Mengo team. They send him up to Acholi to supervise vaccinations in the camps. Médicins sans Frontières can't cope with all of that.'

'Ah. I still think you should rest up this weekend. What does Mother say?'

'The same. But I'd rather be doing something.'

'So as not to remember? Mother told me because I asked. It's obvious you're grieving. I'm sorry.' She laid her hand on Gabriel's shoulder.

Gabriel stroked the puppy with meticulous care, 'I wonder how long it will take for the bald patches on her tail to grow over.'

'What are you going to call her?'

'Salva. I saved her near Gulu.'

'Salva yeGulu. Salva's a nice name. I think she'll turn out well. There's a white star on her chest and when the hair grows on her tail and it springs up again she'll look a proper cheeky *mushenzi*.'

Gabriel nodded and continued stroking, 'They were younger than my grade twos. Two little boys and a girl. We'd gone out to one of the little bush schools in a village about five kilometres from the camp, to take them some books and Dr Pilkington went to vaccinate. They'd been under fire before and when shots came from trees about fifty metres away the teacher shouted to them to stay in the schoolroom and lie flat. But somehow they didn't understand, or they panicked. If only, if only we'd known. If only we'd looked or heard them …'

'Was death immediate?'

'Doctor Pilkington said so. He came straight to them. But they were gone.'

'A mercy, Gabriel.'

'He helped with the burial. The people are very fond of him, and the fathers. They asked him to take part of the service.'

'And the parents?'

'They took it very hard.' At last a tear slid down Gabriel's cheek. 'After this they'll have to leave and go into the camp. They hate the camps. They're so crowded, everyone crammed together. And all the *shambas* for miles neglected and going to weeds and the huts and schools shattered and crumbling. Children killing children. Oh God, if we're still doing that in Ireland, what hope is there for here?'

Frances held Gabriel's head against her neck while she wept until the bell for afternoon classes sounded beyond the garden wall. 'Well, girl, it's O-level paint for me and I'm not in the mood.'

She took the tin plate and opened the door for Gabriel with the puppy in her arms. The pup opened sleepy eyes, looked into Gabriel's face with infinite trust, licked her hands and was not deposited at the kitchen door as usual but hugged all the way to the junior classroom.

In class, Frances's mood did not improve. 'Nantega, you've made a good strong statement there, don't mess it up now. Leave it alone. Kaminda, you've lost your sense of depth here. Remember the use of complementaries and use deep blue there to bring forward the yellow.' 'Ntongo that won't do. You'd never be seen in a *gomezi* that dull. Start again. You can't go into textile design if you mess up good drawing with wishy-washy painting.' Lord, help me, she thought, I'm taking out my fury at those deaths on these innocent girls. No wonder Mother asks Gabriel to keep her experiences to herself.

Head-scratching and puzzled glances followed her ruthless

course through the classroom. 'Remember, this is your last practice, girls. From next week, all work goes into exam portfolios. It's got to be your best from now on. Today's words are my last. Don't make me ashamed.'

It was over at last. She hovered a while over the work drying on the back table. Then she washed brushes, stowed paints in the cupboard and slammed the door.

Over tea in the sitting room Mother Julienne raised her eyebrows at her, 'Any word of Our Lady yet, Frances?'

'Nothing. Daudi and Paulo have asked all round the valleys. It seems no one has heard or seen anything.'

'I'm sorry. Come with me now.' She rose stiffly. 'I want the latest news of Benedicta. Let's go into the garden.'

They all called it Mother's Garden but Mother Julienne had had it made 'pour mes filles'. The walls were of red murram stone grown over with a mass of daisy ivy, golden shower and white, perfumed night convolvulus. Mother had spent many hours designing a refuge where no one but the sisters might come, where there was mystery and privacy, where one could sit in a hidden corner whilst another could say her rosary in a patch of sunlight and someone else could sniff flowers or lure confiding wagtails with crumbs. As they entered, Mother gained a new lease of life. She let go of Frances's elbow and made her way with shuffling determination under the albizias, paused to sniff a velvet gardenia and then sidled to one of the seats beside Teresa's Well. She settled herself with creaking care and smiled at the water. 'I see Gabriel has been clearing the weeds again.' She chuckled. They shared a picture of Gabriel, her habit hitched into her belt, straddling the pond with sturdy legs and fishing out handfuls of weed, tadpoles and a percentage of the frog population which, though rendering nightly praise to the Creator, tended to clog the fountain pump with glutinous masses of eggs. Mother had named the garden pond for Teresa of Ávila. She sighed with satisfaction at the clear depths and the restful voice of water falling from the bowl in the saint's hands.

'So – Our Lady's whereabouts is still a mystery. Well, so be it. Tell me about Benedicta. Is she happy?'

'No. She's cold and lonely and strange. And working in bronze doesn't appeal to her. Mother, I can't help wondering – was I wrong to persuade her to go?'

Julienne turned, picked a leaf off a gardenia bush and placed it on her knee. Then she put her head on one side. 'I think not. So often, I have found that our children, African born but educated 'à l'Europe', they imagine that overseas everything is wonderful. So, they must go and see for themselves. Otherwise they spend their lives yearning for something that exists only in their imagination.'

'I remember how my first English winter shocked me. For those of us who grow up in this continent of light and space, it's the darkness that gets to us. I've arranged for her to go to France and Italy in the summer.'

'C'est bien fait.'

'I gather the offer of a junior lectureship at Makerere still stands.'

'When she returns she will know where she belongs and why. Her talent is very rare. Bon Dieu, we need them – our artists. Everyone extols the sciences these days. They are taking us forward, but I'm not sure what they are taking us forward to. We of the belles lettres, we are superfluous, they say. Is it not ironic, ma fille, it was Einstein who said it: if you wish to have clever children tell them fairytales – lots of fairytales! Him they believe, I hope. Well, le Bon Dieu is nothing if not ironic. Look at me! I took the name of Julienne, hein? It was not until I took the third-year vacances from the Sorbonne to improve my English conversation that I met my Mother Julian of Norwich. Voilà! But here, now, we need our artists. Medicine cannot keep up with our catastrophes, our *Slim*, our guns in the hands of children.'

'Gabriel told me about it.'

'Yes. It is very painful. And so the more we need those who express the soul, its pain, its need of love. How else but through words, art, music? Music most of all when words fail, and so often they do. Worse than the child killed is the child who kills, hein? '

Frances nodded dumbly. Then, at a pricking of guilt she added, 'Mother, please pray for Benedicta.'

'But of course. And for our missing Lady of Sighs. Are you worried?'

Frances pondered. 'I'm … puzzled. I keep trying to think who could possibly … and why?'

Mother held out the gardenia leaf, 'Take it, Frances. If, as Julian tells us, he holds all created things in his hands, small as a hazel nut, only existing because they are loved into existence, then the problem of our Madonna is as light as this. Throw it on the water – there!'

Frances took the leaf and tossed it into Teresa's bowl. It slid over the rim and swooped to the pool where it circled and drifted, feather-light on the shining surface.

'Don't think and don't worry. I shall pray.'

'Thank you, Mother.'

They sat in silence watching the play of light and shadow on water. Clouds floated there, rippling gently pink and golden over blue that was deep and clear as crystal. At last a bell called them back to the world. Frances helped Mother to her feet and they walked through the evening-scented garden, out of the door into a quiet dusk.

It was after ten that night when Felicitas knocked on Frances's door. 'Mother says to come down.'

Frances wrapped her dressing gown round her and went to Mother's bedroom. She was lying propped up on her pillows, one hand still on her prayer book. 'Frances.' She fixed her with a bird-bright eye. 'I asked for a hint, just a little hint, not a big miracle, you understand. But nothing came except – now you must keep a straight face, ma fille. Only a car, d'un jaune affreux et – le bruit abominable! Vraiment abominable. There you have it. I do not know in the least what it means.'

'Mother, really?'

'Just that.'

'But ...'

Mother laid her head back and closed her eyes. Then she peeped wickedly at her. 'Secret, understand? Entre nous deux. Think about it. It is intriguing, non?'

Frances frowned, searching her memory. An appalling yellow car and a lamentable noise. It didn't make sense at all. 'Very well, Mother. Bonne nuit.' She traipsed slowly up to bed.

***

There was an air of Friday afternoon in the quad and Frances suddenly felt as lightheaded as her pupils, looking forward to Saturday with its open tuck shop and a film in the evening. Turning from the fountain, she bumped into Felicitas hurrying head down through the quad and was gripped by tough, rosy hands. 'Oh, it's you! I'm off to Dolosi's *shamba* to talk to her dad about the sewing machine. I've found a respectable treadle at Patel's. I think it'll be just the thing. Feel like a walk?'

'A walk is just what I need.'

They skirted the chapel, crossed the lawns and took the

path into the valley south of the hill. Warm air wafted whiffs of wood smoke, the scent of lemon-gums, the cries of children, goat bells and the voice of a woman scolding. The path wound down through elephant grass and onto a wooden bridge over a stream. A small boy, his rounded stomach and navel hernia bulging over the shorts of an older brother, bounded out of the grass. 'Afernoon Seestah, afernoon Seestah!'

'*Wasusotiano*, Benjamin. How is everyone at your place?'

'*Bulungi*, fine!' Benjamin hoisted up his shorts. 'Umbale is going for siyence, Seestah. He says the show is good, siyence is good.'

'Sister Perpetua will be happy, Benjamin. I shall tell her.'

'Me, I'm going for school next year.' Benjamin ran ahead. 'Can I go for siyence too?'

'Yes, my luv, when you are as big as Umbale.'

'How many years?' Benjamin straddled the path.

'One, two, three, four, five, six years.' Felicitas held up her fingers.

Benjamin contemplated the fingers. 'Is very long time.'

'Are those your goats?' Felicitas indicated a tail-wiggling flock browsing nearby.

'Is my father's,' Benjamin corrected.

'You ask Umbale to help you count them every day and you will be good at science. It all starts with counting.' Felicitas patted the solemn face. 'Now, we are going to Dolosi's people. Greet your family from us.'

'*Weraba*, Seestah.'

'Bless the imp! News travels fast.' Felicitas pushed her way uphill through banana groves towards a group of huts shaded by a mahogany flaunting a shawl of magenta bougainvillea. 'Ah, here we are!' A rutted road gave into a courtyard meticulously swept and abutted on three sides by huts, square, thatched and painted brown to window level and dazzling white above. Goats were milling in a pen beyond and a clatter of plates sounded from the hut on the right.

Felicitas called, '*Wasusiotiano*, Mrs Sebange!' A woman in a mauve basuti came down the steps. '*Wasusiotiano*, Seestahs! Welcome, welcome, welcome, welcome!' She clasped their hands. 'It is tea time. Sit, sit here.' She pulled two wooden chairs from under the kitchen eaves into the place of honour in the centre of the courtyard and disappeared into the kitchen. They heard the pumping of a primus stove and a call out of the back door. A cheerful baritone answered from the goat pen. A short, bow-legged man pushed through the goats, ducked behind the kitchen hut and staggered into the yard with a table hugged to his chest. He put the table down in front of them, greeted them and disappeared into the living room to emerge with two more chairs. Mrs Sebange spread a spotless embroidered cloth over the table. Mr Sebange sat down, rubbed his hands over his knees and enquired with time-honoured Kiganda courtesy, into the health of each sister of St Mary's. Felicitas answered in suitable detail while Dolosi's mother set down a tea tray with rose-patterned cups, milk covered with beaded net and a teapot under a knitted cosy. Finally she produced a plate of tea cakes topped with pink icing. Frances recognized the product of the week's domestic science class.

Tea was poured ceremoniously and Frances sat back to relish her cake. Visits to the valley homesteads were a treat she savoured, rich in scent and sound. She loved to be with people who were not hounded by bells, time schedules and urgency. Who lived according to the rising and setting of the sun, who did not chop time into nano-seconds and who were content to let time flow gently and to pass it without hurry, with one another. They were people who relished presence beyond frantic achievement, who exchanged slow courtesies and allowed long, comfortable silences between them.

Only after her second cup of tea did Felicitas broach the matter of the sewing machine. 'She is a good pupil, Mr Sebange. She will pass well. Sister Theresa has great hopes for her. The girls tell me you have received bride gifts?'

Mr Sebange nodded and put down his cup. 'It is done. His father's brother and I have spoken. He has sent two cows already. The others come in two weeks.' He turned and glanced proudly at a bicycle against a hut wall. 'Also he is giving the bicycle, Sister. It is very new.'

'It has many gears.' Mrs Sebange nodded significantly.

'Goodness, so it has.' Felicitas craned round in her chair.

'That'll save your legs.'

Frances wondered suddenly if the bicycle had not recently belonged to some expatriate boy who was wondering what had become of it. A bike like that was very rare in the *shambas*. Mr Sebange's chest swelled. 'He is a hardworking young man. He is making money.' He permitted himself a small smile.

'And he is giving a new radio.' His wife beamed. 'The music is much louder now.'

'Dolosi's going to be a well set up gal. Now, if we can just get that sewing machine, Mr Sebange, she'll be making clothes for everyone in the valley. You'll never worry about her again.' Mrs Sebange refilled their cups while Felicitas and Mr Sebange reckoned up payments, making shrewd moves and counter moves. Parents and the school shouldered the expense of a sewing machine together. Frances was wondering idly whether it would be possible to make a drawing of the trees on the skyline for the woodcutting class, when a distant throbbing came to their ears. Mr and Mrs Sebange exchanged knowing looks as the throbbing grew louder. Suddenly Frances knew what it was – in Gabriel's words: 'Hi-fi at the max!' Gears ground viciously and the creak of springs bouncing over potholes announced the approach of a car through the banana grove. A vehicle of noxious mustard yellow swung into the drive below the yard, slewed sideways and jerked to a halt. Mr and Mrs Sebange were on their feet, exchanging proud glances. A door swung open, emitting a blast of sound, and a young man emerged. He wore those sunglasses that keep the wearer's eyes a mystery, a purple tie over a dazzling red shirt, a shiny blue suit and socks of luminous green over pointed shoes that glistened like licked plastic. He was rubbing his hands as he jaunted up towards the house. He paused in mid-stride when he saw Felicitas and Frances but his father and mother-in-law-to-be were already extending their hands in welcome. Felicitas had risen from her chair. 'You must be Dolosi's young man. Nice to meet you. This is Sister Frances.'

Frances assumed a guileless nun's smile and swept forward with outstretched hand. 'Delighted, Mr …'

'It is Terence Motongo!' Mr Sebange beamed. 'It is Terence Motongo who is to marry our daughter, Sister. So you come to take Dolosi to the disco? Yes, yes, she has told us and we permit, because it is Friday. The sisters will tell you she is a very good pupil.'

Mrs Sebange turned and sent a high-pitched call up the hill. 'She went to see Kamika about a pattern. She is dressed already. She is coming.'

Mrs Sebange hurried to the kitchen for a beer and Mr Sebange offered Terence Motongo her chair. He sat gingerly on half the chair, as if poised to flee, cracked his fingers nervously in his lap and looked across the valley. Then he looked at Mr Sebange and then, very briefly, at the nuns. He licked his lips once and when Mrs Sebange handed him a glass of beer he took several quick gulps. Frances smiled serenely and encouragingly at him, nodding amiably at the small talk between Felicitas and Mr Sebange on the respective merits of sewing machine brands. Then Dolosi appeared, walking nonchalantly down the path, swaying voluptuous hips and breasts. She was a self-sewn vision in clinging pink, black and silver. Terence Motongo sprang to his feet, consulted a very large watch on his wrist, hitched his arm into hers, saluted her parents and hustled her down to the car. Dolosi, proud and gleaming, bade them all goodbye.

'That's a smart car you're driving, Mr Motongo.' Frances, all smiles, had risen and followed the happy couple. 'Dolosi, fancy you going to the disco in that! What is it? A Ford?'

'Mazda,' said Dolosi. 'With a hi-fi, sister! Look – speakers in the back.'

'My goodness – very big! You don't need to go to the disco.' Frances peered admiringly. 'You could party here all night.'

'But no lights, Sister. You can't disco without the lights!'

'Of course not, silly of me. Well, enjoy yourself. And thank you for the iced cakes. Full marks.'

Dolosi barely had time to smile coyly before the door was shut on her. The driver slammed his door, turned on ignition and all further speech was drowned in a pulsating blast. The yellow Mazda reversed, lurched forward and skidded off down the track. Not before Frances had had time to observe the jumble of crude carvings, rolled barkcloths, *ketitis*, drums and a horn fetish seamed with cowries that had certainly been pillaged from an old shrine. She heaved a sigh and returned to the tea table. Terence Motongo was in the curio business. Was this Mother's vile yellow car and the lamentable noise? The doyen of the curio business in Kampala was Mr Julius Ssemogerere. She had wondered sometimes, knowing the sanctity of some of the 'curios' that Julius Ssemogerere displayed on his shelves, whether he was overly particular about the provenance of his 'Cultural Artifacts: The Real Things'. Perhaps she should call on him tomorrow?

Felicitas was pushing back her chair. 'Well, our business is settled. Time we were getting back. We'll see you again when you come to the school-leavers' service, won't we, Mr Sebange, Mrs Sebange?'

'Oh yes, oh yes. We will be there. Thank you, Sister. I shall send the first instalment with Dolosi on Monday. Thereafter,' Mr Sebange added a little formally, 'it will be done before the end of the term. You may tell Mr Patel the machine is sold.'

***

'Theodora?' On Saturday morning Frances hurried onto the verandah where Theresa and Theodora sat knitting orphans' jerseys. 'Theodora, would you do me a favour?'

Theodora frowned and paused halfway along a row she was counting, 'What is it?'

'Would you please do tuck-shop duty for me? I've got to go to town urgently.'

Theodora forebore to respond until she had made obvious her disapproval of this change of schedule without warning. She nodded curtly. 'I can do it.'

'Sorry – I'll stand in for you next week. Thanks!' Before Theodora could enquire into the reason for this disruption of duty, Frances fled.

'That one is in a big hurry.' Theodora laid a lime-green bundle on her lap and stared with stern disapproval at the figure running to the garage with habit hitched almost to her knees.

***

Hooting shamelessly, like a *mutata* taxi, Frances wove through the traffic making for Kampala market, swerved into a street parallel to the main road and drew up outside 'Ssemogerere's Cultural Artifacts: The Real Things'. She ran up the steps and stood and blinked in the doorway till her eyes grew used to the dark interior, redolent of hut smoke, old wood and hide. She picked her way through the jumble of gaudy cloths from the coast, drums, beaded Kisii stools, Suk headrests, pots, bark-cloth mats, Congolese masks and several cowried horn fetishes, to the back where Mr Ssemogerere sat at a table, smoking a White Fathers' cigar.

'Sister Frances, good morning, good morning, good morning!' He rose, laid the cigar in an enormous yellow ceramic ashtray bordered with green crocodiles and spread his hands. 'How can I help you today?'

'Mr Ssemogerere, have you received a carving of a Virgin Mary and Child – quite big,' she indicated shoulder height, 'made of *majarati*?'

'Yes, yes it came in last Monday. It was unusual, sad, yes, I must tell you it was sad. I have seen nothing like it, it was a 'once off', Sister! The American bought it quickly. I got a good price, very good!'

'Mr Ssemogerere, that Virgin and Child was carved for St Mary's School by my pupil Benedicta Kivengere who passed her degree in Fine Art at Makerere with distinction. That statue is a national art treasure and was stolen from St Mary's chapel on Sunday night. If it leaves the country I am going to lodge a complaint in high places – very high places, Mr Ssemogerere.'

'But Sister, Sister Frances,' Mr Ssemogerere deflated, wrinkling his face into a mask of innocent woe. 'I received the carving in good faith. Theft? No, no, no, no! A young man brought it from Toro!'

'If that young man is Terence Motongo, he brought it, stolen, from St Mary's School, Kubiri Hill, five miles from Kampala, on Sunday night.'

'But the American has left!'

'Then it is your responsibility, Mr Ssemogerere, to trace him before I take the matter to higher authorities.'

'Wait, wait! Somewhere I have it ...' Mr Ssemogerere pawed the litter of papers on the table. 'Here, no, no, no – wait!' Papers flew like wind-tossed leaves. 'No, ah yes, here!' He pounced and lifted a card. 'I have it. There is a little chance – he said he had heard of something Mukono way, maybe ...'

'Please contact him immediately.' Frances folded her arms.

Mr Ssemogerere jabbed a quivering finger and connected: 'It answers! He is still in the country! Sir, Mr Zenowski, it is Ssemogerere here from The Real Things. The Virgin and Child in olive wood, it is with you? You are where? Ah, please hold sir, please hold! There is a lady here, it was stolen. What? Yes, yes. No, no, I had no idea, sir! I will tell her, yes, yes. Oh, sir?'

Mr Ssemogerere slowly put down the receiver and swivelled grieved eyes to Frances, 'He is not happy, Sister. He thinks I lie to him. He is at Entebbe airport. He flies to Nairobi now and then to New York.'

'What time?'

'At eleven o'clock.' Mr Ssemogerere's wrinkles sagged, his yellow eyes awash in sympathy.

She was already at the door. The sunlight fell on her wrist. Twenty to ten! She flung herself into the combi and hooted her way into the traffic. 'Dear Lord!' she prayed, 'help me! The American must be furious. I'll have to go like the wind and the gears are so ...!'

'Gabriel.' 'Of course!' She pushed the accelerator into the floor and barged ruthlessly into the tide of *boda-bodas*. When at last she swerved into the school drive she opened the door and ran.

'Sister Gabriel, where is she?'

'At the fountain, Sister.'

She flew to where Gabriel, awash in tiny pupils, with Salva beside her, was strumming her guitar. 'Gabriel, come! Leave it and come! Madonna's at Entebbe airport, about to leave for the USA!'

'Begorrah! I told you she'd fly!' Gabriel was running beside her. Two doors slammed, gears ground, wheels spun, gravel flew and they hurtled downhill. Frances clutched the dashboard. Nobody could drive like Gabriel.

'Thank God for Museveni's repairs!' she muttered as, at last, Gabriel swung onto the Kampala-Entebbe road. 'At least the dips are shallow now.'

Gabriel's jaw jutted and she played the hooter liberally at the *boda-bodas* and cyclists with bedsteads, *matoke*, chickens, wives and children perched behind them. 'You pray, Frances, I drive!' Frances prayed. The appalling potholes of earlier days were fewer now. Springs creaked as they swerved before advancing lorries loaded with Saturday-morning pilgrims to Kampala market. Frances tried not to look at her watch more than three times a minute. The drive to Entebbe airport took over half an hour. Would a cheated American collector wait out of compunction for a stolen Madonna's retriever? At last the sign for the airport loomed on the left.

'Hang on!' Frances clutched the door hold as Gabriel swung left with a squeal of tyres. Frances looked at her watch. Half past ten. They'd be boarding now. She clenched her hands. Gabriel roared to the terminal entrance and stopped with a lurch that flung them to the dashboard. Then they fled, abandoning the car in the loading zone. Two nuns moving at speed with grim faces were given space with respect.

'Will passengers for flight BA 479 flying to Nairobi please board at exit two. Passengers for flight BA …'

Gabriel lunged towards the BA desk. 'Get me Mr Zenowski, about to board the flight to Nairobi. I have urgent information for him! He must not leave before I have spoken with him!'

'But madam, they are boarding. The last call …'

'Call customs control. He is leaving the country with stolen goods!' Frances drew herself up to her full height and glared. 'I shall demand to speak with the Minister of the Interior.'

'But madam …'

'Do it!' thundered Gabriel, fiery sword in hand. 'The American is eating us!'

The assistant leaped for a microphone, 'Calling Mr Zenowski about to board flight BA 479. Will Mr Zenowski please come to the BA desk. Calling Mr Zenowski. Please come to the BA desk.'

From the remnant of a queue near the exit a tall figure detached itself and dodged its way through the crowd. He wore reflective black glasses, a long greying ponytail, a very bright Afro-shirt over black jeans and his lean jaws were working gum.

'Mr Zenowski?' Frances moved forward.

'That's me, ma'am.' He glanced quizzically at her flabby sandals and habit. 'Can you explain what this is about? I risk missing my flight.'

'Mr Zenowski, I apologize. This is not your fault. But the statue in African olive-wood that Mr Ssemogerere sold you was stolen from our Kampala convent. It was made for the school by a former pupil of mine.'

Mr Zenowski tapped his foot and chewed while she was speaking but now he stowed his gum below his lower left molars where it bulged under a cheek covered in steel-grey filings, 'Can I ask you to describe the thing to me, ma'am?'

'This is the final call for all passengers boarding flight BA 479 to Nairobi.'

'It's shoulder height, a Virgin and Child, sad … and tender.'

'How come it landed up with Ssemogerere? Are you sure you didn't sell it to him and then change your mind?'

Frances swallowed. 'If you don't know already, Mr Zenowski, I have to tell you that theft is a way of life here. Our Mother Superior, wishing to set an example, declines to lock the chapel door where the statue is housed. It was easy enough to steal. You see, Mr Ssemogerere …'

'Didn't he guess where it came from?'

'With Mr Ssemogerere, one never knows. He would certainly not steal himself, but his purveyors … er … it is part of the game, you see. It would be good to keep that in mind, Mr Zenowski.' She could not help a small smile.

The gum leaped from cheek to molars and Mr Zenowski masticated and slapped his jeans. 'Shit! Okay, ma'am. I can't afford to dirty the pen here. Hold my seat!' he slapped the desk. The BA man nodded vigorously, his eyes slewing in delight between the protagonists, and moved away to speak to the controller of the boarding queue.

Entebbe airport is neither large nor sophisticated and Mr Zenowski's cargo was still visible at one end of the building in large cartons being loaded onto a trailer for embarcation. He went swiftly to the tallest carton, extracted a penknife from his jeans' pocket, took hold of a top corner of the carton, sliced into and tore it open. 'Is this what you're looking for?'

Frances pulled aside dense layers of protective wadding and peered. 'That's her! Oh, thank God, Gabriel! We've got her. Oh!' She felt almost faint with relief. She drew herself up. 'Mr Zenowski, thank you. You've behaved with great forbearance. I advise you to give Mr Ssemogerere a stern warning. It will be of help to us all.' She held out her hand. 'I wish you a safe flight.'

'Thank you, ma'am,' he gave her hand a brief clasp. 'I advise you to lock up your treasures. This would go for a small fortune in New York.'

'I shall consider it – but I have to deal with a very determined woman!'

'Good luck to you.' Still masticating, Mr Zenowski proffered a hand to Gabriel who wrung it. Then he turned and loped to exit two.

Gabriel flung her arms round Frances and they did a small clumsy dance beside the virgin in the box. Then they summoned porters who trundled her through the terminus and heaved her onto a back seat of the combi. Several times on the way home, Frances turned to pat the box.

They drove back to Kubiri without urgency. Gabriel hooted and waved to the lorries full of market-day pilgrims, swerving *boda-bodas* and the unsteady cyclists ploughing valiantly towards town, loaded with bedsteads, *matoke*, wives, pawpaws, oranges and chickens. Presently she began to bounce a little in her seat and chant, 'He's got the whole world in His hands!' Frances laid her head against the headrest and silently agreed.

As they approached The Welcoming Mother, Frances looked up into the face of Grace Makubiye and felt the benediction of her approval. A pity she was no longer here to savour the dedication, yes, the dedication and determination of her sisters in education.

Daudi, Paulo and Wiriamu lifted the Madonna from the box

and carried her back to the chapel. When she stood, restored and serene, in the recess between the two back doors, Daudi dismissed Paulo and Wiriamu and faced Frances with folded arms. 'Now we are locking here every night.'

'But Mother ...'

'I am speaking with her now, Sister. You must leave it to me.' He turned and strode down the chapel steps and she heard his boots crunch over the gravel of the path and up the steps to the senior nuns' house. Frances, feeling suddenly a little wobbly in the knees, subsided onto a pew and let out a long breath. She had no desire to witness the battle between two titans.

She slipped out that night, just before eleven o'clock and looked at the chapel doors. A hefty padlock dangled from each bolt and she went up to bed with a heart at ease.

4. Where is Ignatia?

Perpetua, bent over a basin in the staff toilets, lathered her hands vigorously and scrubbed traces of permanganate from under her fingernails. Then she dried her hands and hurried to the dining room for senior supper. Mattea and Theodora were already standing at the heads of their tables and Perpetua strode to the third table, avoiding Theodora's censorious stare for being at least two minutes late. The girls filed in and Mark, who had stayed to prepare slides for a biology lesson, came and stood on her right.

Mattea raised her eyebrows at an empty place at her table.

'Where's Ignatia?'

'She forgot a textbook in the lab for tonight's prep. I gave her the key to go and fetch it.' Perpetua looked at her watch. 'About ten minutes ago.'

'Odd.' Mattea frowned. 'Ignatia's never tardy.'

'I'll go and see what's up.' Mark slid out.

Theodora intoned grace and the meal began. Perpetua was digging hungrily into fish pie when Mark hurried in and bent over her. 'Sister, come quickly! Something's wrong.'

He half-sprinted ahead of her into the quad and flung over his shoulder. 'It's a mess and she's not there.'

They rounded the corner to the science lab door where a shaft of yellow light fell over the lawn. Mark sprang up the steps. 'Look!'

A textbook lay face down on the floor. Toppled bunsen burners strewed the long desk in the centre of the room and smashed test tubes littered the floor. The door to the storeroom was open and there were two conspicuous gaps on the shelves. Mark scanned the labels on boxes. 'Zinc's missing!' He swung round and stared at the other empty space. 'Ammonium nitrate! Oh, my gosh!'

'What are you saying?'

Mark was back at the shelves. 'No mistake. Just the zinc and ammonium nitrate, Sister.'

'Ignatia!' It was a stifled shriek and he turned to see her dash to the back room behind the lab. 'Ignatia! Ignatia-a-a! She's not here! Oh, Mark – could they? Call the watchmen!'

Mark leaped down the steps and up into the quad. 'Moses! Samue-el! Mose-e-es!'

Within a minute torches were bobbing above the thump of booted feet. Perpetua stormed out, 'Where've you been? Haven't you see anyone, heard anything?'

'No, Sister, all is well.'

'All is not well! Look here! Look!'

She grabbed Samuel, who was masticating a mouthful of food, and ushered him up the lab steps. Moses followed and together they surveyed the carnage.

'Where were you?'

Moses backed under her furious glare, 'At the garage, Sister.'

Mark directed: 'Get Daudi! Go back to the garage, Moses. Search the engine room and fuel store and box room. Look everywhere they could tie up and hide a girl. Samuel, go through all the outside toilets, all of them! Quickly! And report to me.'

As booted feet retreated, she took the torch she kept for electrical failures and ran out over the lawn. There were no footprints on the dry grass and no sign of – wait! There was something lying on the lawn near the mango trees. She ran over and picked up a two-inch wide, blue cotton belt. Ignatia's. Just then a strong white beam spiked the darkness on her right. 'Daudi! Mark! I found this! They've taken Ignatia down the hill.'

'Eh, Sister, this is very bad! It is abduction!'

'I pray not, but it's certainly kidnapping.'

'And the chemicals for exploding, Sister. They have taken them? It is theft and abduction!'

'Those boys.' Mark stared over at the mango trees. 'The ones who came to the science exhibition uninvited – they helped carry stuff back to the labs. They poked around didn't they? It must be them.'

'We go after them now! Wait, I bring the pangas.' Daudi thudded up the quad to his workshop.

At that moment Moses and Samuel came panting round the corner. 'Sister, is nowhere nobody! Nowhere, nowhere, nowhere!'

'They've taken her that way, down to the *shambas*.'

Perpetua glanced at them coldly. 'Go back to your watch and, Samuel, stay this end of the school, please.' She twisted the belt in trembling fingers and stalked back to where Mark stood probing the darkness beyond the mango trees. 'How on earth do they think they can get away with this!'

'Kids don't think, they just act. Damn, they've taken the lot. If they play around with that stuff they'll blow themselves sky high.'

'And Ignatia with them. God help us!'

Heavy feet pounded the steps down from the quad. 'The pangas, I have them.' Daudi thrust a glinting blade into Mark's hand. 'We go now.'

Perpetua watched the white beams of their torches flash over the trunks and branches of the mango trees before they plunged downhill. Suddenly her knees buckled and she sat down on the steps to the lab. She rubbed her forehead, took off her glasses, wiped them on her habit and put them on again. The sound of crackling undergrowth faded into silence broken only by the distant cry of a marsh owl. Faintly from a junior dormitory behind her came the sound of a guitar – Gabriel and Helena were singing the nightly hymn. Perpetua heaved to her feet, switched off the laboratory lights, locked the door and walked up to the quadrangle. She paced the perimeter four times, wringing the blue waistband, and then walked slowly past the lighted classroom where diligent seniors bent over their evening preparation. There was an empty desk at the back. 'Now!' she moaned. 'Only three weeks before her finals when she needs every minute.' Then she braced herself and headed for the senior nuns' refectory. As she entered four pairs of eyes rose from piles of marking. 'Ignatia?' Mattea's voice was a little husky.

'She's been forcibly removed from the labs and they've taken all the zinc and ammonium nitrate with her.'

'But that's what you used for the explosion!'

'Precisely.' Perpetua sank onto a chair with her head in her hands.

Agnes crossed herself while Mattea went over and filled the kettle. When it had boiled, she made tea and brought it to Perpetua. 'I kept your supper, by the way.'

Perpetua took the tea gratefully. 'I couldn't eat, thanks all the same.'

'Are you sure they haven't hidden her in the grounds somewhere?'

'The toilets, they always …'

'The engine room!' Theodora broke in. 'Remember that terrible boy!'

'No, she's gone. I found this near the mango trees.' Perpetua dropped the crumpled waistband on the table.

A choking whimper came from Agnes. 'They have assaulted her!'

'I wouldn't put it past Ignatia to have dropped it herself as a clue.' Mattea's cool grey eyes quelled her rising hysteria.

'Daudi and Mark have gone after them,' Perpetua sighed. 'There's nothing we can do now but wait.' She drained her cup. 'If anyone can find her, they will, surely.'

Mattea looked at the clock on the wall and then at Perpetua. 'Mother,' she murmured.

'I know. I'd better tell her now.' Perpetua went through the sitting room and knocked on Mother Julienne's door.

'Come in!'

She took a deep breath and opened the door. Mother was in her chair and Frances was reading the Pensées to her in French. 'Mother,' Perpetua clenched her fists as the bright brown eyes opened. 'Mother, we have a crisis on our hands.'

'Dites moi.' Mother patted the chair on her left but Perpetua strode up and down the small room until she had told her everything. 'Only three weeks till exams, Mother, three crucial weeks. And if … if they … what *are* we going to *do*?' At last she flung herself into the chair. 'And all because of that wretched exhibition. If only I'd never thought of it!'

Mother Julienne was silent for a long moment, her eyes fixed on the crucifix on the wall. 'C'est grave, ceçi.'

'I hate the thought, but if Daudi and Mark don't bring her back tonight, we'll have to call the police, won't we?'

'Hmm. That I wish to avoid if possible. It is not pride. The matter is too grave for pride, the name of the school and all that bagatelle. But that Kakonge!' She shuddered. 'Perhaps it was just that he was looking for a quick promotion, but it was absolutely not necessary to shoot one of our girls. There must be a better way.' She laid her hand on Perpetua's white knuckles. 'You must not blame yourself. You arranged the exhibition out of dedication to your subject and our children.' There were three soft knocks on the door and Felicitas peeped in. 'Time for bed, Mother – oh Perpetua! It isn't true about Ignatia, is it?'

'It is true.' Mother released Perpetua's hand. 'It is time to heave my old bones into bed. Go with God, ma fille. I shall pray.'

Later, Frances found Perpetua at the priedieu in the passage alcove with her head on her arms. Never had the strong, forbidding figure looked so helpless. Frances squeezed her shoulder. Perpetua sighed and rose, stalked resolutely to the refectory table and pulled a pile of marking towards her.

'Tea?'

'Coffee please – strong.'

Frances gave it to her and sat down to finish marking essays on art history. Perpetua glared in concentration, inserting the necessary red marks on paper, only the rubbing of her hand across her high, bony forehead betraying her anguish. An hour later Frances had finished her work. Perpetua was doggedly marking still. Frances glanced at the clock. It was nearly eleven and there was still no sign of Daudi and Mark. 'Are you going to wait up?'

Perpetua raised her eyes and nodded. 'More coffee?'

'Please.'

Frances placed three ginger biscuits on the saucer and brought the coffee. Perpetua raised her cup absently, her eyes wandering to the windows. The scent of night convolvulus breathed softly in from the garden and the frog chorus in Teresa's well clicked and tinkled but no returning footsteps broke the silence of the quad. 'Perpetua …'

'Don't wait up with me, Frances. I'm all right.'

Frances went over to the bookshelf, took out two of Perpetua's favourite reads, laid them on the table and went down the passage to the priedieu. When she rose from it again she peeped into the sitting room. Perpetua was sitting with an open book on her lap, her hands gripping the chair arms, her eyes on the door. Frances went up to bed.

The crunch of feet on gravel came after two o'clock. Perpetua hurried to the door as Mark stumbled over the threshold. His eyes were red and watering in a mask of orange dust, his legs and arms were striped with crimson scratches from elephant grass and lantana thorns. 'Just got back,' he panted. 'Told Daudi to go to bed. Sorry, Sister, no luck. They must've gone at a hell of a pace. We tracked them over the river, heading south-east. At least we know that. Whew!' He collapsed onto a chair and leaned forward over the table. 'We went downhill from where you found her belt but it wasn't till we hit the elephant grass that we picked up tracks. They'd left a flattened swathe. Must have been at least four of them. They'd gone left, round the hill, down to the river. We found footprints in the mud – definitely Ignatia's sandal prints. They went quite a way downstream in the river and came out into the elephant grass on the other side. But the tracks petered out in the bush and the short grass uphill where the banana groves begin. We went along the road, east and west and into the *shambas* uphill but the ground's dry there, too many footprints everywhere. Couldn't even be sure of Ignatia's sandals. We went into the banana groves all along the road and asked a few people still up and about if they'd seen or heard anything. No one had. They'd obviously steered clear of the homesteads. Then we tried various paths going uphill the other side. We even went up the forest rise. No sign of them. All those little paths going nowhere except to shambas. Hell, Sister. I'm sorry.'

'They certainly went fast.'

'And knew exactly what they were doing. Locals. What can we expect?'

'Thank you, Mark. You've done all you can.'

'I suppose we'll have to call the police?'

Perpetua pulled a face. 'Mother Julienne doesn't like the idea. Our local sergeant tends to be trigger happy. The last time we had a scare here, he shot one of the girls. Not fatally, fortunately. For tonight, we'll leave it to God. Tomorrow morning …'

'It is tomorrow morning.' Mark poured a glass of water and gulped it down.

'Time you got some sleep. Don't forget to put Savlon on those cuts. You've no idea how quickly sepsis sets in here. If you're late for the ten o'clock double period I'll …'

'Tell the girls I'm suffering from a hangover. That'll make them sit up.' He managed a wry smile as he closed the door quietly behind him. Perpetua's mouth twitched slightly and then, slowly and wearily, she went up to bed.

***

As morning chapel ended, Mother Julienne came forward to the chancel steps. 'The school may leave the chapel now except for all

A-level girls. First-year and second-year A-level pupils will remain behind, please.'

The school was used to Mother's pep talks and filed out of chapel with envious glances at the forty-six elect in the back pews.

'Girls, you probably all know that Ignatia did not come in to supper last night. When Sister Perpetua and Mark went to the science laboratory to look for her they found that she had been forcibly taken away and that certain chemicals from the laboratory had been stolen. Daudi and Mark followed the people who took her but were unable to find them. However, they know the direction they followed and we shall search until we find her. They went on foot and they cannot be very far from here. The chemicals stolen from the laboratory are those used to make explosives.' There were gasps of horror from the pews and hands flew to mouths.

Mother raised her hand: 'I am telling you what I know about this so that you do not begin to imagine all kinds of horrors. A lot of people came to see the science exhibition that Sister Perpetua was good enough to arrange for our local schools. I think perhaps that some of the young visitors from the valleys, not invited scholars, who saw the exhibition and saw how competently Ignatia demonstrated the use of a fuse and explosives, came to the conclusion that she could help them make explosives for some purpose of their own. But we know nothing for certain. That is only what I imagine. Ignatia is a sensible girl. She will not fight and scream and incite violence. I believe she will remain calm and at least pretend to do what these people ask of her. She knows far more than they do. I do not think they will treat her badly. We shall not call the police about this matter – yet. You all remember, I am sure, what happened last time they came to the school. We wish to avoid that.' This was greeted with wide eyes and murmurs of approval while Namkya rubbed the scar on her arm significantly.

'Now, what I ask of you, each one, is to carry on as if nothing has happened. Look, Our Lady has been restored to us!' she nodded at the recess in the back wall. 'We can be quite confident that Ignatia will be brought back safely. Exams are only three weeks away and you must keep your minds on your work. That will be difficult, I know. We are all concerned for Ignatia. But anxiety and exaggeration will make everything worse. I forbid …' Mother's penetrating brown eyes pierced each girl individually, 'I absolutely forbid you to speak of this to anyone. Not even to O-level pupils and certainly not to the juniors. You may not even discuss it among yourselves. If anyone asks where Ignatia is, you will tell them she is in the sanatorium with a contagious illness and visiting is out of the question. Do you understand, mes filles? I will not have fear or anxiety disturbing the peace of the school at this time. Pray – yes! But if I hear that rumours and talk are flying around I shall deal with them severely. In fact,' Mother lowered her head and above her hawk's nose, her eyes pierced them implacably, 'with the utmost severity. Is that understood?' Nods and murmurs accompanied the 'Yes, Mother Julienne.' 'You may go now and – remember!'

'Yes, Mother Julienne.'

She stood with hands folded over her habit until the girls had filed out of the chapel. Only Nasuna, she noted, paused a moment at the door and looked back at her with spilling eyes. When they were gone Mother Julienne sighed and turned to extinguish the altar candles. Looking up at the Christ she crossed herself and murmured, 'Give me the faith, please, to believe what I have told them.'

When the bell rang for morning tea break, Perpetua stood until the class of first-year A-levels had shuffled out of the laboratory and then sat down and stared into the storeroom. She began to gauge mentally just how much damage could be caused by the quantities of zinc and ammonium nitrate in those missing boxes. How very, very fortunate that, talking to primary children, she had given no mention of relative proportions. Merely named ingredients. Provided the boys – if boys they were – did not play around with the components… 'Kids don't think, they just act.' A shiver ran down her spine. She longed for a cup of tea but she was too tired to drag herself up to the staff room. She was about to lay her head on her arms over the desk when the doorway darkened. Nasuna came up the steps slowly, a cup of tea in her hand. 'Sister, I saw you are tired today. I have brought you tea.'

Shyly, glancing up at her only once, Nasuna laid the cup and saucer on the table. There were two pink-cream biscuits on the saucer.

'Goodness, Nasuna. Thank you, this is kind. Yes, I am a little tired.'

'It is worry, Sister?'

'Well, yes, a bit.' She straightened her sagging spine. It didn't do to let one's hair down. 'Now, run along. I'm sure you want your own tea.'

But Nasuna stood still, her hand on the table, her big shy eyes probing the cool, heavy-lidded grey eyes that to her contained all wisdom.

Perpetua rubbed her hands on her knees in embarrassment. Nasuna made a little choked sound and reached her hand out, almost touched Perpetua's sleeve, then retreated to the door. 'Sister, I shall go to the chapel and pray.' With lowered head she left the room.

Perpetua waited till the girl's footsteps had retreated then reached for the tea. Her eyes left the storeroom shelves and wandered through the doorway, over the sunlit lawn to the brooding trees.

Nasuna crept into the back pew of the chapel and knelt. She could feel Máma Méri, warm and present behind her and she lifted her eyes to the Saviour. 'Jésu Christu, Máma Méri, I beseech you!' She burrowed her forehead into her arms.

'Bring back Ignatia and make Sister Perpetua happy again. She is heavy, so heavy, Jésu Christu, Máma Méri!' Then she lifted her head and held herself straight. That was how you prayed as a child. Now she must pray as an A-level pupil. Mother had taught her in the confessional to examine her heart as she prayed. Praying is loving, Mother said. Did she, Nasuna, love Ignatia? Yes ... now, now she did more. But earlier, no. Always, she had admired her too much, too-too much. When Ignatia won the prize for science, every-every year, she began to be jealous. She was diligent, like her father, she worked hard. But Ignatia was quick. She understood everything straight away. How could somebody be always first in science and beautiful and royal also? She did not talk about it, but everybody knew she belonged to the royal house of Toro.

All through the years Ignatia was the most beautiful and her weekend dresses were shop dresses. She, Nasuna, came with only the dresses Máma made, one pattern for all, the top straight down, no collar just a square neck, too tight, and the skirt bunched out over her big hips. Not hips like Ignatia's. Ignatia and Kamya and Nampa had shop dresses, cool and styled. But then, that Saturday she never forgot, Ignatia gave her that dress. She did it nicely, not like a rich girl giving to a poor girl to show off. No. She called her into her cubicle and held out a pink dress, flared, with a white collar, white belt, white trimming on the sleeves. She said, 'Try it on, Nasuna. If it fits I will give it to you.' She held up the dress and let it sink down over her head, so nicely.   When it was over her head she held her breath praying Jésu, Máma Méri please, please make it fit! And Ignatia, standing behind her pulled the zip right up to the top. Even at the hips it never stuck.

Ignatia said, 'It is a bit long, but not much. Can you hem?'

'Yes, yes, I can hem, I can do it!' And she looked at the dress and stroked it. Smooth, cool, a morning-glory dress not gathered in bunches like Máma's, and she said, 'Yes, please, I like it so much, thank you.' 'Then it's yours, Nasuna.' Ignatia held her head on one side. 'I like it on you – better than on me. Go and hem it quickly in time for the film tonight.' And she, Nasuna, in that dress, she ran to Sister Theresa for the tape measure and pins and Sister Theresa said, 'Eh, you look beautiful, Nasu. Turn round, turn round,' and she tugged and stuck in the pins, 'stand still, now turn again,' talking thinly through the pins. 'Now take it off and bring it to me. I will do the hemming. Yes, yes, leave it with me. I will do it better. Come back after tea.'

And when she went back it was hemmed in Sister's tiny stitches and she'd run to her room and put it on and then she had walked very slowly, proudly, feeling the dress round her, stroking the collar, the sleeves, the belt and all through the film she had stroked her hands over the pink dress. She was beautiful, she was so, so beautiful. Sometimes now she felt bad because never could she be seen in one of Máma's dresses after the shop dress. She washed it carefully and ironed it very carefully every week. Now she could not be jealous of Ignatia.

Even that year when she, Nasuna, had to stay home and fall out of school because Máma's coffee crop failed and they could not afford to send her to St Mary's, and Ignatia and the others got a year ahead. Her people were not rich. Grandfather had run the little Primary and Dáda was now headmaster of the Junior Secondary. When she was a small girl at Dáda's Primary, he used to sit up late with the lamp on the table, marking exercise books and she used to sit with him till she fell asleep over her arms. 'Education is the most important thing for our people, Nasuna. We must be diligent always.'

Máma taught at the Primary and she also sold coffee from the *shamba* and oranges, and made dresses for everyone from her pattern, so Nasuna could go to St Mary's. 'St Mary's,' Máma said every year when she counted her money, 'is the best school for girls in Uganda and it is Catholic too.' Dáda said, 'It is Sister Perpetua's school and that is where you must go so you can teach science one day. Sister Perpetua is the greatest science teacher in Uganda.' Because every year Sister Perpetua came to visit the rural schools in Buganda and Busoga and even sometimes Bunyoro and Toro. She came to give courses to the science teachers and she brought equipment and chemicals, the whole combi full of boxes, and she gave something to each school. She used to walk along the path to Dáda's school, swinging her arms, talking, talking with Dáda and she, Nasuna running to keep up with them. And always when Sister Perpetua drove away with Máma's gift of oranges in a *kikapu*, her father would wave till she was right down the end of the road and the combi was only dust, and say, 'When Sister has been here we are strong again, strong in science!' It was burning in her to be like Sister Perpetua. She pressed her forehead into her arms again. 'Jésu Christu, Máma Méri, bring Ignatia back so that Sister Perpetua's heart is not broken. I will work very, very, very hard to make her happy. I will try for top marks for ever, Jésu, Máma Méri, I beseech you!' The bell clanged in the quadrangle. She started up, crossed herself, blew her nose and hurried to Maths class.

At sunset Daudi knocked on the door of the senior nuns' house. Perpetua turned expectantly from her pile of marking. 'They are back, Sister. They are waiting.'

She followed him out to where Paulo and his three sons stood in the driveway. At dawn they had left to reconnoitre the valleys and lakeshore for news. Paulo was sagging with exhaustion and in his eyes she read ill news. He spread hopeless hands. 'Sister, all day we have been everywhere. Isaiah, he went Masenge way.' Paulo jutted his chin. 'Hezkia, he went to the *shambas* Lubange side. Mattias he went along the water to Wachanga. Nowhere, Sister. Nobody, nobody, nobody knows nothing!' He spat out sideways the coffee bean he had been chewing and his wall eyes devoured her tragically, one into her face and the other over her left shoulder.

'Eh, Sister, what to do?' Daudi's neck and shoulders swelled and he clenched his fists, 'It is worse than the theft of Our Lady. And the police …'

Mattias, Hezkia and Isaiah scuffed the gravel with scratched and bleeding feet, the pangas dangling from cords at their wrists glinted orange in the setting sun and their swift glances at Perpetua's disappointed face were interspersed with longing looks downhill towards their homesteads.

'We are sorry, Sister,' Paulo murmured. 'We are very heavy.'

'*Webali*, Paulo, *webali* Mattias, *webali* Hezkia, *webali* Isaiah you have worked very hard in our cause.'

The tired men drifted away downhill. Daudi shook his head and splayed his arms, 'Eh, Sister, what to do now?'

'I don't know, Daudi. I just don't know. I suppose tomorrow we shall have to call the police. We can't go on like this. Thank you. I shall tell Mother now.'

'Well, so that is that,' Mother stared a long moment at the floor. 'And if Paulo and his sons can't glean any local news, no one can.' She sighed, 'Try and get some sleep tonight, Perpetua. Leave it with me.'

'And tomorrow?'

'Tomorrow will bring whatever it brings, but try and sleep tonight, ma fille.'

Perpetua sagged back to the refectory table, pulled a pile of exercise books towards her and automatically opened the first. When she was halfway through the third, her head suddenly jerked down on her chest. She opened her eyes to meet Mattea's stern grey gaze. 'It's no good, Perpetua. It can wait, you know.'

Perpetua sighed, closed the book, neatly aligned the pile, rose and stalked down the passage to the stairs.

***

At seven in the morning the phone in the refectory shrilled. Felicitas ran. 'Oh, Mr Kaburungu! Yes, certainly. Just one moment.' Mother Julienne was crossing the sitting room and Felicitas hustled her to the phone.

'Ah, Jean-Claude, yes. Yes, I see. I understand. Yes, yes ... ten o'clock. Tout à fait convenable, oui, oui. Certainement. Au revoir.' Mother replaced the receiver and leaned against the table. 'Veronique and Angeline will not be attending school today, Felicitas. Would you please tell the relevant teachers?'

'Yes, Mother.'

'Monsieur Kaburungu will be here at ten, Consolata. Please would you ask Nambiya to bring tea to my sitting room.'

'Certainly, Mother. It is bad news?'

'I don't know yet, but I expect so. Something in the order of a third degree,' she murmured and made her way out towards the chapel.

At ten o'clock sharp she was in her chair in the small sitting room, the tea tray at her elbow. She sat up very straight, wishing she were not of such small stature. Normally she relished a visit from Jean-Claude Kaburungu. He was a tall and very handsome man, the embodiment of urbane authority. His French was exquisite, the product of a Parisian education, a degree in international law, and she rejoiced in his long, eloquent hands. To speak French with Jean-Claude for an hour was one of her indulgences. But today … something in the tone of his voice told her today's interview would be different. At the sound of his knock at the open door, she braced herself.

'Ma mère,' he bent over her hand and pressed it. 'How do you find yourself?'

'Well enough, thank you, Jean-Claude, but − '

'Assez troublée, n'est-ce pas!'

'Naturellement, Jean-Claude, naturellement. Please sit down. Let me pour you some tea.'

For a moment he stood with compressed lips, looking out of the window across the garden and over the valley. She glanced up at him. Under the urbanity was a glint of steel. She poured tea and offered the cake Consolata had provided. He took it with a slight bow and sat down opposite her. He drank the tea, but did not touch the cake.

'Ma mère.' He sat back and observed her. 'Will you speak candidly with me? Veronique has told us what has happened to Ignatia. I know you enjoined silence and that is wise for the school. But we in the diplomatic service, we have to train our children to confide in us absolutely whenever a situation arises, regarding security, that might have political implications.' His eyebrows rose over his teacup and his left hand circled a deprecating apology.

Mother nodded, 'Perfectly understandable, Jean-Claude.'

'You see, we are always in a delicate situation. If anything were to happen to Veronique or Angeline, such as has happened to Ignatia, then it would become known immediately. It is not possible to prevent it because of our high profile. You understand? The press would get it – such things are meat and drink to them, n'est-ce pas? A diplomat's daughter abducted from her school in Kampala.' He put down his cup, lifted his shoulders and splayed his palms. 'They will put a political slant on it. Quite unjustifiably, sans doute, but so often it happens. Everything is turned into something bigger. There would be speculation that might put a strain on relations between our two countries. I cannot afford such an incident. Uganda cannot afford it. And, ma mère, surely the school cannot afford it?'

'Absolutely not,' Mother sighed and laid her head back against the chair.

'So, will you not tell me, exactement, what has happened, what you are doing about it?'

Mother was silent for a long moment. 'I think,' she sat forward again and rang the little bell beside her, 'it would be best if you hear it from young Mark Trevors. He is most directly involved. Sister Perpetua has an important lesson on now – our A-level girls. This has come at the most unfortunate time. Ah, Nambiya! Please would you go to the science laboratory and ask Mark to come to me – immediately. Jean-Claude, more tea?'

'Merci, ma mère. Tell me, what are your security measures here?'

'We have two night watchmen who patrol the grounds from six o'clock in the evening until seven in the morning.'

'That is all?'

'Oui.'

'And the night of the abduction?'

'Perhaps we should call it kidnapping, we have no reason to believe it is abduction yet.'

'I hope you are right, but a girl like Ignatia – what temptation! Imagine!'

'I do not wish to imagine, Jean-Claude.'

'Ah, ma mère!' The eyebrows rose, the shoulders rose, beautiful mushroom-coloured palms splayed. 'You are an idealist, always! But me, I know men!'

'On the night of the kidnapping Moses was at the garage end of the school. Theft of our combi is far more likely than that of a pupil. It has happened four times over the years. Samuel was, I should think, somewhere between the kitchen and the boarding house at the time. He neither heard nor saw anything.'

'Ah, the kitchen! Perhaps that is the answer? I know them! My own guards cause me these headaches, believe me. Ma mère, I do not say this in reproach, but surely this is inadequate? After all, these are young women, very attractive young women you have in your care. You must realize that.'

Mark knocked on the open door and came in. 'Jean-Claude, this is Mark Trevors, our voluntary teacher and Sister Perpetua's right hand this year. Mark, meet Jean-Claude Kaburungu, Veronique and Angeline's father.'

Mark shook hands, 'I know you by sight, sir. Pleased to meet you.'

'Mr Kaburungu is naturally concerned about Ignatia's kidnapping and his daughters' safety here. Any such incident in their lives could have unfortunate repercussions politically, as I am sure you understand. He would like a full account of what happened, Mark. I think you are the best person to give it. Sit down and tell him everything.'

Mark flashed her a glance of sympathy, sat down, hunched

forward and clasped his hands nervously. One look at the formidable countenance of the ambassador and Mother's nervously fluttering eyelids apprised him of tension.

He cleared his throat and launched into an account of the fateful evening, beginning with the visit to the laboratory by 'helpful' youths after the science exhibition and ending with his and Daudi's fruitless pursuit of Ignatia and the stolen chemicals. Jean-Claude Kaburungu placed his fingertips very precisely together, first the little fingers and finally the thumbs, and listened. Mother concluded by telling him of the abortive search by Paulo and his sons for any local information.

'So, I see.' The fingers relaxed and the diplomat's hands flopped over the chair arms, 'Quelle situation! Why have you not called in the police?'

Mother coughed and drew herself up. 'Jean-Claude, two years ago there was a most unfortunate incident. You may remember mention of it. At nine o'clock one morning, I heard dogs bark, in the bush beyond the garage, on that side of the hill. It was deep barking, not the yapping of local *shenzies*. Ah, I thought, Alsatians! Police! A manhunt? It has happened before. I listened. Suddenly the barking was very close and two shots were fired. Near the garage, now. I hurry and press the emergency bell. Grace à Dieu, the school was en classe, except for Sister Frances' art class. They were drawing the statue of St Joseph in the quadrangle. Our emergency drill is to lock all classrooms immediately and order all pupils to sit on the floor with their heads down. So, it is done. The next moment a man runs into the main drive with the dogs close behind. Another shot. Three policemen are running round behind the garage. Again more shots. It happened so quickly – less than a minute. The convict – he had escaped from maximum security, for murder – he ran into the school quadrangle! Imagine! What did he think? To be safe in the school, to get a hostage? I don't know!' Mother's hands and eyebrows made a French gesture.

'I am at the window. The classrooms are quiet, but I see Sister Frances has no time to get her pupils to the art room. I hear her shout and wave her arms and the girls throw themselves flat behind the fountain. The man is running straight towards them and the police continue to fire at him! Imagine! Shooting over children! Why did they not think to wait until the man had run beyond the school? But no. The imbeciles! One girl, Namkya, panics. She does not lie down but runs for the art room. She is shot in the arm!'

'Quel horreur!'

'Do they stop? No, they continue shooting, wildly! The criminal runs through the quadrangle to the lawn beyond.'

'And the girl?'

'The wound is not deep. No artery severed, thanks to God. But what an imbecility! This Seargent Kakonge is an idiot! Just a few seconds more – they could have waited. To shoot into my children – incroyable!'

'Did they get him?'

'Oui. They killed him over there, beyond the science rooms. And that too! I asked them later if they could not have waited. To kill a man there, in front of my children! I ordered them to remove the body but immediately! I told that Seargent Kakonge what I thought of him! I complained, I phoned, I wrote and I also claimed damages for our windows. Sister Frances carried Namkya to Sister Monique. She is very capable. She bound the wound and drove Namkya to Mengo to have the bullet removed. But the trauma! It took a long time for her to get over it – and Sister Frances flagellated herself for weeks: why had she not caught Namkya, why had she not been quick enough, thrown herself over the girl? If only, if only! Quite impossible, naturally, given the speed with which it happened. And my children were very shaken. As for Sergeant Kakonge, he is a buffalo. He has the body, the voice of a buffalo but not the intelligence. If we report this to him, he will go rampaging through the *shambas*, shooting at anyone who runs from him. He will fire at those foolish children, if he finds them. Who knows who will be injured, hein? I will not have his interference, God help me! The only way I can see is to work quietly, to retrieve Ignatia without any violence.'

Jean-Claude Kaburungu extracted a handkerchief from his pocket and wiped the sweat from his forehead. 'Quelle bagatelle affreuse.' He took a deep breath. 'So …. your local news gatherers have discovered nothing and you refuse to call the police. But what are you planning to do? This cannot go on!'

'Non, c'est vrai. It cannot. I do not propose to let it.'

'But – have you no clues whatever? You say you surmise that these young men live not far away. Is that all?'

Mark had been frowning at the faded carpet by Mother's chair. He looked up and cleared his throat. 'You know, there's one thing I remember about the boys that came into the lab. They smelt of fish. It's hit me now that one of them had dry fish scales on his shorts. If it is the same gang, they must have something to do with fishing.'

'But you say that Paulo's son, Mattias, went along the lakeside and found no trace?'

'He said he went as far as Wachanga village,' Mother interposed, 'but there are a few scattered homesteads further along, over the hill in Bulebele bay beyond Wachanga. It is quite a long way, but a possibility, definitely.'

'D'you think they could've taken the stuff, and Ignatia, to blow up fish with, or something? The idea being that she puts the explosives together for them.' Mark leaned forward. 'I know dynamiting goes on occasionally. A friend of mine's doing service with the Fisheries Department. They've banned dynamiting after incidents near Jinja. But these folks along here might reckon they can use lab chemicals to create an explosion and are too isolated to be noticed. And the chances are, they wouldn't be reported by neighbours because they'd all share in the catch. That's my guess, anyway.'

'Hmmm.' Monsieur Kabunguru regarded him thoughtfully. 'It is logical. Can you pursue this?'

'Yes,' Mother's brows arched high, 'I have contacts, very good contacts, among people along the shore. We shall pursue it.'

'Ma mère, have you informed Ignatia's parents?'

Mother shook her head, 'Not yet. I do not want to worry them before it is absolutely necessary. Toro is a long way away. Their anxiety would be very great and Mrs Kawanage is prone to hysteria.'

'But do they not have a right to know? Speaking for myself, if it were Veronique or Angeline, I should wish to know immediately!'

'Jean-Claude, I wanted just one day before – '

'But think, ma mère! If she were to be injured or violated by these youths, what would you say then? Her parents unwarned, the police uninformed. Surely they are not all Seargent Kakonges?' He rose. 'In one thing I can help you. Will you accept the loan of two security guards; no guns, only truncheons – until things are resolved here?'

Mother nodded. 'Thank you, Jean-Claude, yes.'

'But until Ignatia is back and unless your security is permanently improved, I cannot allow my daughters to resume attendance, ma mère.'

'But they have only three weeks before the final exams! Veronique − !'

'I cannot allow it. I will not.'

Two pairs of brown eyes locked. It was Mother who lowered hers. 'Very well. Sister Frances will phone instructions on reading and portfolio work for Veronique. We would be grateful for the guards.'

'Alors. They will arrive this afternoon.' He took her hand, 'Au revoir, ma mère.'

'Au revoir, Jean-Claude.'

As the front door closed, Mark watched Mother Julienne deflate and bury her face in her hands. Presently she looked up again and straightened her back with a sigh. 'He is right, of course, perfectly right.'

'So, what now?' Mark watched the gleaming diplomatic car glide down the hill.

'I shall make the call to Ignatia's father, if he is in his office. Usually he is out. But not to her mother. It would be disastrous. I have had her here working herself up over trifles, mere trifles. And this! Alors, I shall retire for a while.'

'Should I call Sister Perpetua?'

'No. There are second-year A-level classes now. I will not have them interrupted. Bring her to me at twelve o'clock, Mark.'

She went to the phone and dialled the Toro Provincial Administration. No, Mr Kawanage was out in the district and would not return until five, if then. Was there a message? Wearily Mother said, 'Please tell him to phone Mother Julienne at St Mary's convent. That is all.' Then she went back to her sitting room, hung the blue ribbon over the outside door handle, a sign that she was on no account to be disturbed, seated herself in her chair and closed her eyes.

5. Find a Little Blue Boat

The blue ribbon was gone when Mark and Perpetua knocked on Mother's door at five past twelve.

'Come in!' Mother looked decidedly spry. 'It has come to me that we must find a little blue boat.'

'A little blue boat?'

'Mother?'

'I distinctly saw a little blue boat, a *kasese*, but a small one.'

Mark shot a worried glance at Perpetua. Did the old bird habitually 'see' things?

Perpetua seemed unsurprised. 'Was it motorized? What kind of blue?'

'The same blue as Makubenge Fisheries boats, but much smaller.'

Perpetua got up and stared out of the window towards the lake. They often saw Makubenge boats chugging out of the small harbour across the channel that ran north to Port Bell. 'But … that doesn't make sense. All Makubenge boats are big. Even their few *kaseses* are very long and have outboards. And what would Makubenge's want with explosives? They get good catches. Ignatia was kidnapped by locals, on this side, unless Makubenge fellows came over and took her across by boat afterwards. But that wouldn't link up with the exhibition, would it? How would Makubenge's people have known about that?'

'There is only one thing to do now: go to Toni and ask for Jerome's help. He can scout along the shore and see if it belongs to someone there. Immediately.' Mother seemed serenely decided. 'In the meantime, I shall send Daudi across to Makubenge's to look at all the boats, in case there is just one small one. Right, ma fille?'

'Right, Mother.' Perpetua strode out over the lawns beyond the chapel and hurried down the path into the valley. She crossed the bridge over the stream and turned left into the red dirt road that wound through the papyrus, over another bridge and then along a forested peninsula bordered by white sand. Presently the path left the shore and burrowed through shrubs into the shade of a forest garden. Amaryllis and spider lilies spread luxurious carpets under tall mahoganies and albizias, and in a patch of sunlight a brilliant golden bougainvillea sprawled over the house where a game warden's widow lived surrounded by creatures rescued from catastrophe. Perpetua hurried into a creepered verandah, thumped on an open door and peered through a fly screen. '*Hodi*! Anyone at home?'

A distant '*Karibu*!' was the answer before a pack of dogs of mixed breed and size barged through the fly screen followed by a young duiker and two dwarf mongooses. The pack was intent on greeting an old friend, the mongooses came out of curiosity and the duiker considered itself a dog.

'Down, you horrors! Down, Simba, down Mfisi!'

A diminutive woman, brown-blotched as a francolin's egg, came to the door brandishing a fly swatter in one hand and toilet freshener in the other. 'Perpetua! Good show! For heaven's sake don't come in! The dogs have farted all over the sitting room. They've been scrounging avocados again. I've got mountains this year. You must take some home.' She pushed through flailing tails, swatted the dogs out onto the lawn where they collapsed with injured sighs, shoved a serval off a verandah chair and a tabby off another. 'That's better. Whew!' She reached over a dilapidated table and lifted a box made of banana leaves. She selected a small White Fathers' cigar and lit it with an ancient silver lighter, 'The best way I know of countering avocado dog-fart. Well, what's up?' Toni surveyed her shrewdly through a cloud of pungent smoke. 'It's not like you to visit at this time of day.'

'You might well ask! We're worried stiff.' Perpetua told her of Ignatia's kidnapping and ended with Mother Julienne's blue boat.

Toni's nutcracker face split in silent laughter, 'So the Almighty has set you sleuthing!' She threw back her head and slapped her knee. 'I like it, I like it! I quite agree with Mother. Keep the police at bay as long as possible.' Then she frowned, 'But of course, it's not funny. It could get very serious if things went wrong. So you think they might be forcing her to create explosives for them to whack fish with? Quite possible. Problem is, for the folks alongshore here, there's hardly anything left. Makubenge's boats have been encroaching on their traditional fishing grounds. Our people are the old types, using *kaseses* and nets. Very few have outboard motors. Makubenge's boats have been coming into the bays this side and creaming off the catch. It is causing no end of resentment. Jerome's brothers fish only half a mile from here. I get the gossip from them.'

Perpetua looked thoughtfully at the blue smoke curling through beams of sunlight. 'Toni, would it be possible, right now, for Jerome to scout out news of anyone with a little blue boat, from here past Wachanga and over Bulebele way?'

'Yes. He buys our fish twice a week from the locals. He could leave straight away.' She rose and went round the house to the kitchen hut.   Presently Jerome appeared, tall and majestic in a blue *kanzu* and followed by two small grandchildren. '*Memsab mzée* says there is a bad *shauri*. It is true about the girl? And the things to make explosives?'

'I'm afraid so, Jerome. We're scared to call the police.'

'Eh!' Jerome's eyes widened. 'We are all scared, Sister. But what is it for, this blue *kasese*?'

'We don't know. Mother saw it when she was speaking to God, Jerome. We only know that it will somehow lead us to find Ignatia.'

'Ah, the Holy Mother! I shall go now, over beyond Wachanga to the people at Bulebele. My friend Thomasi is there.'

'Take these to make friends talk.' Toni gave him a generous handful of cigars. 'And, Jerome, don't speak about the boat. Don't ask questions. Just sort of look, you know, and smell if there's a *shauri* going on.'

Minutes later a dignified procession was winding through the freckled sunlight on the garden path. Jerome was followed by his small grand-daughter, very erect under a *kikapu* of lady's-finger bananas, and a child of about four trotted after them with an avocado in each hand.

Perpetua was getting up to leave when a buxom girl appeared with a tea tray. 'Perpetua, you can't go without tea. *Webali*, Nazala. And the fruit, the baby's fruit?'

'It is here, *msabu*.' Nazala pushed over a plastic bowl full of chopped pawpaw, banana and mango.

'Tell Muwanga he can bring her now. You haven't met my latest child, have you, Perpetua? No, of course not. I only got her two weeks ago.' Toni filled their cups. 'Another case of illegal chimp export. The mother died of injuries but I got the baby. She's adorable. I'll keep her till she's big enough to go to Maswene Sanctuary. Ah, here she comes.'

Muwanga, gentle and unhurried, without whom Toni could not have managed her animal sanctuary, appeared round the corner hugging a small chimp with a bandaged arm.

'There's my baby! Come to mother, Clementine, come, come!' Gently Muwanga disentangled clinging arms and legs and lowered Clementine into Toni's lap. She promptly buried her face in her shirt front but was persuaded presently, with lip-smackings from Toni, to turn and contemplate a slice of mango. As her long mobile lips pouted towards the gift, Perpetua looked into eyes limpid with sorrow.

'Did she drink the whole bottle, Muwanga?'

'All, *mamsabu*.'

'There's my girl,' Toni planted a kiss on the pale face.

'We're getting better. At first she only wanted to die. It's been a battle. What they need almost more than food is touch. That's what keeps them alive. She sleeps with me – in plastic panties of course, but we snuggle up together. Now, my lovey, time for lunch. Nyummy mango …'

Perpetua sipped her tea while Toni coaxed Clementine, taking little bites of fruit herself and proffering them. 'We'll be playing the garage game soon, won't we? Worked like a charm with my kids. There, that's gone down.'

'What happened to her arm?' Perpetua put down her empty cup and rose.

'The brutes tied them up with leather thongs. They cut deep into Clementine's arm, almost to the bone. We're treating it.' Another kiss was planted on a groping hand.

'Well, I must be off, Toni. Thanks for the help.'

'I hope to God Jerome gets news for you. I'll send him up the moment he's back. He's got a good nose for a *shauri*. Just one more, Clementine, my darling, just a teeny bit ...'

Perpetua was smiling for the first time that day as she launched herself down the steps into the garden and hurried back to St Mary's. Daudi was waiting in the quad. 'All the boats at Makubenge's are big, Sister. There was no small one anywhere. I looked everywhere, I asked everyone.'

'Daudi, thank you. So it can't be one of them. Jerome's gone off to Bulebele to see if he can discover anything. We'll just have to wait.'

Daudi strode away to his workshop and Perpetua stood alone beside the fountain. 'Where is she and what are they doing with her? Any mistake with those components ... Better not think, must not think.'

Frances came hurrying past and stopped. 'Any news of Ignatia yet?'

'Mother has seen a blue boat.'

'Oh, good! Much nicer than a foul yellow car with hifi at the max.'

'When was that?'

'It helped us find the Madonna, so take heart. I must run. I've a lunch date with an unknown man.'

'Still dating? I am beyond surprise.'

'I'm glad you don't think I've lost my touch.'

'Hmph! Who?'

'Didn't give his name.'

'Up to no good, then.'

'Possibly. Actually he rang to say he had some deal that might be of profit to the school and would I be prepared to discuss it.'

'Sounds like *magendo* to me.'

'It probably is.'

'Be careful then.'

'I will. I must rush. I've got a class at two-thirty.'

Frances entered the dining room of the Kavirondo Hotel and surveyed the lunching couples and small parties. Eventually in an alcove she saw a single man sitting with his back to her. It was a very broad back in a tight blue suit and there were three gleaming rolls between head and collar. She made her way to him and held out her hand. 'I'm Sister Frances from St Mary's. Am I speaking to my mysterious caller?'

The man rose and extended a large pulpy, starfish hand. 'Ah, you have come, Sister Frances. Good, very good. Please have a seat.' He pulled out the chair on his right and she realized that luncheon was to be tête-à-tête. As she sat down she murmured, 'Tell me your name again, I think I missed it.' There was an instant's hesitation, but only an instant's.

'James Mujaju, Sister Frances. I am very pleased to meet you. Shall we order?' He flapped at a hovering waiter and asked for iced lemonade and beer. He informed her that the chef's special for the day was an Indian curry and would that be acceptable?

Frances expressed delight and Mr Mujaju wiped his face with a handkerchief. 'It is hot today, very hot.'

'I always find Kampala hotter than Kubiri, Mr Mujaju. We catch a little breeze off the lake, while Kampala's like an overheated stew.'

'That is true! "An overheated stew", it is true. That is just what it is like. Ah, the beer and the iced lemonade for you, Sister.'

They drank in silence a moment and then Mr Mujaju contemplated the foam on his beer. 'Sister Frances, it has come to my ears that at St Mary's School you have a very fine piece of sculpture, made by one of your pupils.'

'The Madonna and Child made by Benedicta Kivengere, yes, that's right. I expect you know that she graduated with first class honours at Makerere?'

Mr Mujaju nodded in as far as he was able over the rolls of fat and his tight collar. 'I am also aware of the commissions she has accomplished. The sculpture in the University Hall, the one in the Minister of the Interior's residence – yes. Very valuable, very valuable.'

'How did you hear of our Madonna?'

Again the fractional hesitation. 'My good friend Julius Ssemogerere keeps me informed. Yes, we both share an appreciation of the arts, Sister Frances.'

A steaming platter of red-gold curry was placed before them. 'Help yourself, Sister!' The starfish waved magnanimously at bowls of chopped fruit, peppers and grated coconut. Frances helped herself though her mouth felt a little dry. She sipped lemonade while Mr Mujaju heaped his plate.

'Did Mr Ssemogerere also tell you that the statue of the Madonna and Child was stolen from our chapel?'

'Ah, Sister, it was an embarrassment to him! A great embarrassment. He is concerned for the good name of his business. Also, he had to pay back the American a lot of money.'

'Ah. Indeed.'

'And that is why I have a proposition to make to you, Sister. This sculpture: somebody who knows art would pay a lot of money for it. It is not safe in your chapel. To have been stolen by a novice like that! It is not kept locked up at night?'

'Yes, the chapel is locked now, after the theft.'

'Ah. And the statue? It is attached? It is fastened to the floor or to the wall?'

'The statue is free standing. Our Lady is taken out for religious processions. The Catholic people from the valleys round the school come to pray beside her and when the chapel is too full for them to come inside for Easter and saints' days we take her into the gardens where they can see her. We cannot deprive them of that, Mr Mujaju.'

Mr Mujaju engulfed a mouthful of curry, looked pensively at the bowl of pawpaw and speared a glistening slice. Then he said, 'I have an offer to make, Sister Frances. This statue is unprotected. Who can say, now that it is known, that somebody else will not try to steal it? I am willing to buy it at a good price and surely the money will be welcome to the school?' Fat-encased eyes gleamed at her. 'You see, I know the school needs a new generator and that old combi!' The starfish flapped contemptuously.

Frances speculated on how he knew. The wheels within wheels had many small cogs.

'Mr Mujaju, we could not possibly sell Benedicta's Mother and Child. It was made for the chapel. It was a gift from Benedicta and it belongs where it was made.'

'Ah, I see. You worry that it will leave the country – like an artefact sold to tourists. No, Sister, that would not be the case. I myself would see that it was displayed in a prestigious position. I care for the honour of our artists here in Uganda.'

And you would make a hundred percent on the deal, too, thought Frances. She shook her head and gave a bland, ingenuous nun's smile. 'You are very kind, Mr Mujaju. I appreciate your concern for our welfare and your respect for Benedicta's work. But it would break Mother Superior's heart. She sets great store by the statue of Our Lady. I am afraid I must refuse your kind offer.'

Mr Mujaju's eyes wavered an instant as he reached for his beer and Frances looked at her watch. 'Oh, goodness – look at the time! I'm so sorry, Mr Mujaju, I must leave now. Afternoon classes, you know!' She rose and stretched out her hand.

'I will be amenable if you should change your mind, Sister. A new generator, a new combi? Exchange could be made without money passing hands. That way we save trouble.'

A new stolen generator and a stolen combi, thought Frances, could cause a great deal of trouble. 'I will keep it in mind, Mr Mujaju. Thank you. Goodbye.' Bestowing a last sweet smile, she fled the Kavirondo Hotel. 'Snake,' she muttered as she swung into the stream of traffic, 'blatant, bloated puffadder!'

***

Perpetua, summoned from the labs, found Jerome sitting on a bench under a tree in the quadrangle. At his feet reposed two *kikapus* bulging with avocado pears. She hurried over to sit beside him, 'Jerome! Did you find anything?'

'I did, Sister. It is like this. I go asking for *ngege*. *Ngege* is very hard to find these days, so I have to go very far, asking everybody, looking at what they are doing. That way I talk to everybody. Everybody says the *mamsab mzée* is mad asking for *ngege* and I tell them, yes, but I must do my best for her. So I go far, to the last people at the end, at Bulebele where my old friend Thomasi is living. I go to him with the cigars because always we smoke together. They have no *ngege* there but I ask for Thomasi. Now every time when I visit he tells me "come inside". We sit and smoke in the sitting room. But today, no. Thomasi comes outside, he shuts the door, and we go far, to sit under the mvuli to smoke.

But Thomasi is not happy. He is looking at the house, worried, and at the boat shelter where the mats are hanging down. I send the children with bananas to visit his sons' children, out at the back, there at the boat shelter, to give the bananas. They come back and we go home. I ask them "Those children at the back, in the boat shelter where the mats are hanging down, hiding everything, what are they doing?" They tell me the big boys chase them away, all of them, because they are busy there. Something they don't want people to see. "What something?" I ask. "Painting" the children say. They are painting a *kasese*. "What's wrong about the painting, to be hidden?" I ask. The children don't know. "What colour is the painting?" "It is sky colour." Jerome paused significantly, his eyebrows raised, 'You see, Sister? They are painting the small *kasese* blue.'

'Whew!' Perpetua sank back. 'Jerome, thank you! You didn't make them suspicious, did you?'

'Me, no. I see nothing. I do not look at the boat shelter, I do not look at the children. I do not ask Thomasi why he is a man with a snake in his stomach. I just buy some fish from him and I go home. It is all.'

'Well done. Thank you! Let's take the avocados to the kitchen. And thank Mrs Thompson for the help. We shall come again soon.'

She arrived out of breath at Mother's door. 'Come in!' Frances and Mother had their heads together. 'Ah, here she is! Any news?' Four anxious eyes scanned her face.

'Jerome's traced the little blue boat! In Bulebele Bay. A friend of his, Thomasi, lives there. Jerome said his older grandsons were painting a small *kasese* blue, behind hangings in the boat shelter. The children saw it while he sat and smoked with the old man.'

'Voilà!' said Mother. 'And while you have been busy, so have I, or rather, le Bon Dieu. I have just been telling Frances. I saw that old woman, a rather beautiful old woman, you said her name, Frances …'

'Namugasi.'

'Yes Namugasi, the one who gave Frances information about ancestral shrines and fetishes in her research on local artefacts. Well, I saw her standing singing. Like this,' Mother produced a thin quaver, 'bah! not like that – I cannot do it. Something about gifts, I think, and neglected shrines and spirits of the forefathers. It was rather an eerie sort of singing.'

'She may have learned it from her father who was a bit of a diviner, I think,' Frances suggested.

'Good grief, surely not!' Perpetua's eyebrows shot up her forehead. 'Mother, you can't take this seriously!'

'Mais oui. It is what I heard.'

'You don't mean to involve us in heathen spiritism!'

'Namugasi has been a devout Catholic for years,' Frances reminded her.

Mother put her head on one side and frowned. 'I had the impression there was nothing wrong with what she sang. It was more like a tender regret for something lost.'

'Shrines and spirits — for crying out loud!'

'Family shrines do not harbour evil spirits.' Frances sighed patiently. 'Only those of the family who have passed on and watch over their children. The living family members leave little gifts at the shrine as tokens of respect and remembrance, just as our girls leave flowers and sweets for the Madonna.'

'A beautiful gesture.' Mother nodded approvingly.

'No, I'm sorry. We cannot get mixed up in ancestor worship!'

'Perpetua — we know perfectly well that "ancestor worship"

was a crude misnomer coined by nineteenth-century anthropologists in the early days of the discipline. It has been discredited and replaced by, "Reverence for family ancestors."'

'Hmph! Anyhow, what does it have to do with those wretches and Ignatia?'

'I do not have the faintest idea.' Mother shrugged. 'I only know what I saw and heard. Frances, you know where Namugasi lives. Would you find her for us?'

***

Namugasi was sitting on the ground against a hut wall, warming her legs in the afternoon sun. She was helping a small granddaughter weave *makeka* matting. Namugasi sent her scuttling for a chair and Frances sat down. It was discourteous to skimp Namugasi's solicitous enquiries into the health of St Mary's staff, but Frances did her best to make it brief. At last Namugasi said, 'You are looking for Nampa? She is hoeing *enjugus*. The children are in trouble at school?'

'No, no, not at all. It is you I have come to speak with, Namugasi. Mother Superior needs your help. Can you come to her now?'

The beautiful old face lit up in surprise, 'The Holy Mother is calling for me?'

'She is.'

'Then I am coming. Namiri, tell Máma I have gone with Sister Frances to St Mary's School. To speak with Holy Mother,' she added.

When Frances brought Namugasi into the refectory Perpetua, who was marking physics homework, looked up briefly and then down again in stony silence, ignoring the old woman's shy smile and greeting. Frances led Namugasi into Mother's sitting room and closed the door. In fluent Luganda, Mother told Namugasi of Ignatia's kidnapping, the explosives and the small blue boat while Namugasi smothered her exclamations behind her hand as elderly Baganda women still do. 'We don't know what the boys want to blow up, or why they're painting the small *kasese* blue, Namugasi. What matters is that we get Ignatia back very soon. The exams are close. She has to do well if she wants to become a doctor.'

'To study for doctor is very good. We need the doctors for our women and children very much, Holy Mother. I will help. Thomasi, I know him. We are old people. Sometimes he comes to our place and we talk. We remember together about the old things. But today the young people forget the spirits of their family. They leave one egg or two eggs only at the shrine instead of a chicken as we did before. Thomasi tells me his people are forgetting. He tells me the spirits are sighing. We old ones, we still hear them sigh among the banana trees when the sun is high.'

'Your father was one who could sing the spirit songs, wasn't he?'

'You remember that, Holy Mother?'

'Can you do that, Namugasi?'

Namugasi looked at her feet and then glanced up at Mother. 'Yes,' she whispered and hid a smile behind her hand.

'Could you do it for us? To bring fear into the hearts of those people who have stolen Ignatia? So that they let her go without violence, with respect?'

'If Holy Mother wishes, I can do it.'

'You must help us tonight, Namugasi. The time is very little now.' Mother turned to Frances. 'If you could go and find Nambiya, we can organize a light supper for Namugasi and all of you. I think Namugasi must stay in here with me.'

Frances came back with coffee and a plate of sandwiches and

Namugasi was lifting a sandwich to her mouth when there was a sharp rapping on the door. Mother looked startled,

'Take Namugasi into my bedroom,' she whispered. 'I don't want anyone to see her.' Frances led Namugasi with her supper into Mother's bedroom. As she closed the door behind her, the rapping was reiterated imperiously.

Mother composed herself. 'Come in!'

The door burst open and Theodora marched in, dragging Perpetua with her. Her eyes were blazing and her right fist was clenched round something, held with disgust in front of her.

'I have it, Mother! I have it – what is behind all this with Ignatia. I have it here!' She thrust out her hand. In it lay a packet of condoms, a tattered note and a folded letter. 'I found them in her drawer, hidden in the underwear. Read it!'

Mother took the note, pushed her spectacles down her nose and unfolded it. Then she read the letter. When she had read it she handed the note, letter and condoms to Perpetua who gasped, turned red and began to rub her forehead. Frances took the papers from her and read: 'To that beautiful one, Ignatia Tawanage. I am burning for you. I wish to meet with you. I have seen your beauty and your cleverness and when you dance it is the best in the world. My heart is very full of feelings. I give this to my sister to arrange it. Basilio.'

The little note replied: 'Meet me at the big tree at the end of the netball pitch.' Frances handed letter and note back to Mother.

'It is Ignatia's hand writing, is it not?' Mother held up the note.

Perpetua nodded, 'Yes, it is but – '

Theodora glared at her with contempt. 'It is obvious. She made an assignation. For sex, yes for sex! It is to be sex with one of those boys who have taken her. That is what it is. The condoms are the evidence.'

'Impossible.' Perpetua was rubbing her forehead. 'Ignatia would never do such a thing. Why did they trash the laboratory and steal zinc and ammonium nitrate if they only wanted ... wanted ... er – '

'If a girl writes a note to someone else to meet her at the tree, the note doesn't end up in her locker.' Frances pointed out. 'It's left in the hands of the receiver. Anyway, the girls always go to that tree when they want to share secrets. There's nothing strange about that.'

'Huh!' It was a triumphant snort. 'That note could have been dropped by the boys after they met at the tree.'

'But how on earth could Ignatia have got a note to them in the first place? None of this makes sense.' Perpetua was attempting patience but her knuckles were white over the chair arms. 'If this lout Basilio's sister is arranging it, she must be something to do with the school.'

'There are always ways,' Theodora fixed her huge eyes behind their magnifying glasses on her, 'for those who plan evil. The devil has his servants and that girl always has money. She could have bribed one of the kitchen staff.'

'But those boys live miles away at ...' Frances stopped as Mother gripped her arm.

'Theodora.' Mother sat up very straight. 'Leave this evidence with us. I will examine the matter thoroughly, I promise you. I would ask you, please, to keep it strictly between these walls. Thank you.' She nodded dismissal. Theodora gave her one long stare, then slowly turned to the door, let herself out and closed it behind her, not quietly.

Mother looked at Perpetua. 'You are right. It does not make sense, any of it. We have no time to go into it now. If we don't get Ignatia back tonight, tomorrow I have to call the police.

104

You have informed Gabriel, Frances? I trust her fortitude in unusual situations. Mark, I know, is willing to accompany you. I have explained to Daudi who will bring his sons. Dark clothing will be suitable. Perpetua, you wish to accompany them?'

For a moment Frances thought Perpetua's anger at the slur cast on Ignatia would spur her to her swift defence but she rose and shook her head. 'I want nothing to do with this tomfoolery. I cannot be involved in what that old woman stands for.' She turned and left the room.

Mother shrugged. 'Alors, time to get going, Frances. I have ordered sandwiches and coffee for you, Mark and Gabriel on my private verandah, out of the way, you understand.'

Frances hurried up to her room. When she came down and slunk out to the small verandah outside Mother's windows, Mark and Gabriel were there, wolfing down sandwiches. Mark smiled at her black slacks and shirt and old green bush hat.

Gabriel poured coffee and passed her a mug. 'Sure, Perpetua'll be sorry to miss the fun, won't she?'

'I doubt if it will be fun,' Frances sipped her coffee. 'I'm sorry she won't be with us for Ignatia's sake – especially if she's in distress of any kind. Heaven knows what we'll find when we track her down.'

Gabriel dug her with an elbow, 'Try her one more time.' Frances slunk round the corner into the main verandah and peered into the refectory window. All other sisters were away on supper and preparation duties but Perpetua's stern profile was bent over a pile of exercise books.

Frances summoned her courage and went in. 'Perpetua, won't you think again? For Ignatia's sake, you could show some solidarity. If she's scared or hurt, it's you she'll need more than anyone else, don't you think?'

The marking hand did not relent, though Perpetua's left hand began to rub her forehead.

'No one else will ever know what we do tonight. We do realize what it means to the school's reputation.'

Perpetua did not quite slam down her pen but Frances felt the table wince.

'Come on. We won't let anything un ... unseemly happen. It's only an old ghostly voice chanting to scare some silly kids, that's all. When it's dark we'll go. There's coffee and sandwiches on Mother's verandah. No one will see us.'

Perpetua pushed back her chair, rose, stalked out of the room and up the stairs. When she joined them on the little verandah she was wearing long black slacks and shirt, black canvas shoes and a dark green cotton hat rammed over her short grey hair. Without smiling she accepted a sandwich and coffee held out by Gabriel. When she put her mug back on the table she sat and twisted her fingers between bony knees,

'Well, where's Daudi? Can we really trust George and Michael to keep their mouths shut? Where's the old woman?'

'She's with Mother. I'll fetch her when they come,' Frances murmured.

Mark looked at his watch and then into the night sky.

'Seven-thirty. They should be here any minute. We're lucky there's no moon tonight.'

Presently they heard the crunch of boots on gravel. Frances ducked inside to retrieve Namugasi as Daudi, George and Michael, clad in dark green bush-clothes with *rungus* in their hands, strode purposefully to the verandah steps. 'Sister Perpetua, we are ready. We must go now. It is far to Bulebele.' Perpetua stood on the steps and peered past them. Beyond the lawns the mango trees hulked black. Stars winked over them. The only other light was the very faint luminosity of the lake that never quite died. 'Is it really dark enough, Daudi? We *must not* be seen!'

'It's not going to get much darker,' Mark muttered. 'No one's going to see us going over the lawns past the chapel, for sure.'

'Alright,' a deep dry sigh. 'Lead the way, Daudi.'

Daudi headed across the lawns and then into the black shadows of the mango trees. Michael and George walked behind him. Frances followed them, carrying a dark cotton bag in one hand, with Namugasi beside her. Gabriel and the reluctant Perpetua trod at their heels while Mark brought up the rear. Once they were over the crown of the hill Daudi switched on a powerful torch and its ray led them without stumbling down the twisting path to the bridge in the valley. Here the tinkling chorus of frogs fell silent and resumed again as their footsteps died away in the dust of the road leading to the lake shore. When they had passed the last *shambas*, Daudi took a little path to the right, skirting banana groves. They climbed steeply to the high, flat summit of a hill and the evening sounds of the homesteads receded. A distant radio buzzed like an insect, singing and laughter dimmed to small bird voices. The lower slopes and the valleys were where people lived, close to roads and water. The lonely hilltops were where goats browsed and cattle grazed. They walked into silence and a soft breeze. No one saw them except startled plovers that rose and bleated overhead.

It was easy walking until Daudi led them into a narrow, forested valley and over a small river with five fording stones. They climbed another hill and then descended into another valley where the path narrowed into a runnel through papyrus. Here Daudi helped Namugasi with solicitude over quaking logs in deep black mud. They climbed again onto a long ridge running east towards the lake. Half an hour later they stood on the crown of a lumpy, forested hill. Here the path petered out. Daudi stopped and extinguished his torch. 'Máma Namugasi says down there is Thomasi's place.' He pointed between two trees.

At their feet, the forested slope plunged steeply to where banana groves and cassava beds surrounded a cluster of huts huddled dark against the dim white curve of Bulebele Bay.

'Now we must go down. Carefully, Sister, carefully. Walk just after me.' Daudi beckoned Perpetua to his side. 'Putting your feet sideways, like this, like this. Michael, hold Máma Namugasi so she does not fall. George, help Sister Frances.'

Slowly, a hen ushering chicks, Daudi pushed his way downhill through saplings, lianas and thorny undergrowth while they slithered behind him. When they stood at last at the edge of the banana groves Daudi raised his hand. 'Now it is time. Máma, come. Begin!'

Namugasi, a translucent ghost in her *basuti*, stood a moment looking down at the dark huts. Lights glowed dull orange in two windows. A dog barked. Mark scuffed his foot on a root and cursed softly. The dog barked again and then silence fell. Muttering to herself, Namugasi stepped into a path that descended into the banana groves. At the edge of the forest, Frances spotted what she was looking for and left the cotton bag containing a white chicken under a tiny thatched mushroom on stilts.

Suddenly, from the groves below, rose an eerie wailing. The hair crawled on Frances's neck as the lamenting of ghosts shivered under the black trees near the huts. Perpetua stopped with a jerk and Frances walked into her. The shivering wails increased in intensity. A door flew open and a figure dashed from a hut. Shouts and cries came from an open window. Two dark figures broke from a hut on the far right and fled along the shore. Presently they heard the crunch of wood being dragged over sand.

'Damn, they're getting away!' Mark pushed forward, 'We must stop them!'

Daudi grasped his arm, 'Not yet. It is less trouble if they run away.'

'But they've got explosives!'

'It is good they go with the explosives. Now nothing bad can happen here.'

The eerie quavering floated between the huts as Namugasi approached them, hidden in deep shadow. Another door banged open and two more figures fled along the glimmering sand.

'Now we go!' Daudi switched on his powerful flashlight. With his sons at his heels, brandishing *rungus* with bloodcurdling shouts, he plunged through the banana trees.

'Better stay here!' Mark cautioned the sisters, 'Till the worst's over.' He ran round the huts to the right and sprinted for the shore. 'Come back, you idiots! Come back!' But when he reached the spot where the furrows of two prows had gouged the sand, only a distant slap of paddles answered him.

There was a shout as Daudi wrenched open a door and lamplight fell over peanut beds and orange cannas, 'Come! She is here!'

Perpetua pushed through slapping banana leaves with Frances and Gabriel at her heels. As Perpetua reached the huts, a familiar form stood etched against yellow light. 'Ignatia!' Perpetua stumbled towards her. 'Ignatia! Oh, thank God we've found you!'

Frances witnessed something she'd never thought to see, as Perpetua sprang to clasp a lost daughter to her heart. 'I've been so worried. I couldn't forgive myself. Oh, dear God, what a mercy! You *are* all right, aren't you? They haven't hurt you?'

Gracefully Ignatia disengaged from Perpetua's embrace and

smiled. 'But, Sister, you trust in God! Surely you knew I would be all right.'

'But the exams! I was so worried you'd be too upset to think and ...'

'Sister, you will not be ashamed.' She drew Perpetua into a square hut with white-washed mud walls. Gabriel and Frances stood at the door and peered in. At the far end of the room a lamp stood on a small square table. On each side of it stood a chair. Against the right and left walls were beds raised high on bricks and covered with bright cotton bedspreads. In the middle of the room Daudi was kneeling over an old man lying in a foetal position and groaning loudly. Daudi wrestled thick twine loose from his ankles and wrists and helped him up to sit on a bed. He turned as they came in. 'It is Thomasi. They tied him.'

The old man moaned and rocked, rubbed his wrists and wailed. 'They tie me. I am father's father and they tie me like a chicken!' Then he sat up straight and stared at the nuns in the doorway. 'Eh. It is everybody here! It is the sisters. They have come to find her. They have come here. It is good. See, she is well. Nothing has happened to this girl. She is well, Sisters. I am taking care.'

Ignatia had gone to the table and lifted a tattered child's exercise book. She held it out to Perpetua. The pages were covered in neat mathematical and chemical formulae.

'Those stupid boys!' Ignatia laid down the book and clasped the old man's hands. 'They tied him up when he tried to stop them. But they did not hit him.'

'Máma Namugasi, where is Máma Namugasi?' Daudi peered outside. Namugasi was standing, shyly illumined, beside a bed of cannas. 'Máma, come inside to comfort your friend. He is much shaken up. Thomasi, it is Máma Namugasi. She has helped us.'

With gentle dignity Namugasi entered and sat down on the bed next to Thomasi, 'Bába, who does this to you?'

'Sons of my sons!'

'Eh, that is bad.'

'They do not respect me,' the old man moaned. 'They do not listen.'

'They hurt you very much?'

Thomasi looked briefly at his scuffed wrists and ankles,

'No. That does not worry a man. It is here,' he patted his shirt front with a fist. 'It is here it is hurting.'

'I know,' Namugasi sighed. 'I know, Bába.'

'Grandfather,' Ignatia bobbed before him, 'shall I make tea?'

'Yes, make tea. For our visitors, for everybody!'

'Is it safe?' Perpetua clutched her favoured chick. 'Where are those boys of yours?'

'They are gone!' It was almost a wail. 'They are gone away to do this thing.' Again he beat his heart and his head fell over his chest while Namugasi clucked and soothed. At last he looked up again. 'Yes, my daughter, make the tea.'

Ignatia lit a candle in a tin holder on the table and went out to a hut at right angles to the bedroom. Perpetua stood outside to watch over her, peering now and then into the dark gardens while Ignatia remained in the kitchen hut. Presently they heard the pumping and then the hiss of a primus stove. Perpetua remained doggedly on guard.

Mark looked at Thomasi, 'Where have the boys gone?'

'They go to blow up the boats at Makubenge's. They bring this girl to make the explosives. They paint one *kasese* blue to hide it with those boats of Makubenge's, to look the same. They put the explosives in the blue *kasese*. They take the other *kasese* for coming back. They are gone. When they hear the spirits they go quickly. I tell them, you cannot do this thing. It will bring trouble. But they do not listen. I run to them, I try to stop it. But they tie me … you see how they tie me. Me, father's father.'

'So …' Mark whistled. 'That's what it's all about. Blowing up Makubenge's boats.'

'Sure,' Gabriel murmured. 'I hope it's a very long fuse. How much explosive have they got?'

'Enough to do a lot of damage.' Mark looked at Perpetua.

'D'you think there's enough time to phone Makubenge's and warn them?'

'We could try,' Gabriel looked at her watch. 'We could go back along the shore, it's much quicker, and phone from Toni's.'

'Strewth! So much for science. This could have repercussions. The school's involved whether we like it or not,' Mark muttered.

Just then Ignatia entered with a tray of tin mugs and a large enamel teapot. She poured and gave the first mug to Thomasi and offered sugar. Thomasi put in six spoonfuls, stirred and sipped with a deep, comforting slurp while Namugasi stirred her tea. An assuaging silence fell over the room. Enamel mugs winked in the light of the hurricane lamp that sent shadows gesticulating up the walls. Daudi and Perpetua, his lady of honour, sat on chairs at each side of the table. Michael, George and Mark hunkered on the floor. Thomasi and Namugasi sat on one bed, facing Gabriel, Frances and Ignatia on the other.

The silence was long and grateful until Mark looked at Ignatia. 'How much explosive *did* you put together for them?' Ignatia lifted a smiling face from the blue mug in her hands. 'Those boys!' she shook her head. 'Bába, have you told them?'

'I tell them everything. I am ashamed.'

'No, Bába. Not everything. But I am free of the oath now?'

'You need not fear. I have told for you.'

'Then I can tell them what I did not have to swear not to tell.' She sipped her tea again. 'They brought me here, telling me they would not hurt me if I made the explosive. Why, I asked, what for? They said they wanted to blow up some of Makubenge's boats because Makubenge is eating them, taking their fish, coming into their water. They said they had complained but Makubenge does not listen, so now they must do this. They said everybody is blowing up other people when they do not listen. It is on TV, on the radio, in the films. It is the best thing.'

'Idiots!' Mark groaned. 'What sort of fuse did they make?'

'Wait.' Ignatia smiled again. 'I have not finished yet. Those boys are not too stupid, really. They read well. They took the right boxes. But they didn't know how much ammonium nitrate, how much zinc to use. If I made it the right way, they would be nice to me. If I refused to make it, they would hurt me. What could I do? It is nearly time for the exams. I must not delay. So I tell them I must do many calculations on paper to get it right. They bring me an exercise book and I practise my theorems and my chemical formulae. I tell them it takes a whole morning to do these calculations. Those boys do not understand higher maths. It is all right. I know you will come looking for me. I play for time. In the afternoon I pretend to start putting the components together. I work very slowly, very exactly. But of course I am not going to let those silly boys get into big trouble. I pretend to do it right but I put too little ammonium nitrate with too much zinc. Then I package it very carefully, making a big story about working very slowly with chemicals. The boys are painting the *kasese* with blue paint they have bought from town. They are cross with everyone. They keep looking in at the door telling me to hurry. I tell them, if I hurry there will be an explosion in the house. I ask them if they want everybody here to die. I say, "Leave me alone, I am getting on with it!"' Ignatia beamed into a shocked silence.

Mark started laughing first. Perpetua's exhalation of relief was followed by a chuckle from Gabriel. 'You're a bright girl, dear.'

'So the ruddy thing won't go off at all?' Mark raised an eyebrow.

'It will not explode. Those boys are going to be very tired for nothing.'

'They won't come and get revenge, will they? I mean when the thing doesn't go off, when they realize you've tricked them?' Perpetua gripped Ignatia's arm. 'Perhaps we should set guards all around the school now?'

'Thomasi,' Frances put her hand on his arm, 'what do you think the boys will do when the explosion does not happen?'

Thomasi rocked back and forth. 'I do not know. I am ashamed. Too much ashamed.'

'Should we tell the police? Get Seargent Kakonge to put the fear of God in them?' Perpetua suggested.

'Sure, fear of Seargent Kakonge himself would be enough,' muttered Gabriel.

'It's all so complicated.' Perpetua frowned and looked thoughtfully at Thomasi. 'Surely, they must have known that if they let Ignatia go, as they promised, that she would be bound to tell us. Especially if Makubenge's boats were badly damaged.'

'Eh-eh!' old eyes held hers with confidence. 'She will die if she does it. They made her swear the oath. It is a very strong oath.'

'Good gracious! They surely don't believe in that rub− !' Frances broke into a fit of coughing and gripped Perpetua's arm.

'Oh yes, they believe.' Thomasi was unshaken. 'I teach them. That they believe. They like to forget other things, but they are afraid of the oath. They know that if Ignatia tells anybody she will die.'

It was Gabriel who broke the silence, 'Well, sure then, Bába, they are happy because they know she will not tell, and we are happy too because Ignatia is safe.'

'Yes, we are all happy. Jésu Christu-Máma Méri *webalî*! She is safe and everybody is happy and Thomasi's son's sons will not die.' Namugasi's smile lit the room.

'Máma, the spirits are still with us and they will be happy too. I thank you for calling. We have shown respect. It will get better now, from the respect.'

Suddenly Daudi yawned cavernously. Then he fixed Thomasi with a stern gaze, 'Bába, from not reporting this thing to us, from not telling us where Ignatia was, you have caused great fear, great heaviness to Sister Perpetua, to all the sisters and ...' with slow and deadly emphasis, 'to the Holy Mother. Is that good? Why did you not send a small boy with a *kipandi* telling us, do not worry she is safe?'

Thomasi writhed for a moment, struck to the heart. Then he lifted yellowed eyes and returned look for look. 'Because now, today, she is going back to school. They promise me, those boys, as soon as they go to Makubenge's, I let her go back. In the morning, very early, with the torch Namutange must take her back, Wachanga way, to the school. Only two days, she is missing.'

Daudi held the old man's eyes for a moment. Then he looked at Perpetua. His shirt began to flutter, his huge chest rose and fell in suppressed laughter. 'All this!' Spade-wide hands slapped his knees. 'All this trouble for nothing! This girl would have come back to school this morning!'

'Hell's bells,' Mark groaned. Gabriel's chuckle shook the bed and Perpetua sank her head in silence.

'Ignatia,' Frances held out her mug, 'is there any more tea before the walk home?'

The star pupil of St Mary's lifted the teapot with maidenly modesty and poured more tea into thirsty mugs.

Thomasi's eyes followed her with glistening devotion. 'This girl will be the good daktari, Sister Perpetua. She is a clever girl. Also, she is kind and she is respectful. Yes, she is respectful.'

'Eh, eeeeh!' Namugasi, wagging her head, sighed beside him. 'She is daughter of Máma Méri. She will do well.'

***

They left the quiet homestead where Thomasi now lay on his bed under a blanket spread by Ignatia and Namugasi, his heart and spirit at peace. The rescue party tramped homeward along the shore, their tired feet crunching in still-warm sand. Daudi and George strode in front, a powerful torch beam probing the darkness before them. Close behind them walked Ignatia with Perpetua's arm linked protectively in hers and Michael safeguarding her right hand. Gabriel and Mark ambled behind them, relishing the sand under their feet and walking without torchlight in the gleam of sand and low white waves. Frances linked her arm with Namugasi's. The old woman, thin and agile enough for the long walk to Bulebele, was feeling her age now and tottered slightly over tussocks of grass in deep sand.

Frances let her pause to regain her breath. 'It is heavy, this walk. Me too, the grandmother, I wish to rest,' she murmured, quite truthfully, in Luganda.

Namugasi rested one hand on her knee and kneaded her lower back with the other hand. Then she straightened up and stared resolutely ahead to where Mark and Gabriel had stopped to wait for them. 'It is nothing. We have done it. This girl is safe now. Holy Mother will be happy.'

Presently they climbed the promontory at the end of Bulebele Bay and passed the silent village of Wachanga where a couple of *shenzies* barked at them. They were passing a cluster of beached *kaseses*, black pods on silver sand, when Mark suddenly said, 'Sister Frances, this thing of the little blue boat that Mother Julienne saw – I mean, is she a psychic or something?'

'Well ... charismatic,' Gabriel interposed. 'Ever heard of the charismatic movement?' Mark shook his head. 'Ach, the pagan English,' she glanced mischievously at Frances.

'Well, it was when the Holy Spirit ...' Frances began.

'Ever heard of that?' Gabriel teased.

'Erm, not really. My family aren't church goers. But my grandmother was and I vaguely remember her mentioning a Holy Ghost.'

'That's the one but they've updated the name.' Gabriel dug her elbow into Frances.

'Well, in the seventies,' Frances dutifully began again, 'there was a great outpouring of the Spirit on the churches and there were healings and the ability to prophesy, and things like that. Mother once told me she'd been rather psychic as a child but had had it beaten out of her by a good, rational French education. But in the seventies the gift was given back and ... sort of amplified, I suppose. She learned to pray in a certain way and ... well things come to her that are very helpful. Does that make any sense to you?'

'Well, it wouldn't if it hadn't been for the little blue boat. But what was the point of it all if Ignatia would have returned safely today anyway?'

Gabriel, carrying her shoes and twisting her toes luxuriously in the sand, grinned. 'Ah, sure, the Lord likes a bit of fun. It made it a team effort – Jerome and Toni, Namugasi and Daudi and George and Michael and all. I've enjoyed meeting Thomasi and Namugasi.'

'And it saved Perpetua and Mother from desperation,' Frances added. 'Jean-Claude Kaburungu would have insisted on police intervention today. Think what would have happened if Kakonge had got involved. Imagine what he'd have done to Thomasi's boys. Instead we've had a lot of fun and got to know each other. And nobody who doesn't need to know, will ever know about it.'

'I guess you're right.' Mark stopped a moment and looked back at the fishing boats. 'Thomasi and Namugasi and these folk here … They're sort of unique, aren't they? It seems a pity.' He turned and they walked on again.

'What's the pity?' Gabriel prompted.

'It's unfair, what Makubenge's Fisheries are doing, destroying something so – ' He waved an arm at the graceful boats.

'Timeless and in harmony with this place.' Frances supplied.

'Yes. Greg, my friend working for Government Fisheries, says the whole lake ecosystem has been destroyed by the introduction of Nile perch and encroaching hyacinth and now over-fishing in areas like this … it's a dim show.'

'At least those fool kids are not going to be had up for murder or malicious damage to property. Ignatia's seen to that,' Gabriel muttered.

At last Daudi's torch illumined the papyrus of the tiny estuary ahead and swung left into the red dust of the road along the valley. They followed him until he stopped and detailed George to escort Máma Namugasi back to her home along the hill and they thanked her for her help and watched her walk away, a slender ghost beside the forbidding George with his sword of light.

As they turned to the bridge over the stream to follow Daudi uphill, Mark hesitated. 'That old woman's singing was weird, wasn't it. I mean, if I hadn't known it was her, it would have scared the hell out of me, even though I don't believe in ghosts and spirits.'

'Belief in the spiritual world is very strong in Africa.'

Mark nodded a little dubiously and picked a flake of bark off the wooden rail. 'But the shrines, these little huts on stilts – I saw you, Sister. You dumped that bag on the one at the edge of Thomasi's place.'

'Oh, you did, did you,' Frances snorted. 'It has a chicken in it. I snitched it from the back kitchen, before it got plucked. I thought it would buck Thomasi up. He's had a thin time of it. At least someone must respect his reverence for the ancestors.'

'But you don't believe in all that, do you?'

'I respect other people's beliefs. Think of the Roman shrines to the lares of the family, and the Shinto shrines in Japanese homes. They're exquisite and surrounded by photos of the beloved deceased. Rituals and symbolic offerings – there's nothing strange about the little shrines here.'

'Hmmm.' Mark stripped another piece of bark from the rail of the bridge.

Frances giggled. 'I have my own private family shrine in a shelf in my cupboard – photos of my parents and grandparents, my husband and my two sons. I sometimes tell them goodnight.'

'You didn't know this old nun was a widow, did yer?' Gabriel interrupted.

Frances gave her a dig with an elbow. 'Don't get personal now.'

'You started it.' Gabriel jabbed her back.

'True. But Thomasi and Namugasi have been steeped from

childhood in reverence for the spirits of their family. For the old people to be forgotten by their children was to die altogether. Only the remembrance of children and grandchildren kept their spirits alive after death. To forget your family ancestors was to cause their final death.'

'You don't believe that, surely?'

'I respect the dearly held beliefs of others.'

Mark gave her a skew look and removed another strip of bark, 'Africa's something else, isn't it.'

'Sure is.' Gabriel grinned. 'A big something else, and mind you don't turn up a scorpion under the next bit of bark.'

A beam of light from up the hill blinded them. Michael called, 'Are you very tired, Sister Frances? Can I assist?'

'I'm all right, thanks, Michael. We're coming.'

They trod the rough path illumined by a tutelary beam from above and found Michael waiting to light them home. Daudi was already striding over the lawns past the chapel taking Perpetua and Ignatia towards the school sanatorium where Sister Monique waited to smuggle her into the 'infectious' room. Mark sneaked to his car and drove off downhill with his dims on while Michael ushered Frances and Gabriel solicitously to the door of the nuns' house. As Gabriel opened the door, he flashed them an impudent grin and shook his head. 'All this trouble, all this trouble – and today the girl is home! Sister Perpetua is happy now!'

Frances stopped at the refectory table, wrote a note and pushed it under Mother's door. Then she dragged herself upstairs and fell asleep in mud-spattered clothes.

6. Home and Dry

Ignatia spent the following day in the sanatorium. She slept until three in the afternoon and was visited only by Perpetua who arrived with afternoon tea and homework.

The few who noted the heavy eyes and frequent yawns of three sisters during morning chapel put it down to late-night marking and passed no whispered comments. At the end of the little service Mother asked first- and second-year A-level pupils to remain seated. She informed them that Ignatia had returned safely to school, that she had not been harmed in any way, that nothing more was to be said of the matter, and no questions asked. Frances noted that Nasuna's eyes suddenly brimmed with tears. She bowed her head, crossed herself and gave Perpetua a shy and adoring smile as the girls rose and filed out of the chapel. Frances also darted a covert glance at Theodora who pursed her withered mouth as she rose from her stall and stalked down the aisle staring grimly at Mother's head preceding her towards the chapel door.

Frances sighed as she headed to the art room. Once Theodora sank her teeth into someone ... Hopefully Mother would untangle this knot before bitter upsets occurred.

They were all settled with their cups of mid-morning tea in the staff room when Theodora cleared her throat and fixed her huge eyes on Mother Julienne: 'You are taking the matter in hand, Mother? It cannot wait too long. It is a serious threat to the school.'

Such was the ominous portent in her face that Annunciata, sitting beside her, looked anxiously from Theodora to Mother and whispered, 'What is this threat?'

Mother put down her teacup. 'The matter will be attended to.'

'We must erect a fence round this school. I have said it before. It is time now.' Theodora bit into a biscuit and continued to stare Mother down.

'A fence round the school? Absurd!' Mattea raised a sarcastic eyebrow.

'How will people come to mass?' Agnes cried.

'A fence would mean gates with guards at them and – '

'Yes, I like it! Nobody will steal my chickens again!' Consolata leaned forward eagerly.

'We could never afford it!' Felicitas shook her head. 'Never in a million years.'

'You will see,' Theodora munched and nodded significantly. 'When you know what I know, you will see. It is only the blind who do not see what is happening to this school.'

'Enough!' Mother rose, lifted her chin and pronounced, 'There will be no further discussion of this matter. We have been alarmed at what happened to Ignatia. From now on we shall employ two more guards, as Mr Kaburungu has suggested. I give my word on that and there it ends.' A bell sounded the end of tea break and Mother left the room without looking back but Theodora stalked out after her, shaking her head and muttering under her breath.

Perpetua returned her cup to the table. 'Please, everyone, don't talk about Ignatia, especially in front of the girls. Calm is needed now, with exams coming.' She went out, rubbing her forehead, her eyes on the floor.

***

During the next few days, after giving French lessons and creative writing in Luganda, Mother interviewed A-level pupils, one by one, and sat cloistered with them in her classroom. On Thursday evening, after preparation supervision, she called Theodora, Perpetua and Frances to her sitting room. She was sitting very straight in her chair and holding a letter in her hand. When they were seated, she handed the letter to Theodora. 'This is from a pupil of yours, Sister. It is a confession and an apology.'

Theodora read in silence and then laid the letter on her lap. 'It is true?'

'I'm afraid so.'

'But ...'

'Please let Sister Perpetua read it.'

Very slowly Theodora handed the paper to Perpetua who read it and passed it to Frances. 'Sister Theodora,' she read, 'I am making my confession now. I have made it already before Mother. It is I who put the letter and the note and the condoms in Ignatia's drawer. It is Pretty Mukasa who brought the note and the condoms from her brother Basilio who is very hot for Ignatia. He has seen her many times at the school prize giving and the concerts and he wishes to speak his heart for her. He is a man now and is going with girls and he knows about the condoms so no danger can come.

'It is I who added the note from Ignatia to Namkya for meeting at the tree. I found it fallen under Namkya's bed. I did it for a joke to pull Ignatia down because she is always so high. Mother tells me it is jealousy that made me do this joke and it could make big trouble for Ignatia. I am sorry for it now. I offer my apologies for causing this worry to you, Sister Theodora. I am yours sincerely, Joyce.'

Frances looked up at Mother. 'Joyce Kalema?'

Mother nodded and Frances understood – poor unattractive Joyce with her square, sullen features. No, it had not been a joke but long-simmering resentment that had found an outlet in malice, bound to lead to trouble. All the girls were aware of Theodora's snooping and were afraid of it. But what a useful weapon it could be. And now the foolish Joyce would be a victim of Theodora's wrath. She handed the letter back to Mother who took it, leaned forward and put her hand on Theodora's knee. 'My dear, now we know the truth, we must forgive this poor, silly child.'

'It is that Pretty Mukasa who is behind it! I have warned you! I have warned you many times of the danger these day-girls bring to the school. I am going to phone her parents and tell them the bad influence that girl is here!' Theodora rose and reached for the door.

Kindness had failed. Mother rose. 'You will do nothing of the sort! I forbid it! Sit down, Sister!'

Very slowly Theodora took her seat again but her mouth was an indrawn trap and her eyes blazed enormous. Mother's eyes met them, implacable, and she remained standing. 'You are trespassing on my authority, Sister. It is my prerogative and mine alone to speak with the parents of my girls on their performance here. I and no one else shall speak with Mrs Mukasa about her daughter's behaviour. Do you understand?' Theodora gave a slight inclination of her head and looked at a hole forming in the threadbare carpet under Mother's chair.

'Very well. And one thing more. You are to treat Joyce with kindness. Her final exam results are as important to you as they are to her. Do not spoil the years of excellent tuition you have given her, by making her a victim of your anger now. Forgive her and show your forgiveness to ease her mind so that she may do herself justice in her finals. Your own reputation is at stake. Understood?'

Only Frances understood Mother's despair at having to appeal to a nun's reputation as teacher, rather than her compassion for those she taught.

Theodora heaved a weary sigh. 'I will do it.' She rose and gripped her hands together. 'But I will return to discuss discipline, Mother Julienne.'

'Thank you, Sister Theodora. And we must remember that discipline begins with self-discipline, doesn't it?'

Theodora drew herself up and made for the door. When it had shut behind her, Mother slumped back in her chair and sighed. 'I have failed. Still I fail with that poor Theodora. Bon Dieu, can anything be done? I do not know. Well, it is finished now, this little affair. Perpetua, how is Ignatia – in herself, I mean?'

'I think she's come through it better than I have.' Perpetua gave a down-turned smile. 'It hasn't affected her work at all.'

'Très bien.' Mother smiled. 'Apropos of that, Toni Thompson phoned me the morning after, asking if we'd got her back safely. She was overjoyed to hear that Jerome's information had been of help. In fact, she has invited all who participated in Ignatia's rescue to tea with her, to hear the end of the story from Jerome. I said that two hours next Friday afternoon, from four to six, would be permissible. You are agreeable?'

'Oh, definitely!' Frances grinned and rose.

Perpetua merely shrugged. 'It would be the polite thing to do, I suppose.' But Frances thought she caught a slight gleam of suppressed curiosity in her eyes.

Mother hid a yawn behind her hand. 'Alors, bonne nuit, mes filles!'

***

Frances sank into a deck chair on Toni's verandah and breathed a glad sigh. The huge flowers of a goblet creeper were dripping vanilla-scented sunlight over the low wall where the two mongooses lay soaking up its warmth. A murmurous benediction of laughing doves surrounded the guests assembled to celebrate Ignatia's retrieval. Toni presided in a battered cane chair with Clementine asleep on her lap, while dogs banished to the lawn for pungent offences regarded the company with longing eyes. George and Michael had business in town, but Daudi and Mark had accompanied the three nuns, on Toni's insistence.

Jerome, in major-domorial magnificence – white *kanzu*, gold-embroidered waistcoat and scarlet fez – had laid a feast over a spotless tablecloth on the battered verandah table. There were platters of mashed avocado on biscuits, whipped avocado dips with wafers, his own famous cheese straws, milk-sweet peanuts from the garden, anchovy eggs and curried fish garnished with green pepper, mango and avocado slices.

Beaming at his guests, Jerome poured his homemade lemonade, clinking with ice, into three tall glasses for the sisters and handed them with small bows. Then he opened Tuskers and poured beers for Daudi, Mark and himself. Finally, with a flourish, a whisky and soda for Toni. She winked at him and raised her glass. 'To Ignatia. She seems to have shown great presence of mind in her trials.'

Perpetua smiled primly and even raised her glass while murmurs of 'Here's to Ignatia, God bless her!' and the clink of glasses passed among the guests.

'To Jerome,' Mark piped up, 'who traced the blue *kasese!*'

Jerome permitted himself a small smile and raised his own glass of Tusker.

'First class recce!' Mark added.

'To Daudi of the mighty arm!' Gabriel cried. 'To George and Michael!'

'To Namugasi – fearful haunter!' Frances murmured.

'Me,' Jerome nodded, 'I drink to the Sisters of St Mary's School!'

'To si-yence!' Mark cocked a mocking eyebrow at Perpetua. He turned to Jerome. 'Tell us what happened afterwards. Did those boys get to Makubenge's?'

'They arrived.' Jerome leaned back against a pillar and shook his head. 'Eh, they arrived there. Thomasi tells me everything. They tow the blue *kasese* and leave it between two boats of Makubenge's. They light the fuse and they paddle away and wait in the bush there by the swamp. They wait, they wait. They hear nothing. No explosion – nothing! The sun rises. Makubenge's boats go out. The boys go back to Makubenge's, to the *shambas* there. They look for the blue *kasese*. It is not there. They ask people, have they seen a small blue *kasese?* Yes, some boys have found a blue *kasese* with a box. They have thrown the box away and they are happy to have a new boat. These grandsons of Thomasi, they find those boys and they tell them, "This is our boat."

'Those that found the boat say, "Where are you from? You are not from this place."'

'"We are from over there, that side." '

'"Then this is not your boat, you are lying. How is your boat here?" Those boys of Thomasi's, they don't want to tell them. So they come home and their *kasese* is taken. It is all trouble for nothing.'

'Good old Ugandan justice!' Toni croaked.

'God sees.' Daudi nodded over his beer.

'Thomasi is happy now,' Jerome continued. 'He says a gift has been left at the shrine, a chicken, a white one, and the spirits will guard his children now. Also, the family are giving as they used to give. Not one egg, but six and pawpaws and sweet bananas. From now on it will go well at his place.' Jerome chuckled and shook his head again.

'I'm sorry for them.' Mark helped himself to another cheese straw. 'Why is it that small initiatives always get squeezed out by the big sharks? I'm not surprised Thomasi's boys are fed up.'

Jerome shrugged. 'They must go and find work in Kampala. There are factories now. Maybe,' he gave a sly hitch of the shoulder, 'maybe they can ask for work at Makubenge's?'

'I agree, it's a shame.' Toni held out her glass and Jerome ceremoniously tipped a bottle and pumped an aged soda siphon. 'These families have fished here for generations. Makubenge's have the motor power to take them right out over the lake. In spite of the water hyacinth there's no need for them to encroach on our water here.'

Mark examined a stuffed egg thoughtfully. 'My friend Greg Turner's doing a two-year research stint at the Fisheries

Department. I wonder, what's their take on traditional fishing communities?'

'Try and find out,' Toni said. 'I wouldn't be surprised if they're sympathetic. There've been reports of serious overfishing in some areas, while the fish-export boom was on. Now it's declining and they're in trouble. At least our locals only fish to support their families and are not responsible for the overfishing. Find out and let me know. Maybe we could make a plan for the chaps along the shore, if we could get their co-operation. I think they trust me, don't they, Jerome?'

'*Mamsab*, they think you are very strange – all these animals. But they like you. You don't buy Makubenge's fish, you buy only from our people, only our *kikapus* and bananas and you take the children to hospital and give them small medicines. And always you pay for the animals from the snares.'

'Well then?' Toni cocked her head at Mark and he nodded.

'Jerome.' Perpetua's forehead creased. 'Are Thomasi's boys angry with Ignatia? I was afraid they might be resentful and try to get their own back on her? Did Thomasi say anything about it?'

'They say only that girl is stupid. Too stupid to get it right, the explosion. She will fail her exams.'

Perpetua relaxed into her chair. Ignatia was safe and exams could proceed in orderly calm.

'I tell Thomasi, seeing the great worry of Sister Perpetua, that if the boys from his place come near the school again, we will call Sergeant Kakonge to their place.' Jerome gave her a sly grin.

'Thank you, Jerome. I don't suppose they like him any more than we do. Here's to Sergeant Kakonge!' Toni raised her glass.

'Thank the Lord we did without him this time!' Gabriel clinked her glass against Toni's and took another forkful of curried fish. 'Jerome, would you write down this fish recipe for Consolata? It's delicious.'

'We mustn't forget to thank Namugasi,' Frances murmured in her ear. 'What would we have done without her? Some chickens would be welcome, I think, and cloth for a *basuti*?'

'Kampala market?' Gabriel's eyes kindled. 'Tomorrow?'

'I think we'll find everything there.'

Toni bent over Clementine and tinkled the silver bell at her elbow. 'Time for drinkies, my love. She's only been taking half her bottle. I keep trying bits in between.'

'It's not like Clementine to sleep when there's company, Toni,' Perpetua frowned, 'usually she sits up and takes notice.' Toni shook her head and stroked a small, folded arm. Black-haired fingers reached languidly for her hand and then fell back on Toni's lap. Clementine opened her eyes and then closed them again. 'She's not herself. I'm worried.'

Nazala appeared on the kitchen path and passed a bottle over the low wall to Toni. 'Come now, lovely, just try ...' Silence fell as all eyes turned to the woebegone face of Clementine who sucked for a moment, then turned her head away and buried her face in Toni's dress. Frances sniffed the aura of a very sick child, an old, familiar smell, but Gabriel's eyes were melting and she inched closer till her knees touched Toni's. Gently she reached out and stroked long toes that curled under at her touch. 'She's so human, such a little babby, aren't yer darling.' Sad eyes swivelled to hers and toes fastened slowly over her hand. 'Ah, mother, if ever you want a baby-sitter, you've found one, Mother Julienne permitting, of course. But if she set eyes on you ...'

The reverent silence of Clementine's audience was broken by footsteps on the path. Toni peered expectantly. 'Ah, here he is. Doctor Pilkington's come to do your arm. You won't be naughty this time, will you? He's such a nice doctor ...'

Frances turned to see a dark-haired man with a short beard. His face was solemn but his eyes creased with humour as he surveyed the gathering on Toni's verandah. He came up the steps with a canvas bag and paused between the serval and the reposing duiker. 'I'm sorry to butt in, Mrs Thompson. How's my patient today? I see she's made friends with Gabriel – Sister Gabriel. Good afternoon, Sister?' He held out a hand to Perpetua.

'Sister Perpetua and Sister Frances and Mark,' Gabriel introduced them and Dr Pilkington shook hands and was offered a drink. 'Thank you. A beer would be nice. But I'd better look at Clementine first. I'm sorry, Mrs Thompson but it won't be pleasant for your guests. Shall we take her inside?'

'Don't take her away,' Gabriel refused to release the toes round her fingers.

'Well, if you don't mind then, on the couch, but a clean sheet over it would be best.' Dr Pilkington surveyed the moulting dog-haired couch without misgiving, but they could see he was definite about the sheet.

Jerome disappeared, returned with a folded sheet and spread it over the couch. Toni sat on the sheet, cradling Clementine, while the doctor fished in his bag for a box of medications and a clean bandage. Clementine knew what was coming, drew her lips back in a grimace and hid her face. Dr Pilkington unwound the bandage on her arm, bent over the wound and sniffed. 'I don't like the look of it. You've applied the antibiotic ointment four times a day?'

'Yes, absolutely.'

'You see, chimps, unlike us, have no subcutaneous fat. When they bound this little one, the cords cut to the bone. If we're not careful this could become a generalized infection, even osteomyelitis. Has she been off her food at all?'

Toni looked stricken. 'Yesterday and today she's only taken half. Should I have called you yesterday?'

'Hmmm. Hold her firmly.' He extracted a stethoscope and warmed it against his inner arm while he very gently took Clementine's pulse, drew down her lower eyelids and felt her forehead and under her arms. Then he felt the glands in her neck and put the stethoscope to her heart and chest. Not a soul moved. 'Hmmm. I'm afraid the infection's spread. I'll anoint the cut again and give her a jab. I'll come and give her another tomorrow morning – very early, Mrs Thompson, before ward rounds, if you don't mind. I'll leave you something to give her tonight.' He deftly cleaned, anointed and re-bandaged the wound. 'Now, I'll give her that injection, if two of you will hold her.'

Toni laid Clementine over her shoulder and Gabriel, to the manner born, Frances thought, held her round back and chest. The doctor opened a syringe and regarded her thoughtfully. 'Hmmm. Human infants are so much easier. Nice fat arms and buttocks. What do we do with Clementine, hm? A thigh perhaps?' He rubbed a spot on the back of her thigh with cotton wool and spirit, flicked it with his finger and slid in the needle. Clementine squirmed and whimpered and afterwards Gabriel gently massaged the insulted thigh.

'All over now, my love.' Toni rocked her child. 'Nice doctor, I told you so. She didn't scream at you like last time, Doc.'

'That's because she's too weak, Mrs Thompson. I'll be glad when she does scream.'

Frances noticed that Gabriel had moved away and was staring into the trees. Her face had turned strangely blank and Frances wondered if she was seeing those same long-fingered hands closing the eyes of dead children.

'Well, that's done.' Toni settled back in her chair and let

Clementine hide her face in her neck. 'Good job, Doc. She hardly felt it. How about that beer?'

'Yes, please.' He sat carefully in an old wooden deck chair, eschewed by earlier comers as being of dubious integrity and Frances held her breath as the canvas groaned, but just held. His eyes wandered to the half-empty platters and she rose and brought him a plate and snacks. 'Heap them up.' She winked.

'I recommend Jerome's cheese straws.' Her heart melted as he helped himself like an eager boy. 'I wonder if you had any lunch today?' He shook his head and swallowed a mouthful of anchovy egg. 'No time.'

'I thought not. Try the curried fish, it's excellent.'

Mark kept him company with another cheese straw. 'Do you often treat animals as well as humans?'

'Chimps are human!' Toni cried.

'You know what I mean.'

'With only one doctor to so many thousand of the population, I don't often get the chance. But when Mrs Thompson called me for Clementine, I couldn't resist. They are human, or rather, better. In my book the word "human" is a dubious compliment. Clementine's my first, but I often watched the vet treat them when I was a boy.'

'Where was that?'

'Here, in Kampala. My father was in the zoology department at Makerere and a bit of a primate enthusiast. Two orphaned babies found in Budongo were brought to us and we fostered them for a couple of years. We lived out at Kabonyolo, the agricultural campus, which made it possible. My mother did most of the work, of course. She dubbed them Mo and Minnie and we kept them till they were about two or three. Then they joined another couple of chimps at the Entebbe animal orphanage where they had a lot of fun – neat little sleeping quarters and a big run. They were a couple of hellions, actually. They used their plastic food bowls, red and yellow ones, as hats, seats and projectiles. They loved to hide round a corner, or behind a bush and jump out at us. I was just a small kid and they tackled me to the ground and jumped all over me. Or I'd be innocently mooning round the garden after butterflies and a flying banana or pawpaw peel would hit me smack in the face. I'm afraid I went howling back to Mummy, till she taught me to throw them back. I was allowed to aim a catapult with a squash ball at their backsides, only their backsides, when they got above themselves and messed up my dinkie games. But, actually, we had grand times with them. You won't believe the sense of humour chimps have. Warped humour, sometimes! Banana-skin humour. It's only when they get to about four that they get so strong they can be dangerous, especially if they throw a tantrum.'

Toni sighed and looked into Clementine's eyes. 'That's the trouble, my darling. In a few years this little person will tumble Jerome if she doesn't get her way. I'll have to say goodbye and you'll go away to the sanctuary and become a big, strapping girl with playmates and lovers. Provided Doctor gets you right again.'

Doctor smiled over a plate of curried fish. 'I'll do my best. Talking of Budongo, Mrs Thompson – '

'Toni, to you.'

'I'm Jeremy. Have you been there lately?'

Toni shook her head. 'I don't get away much from my waifs here. I hate going back to the Parks. Old memories … silly, I suppose.'

'I know what you mean, but I'd like to see Budongo again. My father collected butterflies. Have you ever seen the charaxes there? We used to take rotten bananas and chimp faeces and put them out as bait. We'd wait, very still, and they'd come down from the canopy. Sort of a flipping flight, like a leaf falling. Do you know the species?' He turned to Mark. Mark shook his head.

'Well, they're very interesting. They prefer decaying matter to flowers. Camouflage is their speciality. When the wings are closed you only see a dead leaf – yellow-brown, dull green. There's a seam running up them, like the vein of a leaf. But when the wings open – mother of pearl, golden orange, blue. My favourite was the tomato red as we called it. Bright red all over the upper wings. You know,' he turned to Toni, 'we caught those butterflies when I was a kid, but my father set them well and when I went to medical school in Edinburgh I took a case of charaxes with me and I used to open it and stare at them and I was back in Budongo again. Hot as an oven, smelling of stink ants and orchids, chimps calling and tree hyrax rasping all night. Those were holidays. We caught one of the largest butterflies in the world there. An acraea with a wingspan of two hands. They're a savannah species, but we found one on the forest outskirts. That has a case to itself.'

'Lucky devil,' Mark was far forward in his seat. 'Would you take a guy there if you went again?'

'Certainly. The only problem is when.'

'Perhaps even doctors take holidays?'

'If we get something nasty to deserve it. Cerebral malaria's in fashion right now but hardly worth the holiday. At this rate,' he lifted his glass as Toni proffered another Tusker, 'I'm not likely to qualify for beri-beri. Here's to beer and vitamin B!'

But Mark was not to be deflected. 'I wish I could get over to Western Uganda, to the parks and see the wild life. I've only really met it in textbooks and zoos. The thought of it all out there! I enjoy the teaching.' He turned quickly to Perpetua. 'But, wow, would I like to get in with a research team one day! Look at you, growing up with all that. What made you take up medicine, I mean, after living with chimps!'

'We had to leave Uganda in sixty-nine. Obote had been gunning for academics in the late sixties – you know, getting rid of critical intellectuals. Some were given only forty-eight hours to leave the country, families and all. My father did his best to work under the radar – animals being more important to him than humans. But we got out before Amin's men began on Makerere. We went to the Nairobi campus for a couple of years and then to Bristol where my father took up a zoo post. A bit of a living death to Dad, but at least he was with animals. He never stopped missing Africa. It gets under your skin. "Those who drink the waters of the Nile," sort of thing. By the way, be careful where you drink the waters of the Nile. I just grew up with an interest in things biological and opted for medicine. Somehow I couldn't opt for the UK. After med school I went to Cairns hospital in Australia and then to Papua New Guinea. I felt at home there. Same bush, tropical forest and same complaints as here.' He fell silent and stared into the garden.

'What about the fauna?' Mark asked.

'Oh, taipans, pythons of all types and flying foxes. You should go there.'

'Thanks, but I'm not finished here yet.' Mark shook his head and scowled. 'I don't see how anyone can want to spend time on people who bring disease on themselves, when there are all those animals out there that need protection from over-populating humans. I just don't see it!'

Gabriel had wandered back from the far end of the verandah and plumped down defiantly next to Frances. 'Well! If you don't, you don't, but someone has to think of two million AIDS orphans!'

Toni, alerted to looming debate between two irreconcilables, put down her glass and cleared her throat. 'Talking of AIDS, I notice a sudden flurry in the papers about how wonderful Uganda has been about AIDS awareness. Bit of an about-turn, isn't it, after all the years of neglect, the banning of condoms by churches, etcetera? Why the sudden self-congratulation now? It's common knowledge that Museveni only got concerned because UPDF soldiers proved to be infected. I mean, as late as '93 he was saying: "AIDS is not really such a big crisis. Voluntarily you go and look for it. What will happen is that many people will die and then others will begin to fear ... The population of Uganda is now seventeen million. Even if you assume that two million will die, you will still remain with fifteen million which is higher than the population of 1956". And: "Undisciplined sex is like sticking one's hand into a hole with a snake in it." If you get bitten that's your *shauri*. Now, suddenly, all this tender concern.'

Jeremy nodded. 'I can't help agreeing with his hand in the snake hole bit.'

'But we're left with millions of orphans. The affected ones are dying but it's the rest – not enough parents to go round, not enough food, pretty well no education, no chance to get on and make a life, except for crime. It's a huge social disaster!' Gabriel was on her high horse. 'How will the government cope with that?'

'It can't and it won't,' Toni said. 'Governments seldom do that anyway. They leave that problem to individuals from the rest of the willing world. It's good old *shauri ya Mungu*. Well, maybe that's just what it is. *Mungu's* will seems to me to be the ordained laws of nature, which programmes the death of all living things. Human death has become anathema to the so-called "developed" world.

'Oh well, better keep off that subject!' Jeremy leaned back and folded his arms. 'Some informed opinion has it that Museveni's facing international disapproval since the Kisangani affair.' He turned to Mark. 'Museveni's UPDF went into the Congo after '94, legitimately, to root out Rwandan genocide perpetrators who escaped there. Instead of leaving the Congo, the UPDF, Museveni's main power base, has got involved in exploitation and self-enrichment which, needless to say, has trickled into the upper echelons in government, not to mention the Museveni family, particularly his brother. The army refused to leave when Kabila told them to, and are helping to keep the civil war in eastern Congo on the simmer. The UN are not pleased with our president. He's got to produce some good copy or massive aid will be withheld. And our economy can't do without it.'

'It's the bad boys who need good press.' Toni fixed her eyes on Mark. 'Our economy is totally underpinned by international aid. Because of huge spending on the military – it went up to about a hundred and fifty million US dollars – and on an overweight admin and élite cronies, not to mention the inept redistribution of previously-owned state land to friends, our economy's not doing too well. Since a deficit of two hundred and fifty-two million dollars in '96 it's gone to about four hundred and seventy-seven now, while our GDP growth's declining. Very little's been done about poverty eradication. Free primary education's all very well but with all these AIDS orphans who can enforce that anyway?'

Perpetua sighed. 'Oh well, it's always been a bit of a mess, hasn't it. One just has to plod on and do one's best for education.'

Frances laid her head back on her chair and closed her eyes. After its bright beginning, this celebration was becoming just another East African verandah conversation. She smiled grimly at memories of her grandfather and his friends, her father and his friends, her husband and his friends, stalking up and down verandahs, knocking out pipes, lighting them again, knocking them out, discussing the current state of affairs: crops and prices, East Coast Fever, coffee berry disease, foot-and-mouth, droughts and floods, Mau-Mau ... independence then land redistribution ... staying or leaving ...

She heaved a very audible sigh, opened her eyes and smiled at Jeremy. 'Somehow we survive, don't we. We even survive doctors. Did you ever hear of our famous old Doctor Burkitt The First – not his nephew, Denis, or William, his son, who both worked in Uganda?'

'You mean the lymphoma Denis?'

'Yes. William was "the eye man". He worked a lot on blindness in Karamoja. But Burkitt The First treated my grandparents and their horses with brutal cold water. Patients with high fevers were plunged in cold baths and made to stay in them till their temperatures came down. Settlers without baths were slung in hammocks and doused. Relays of buckets were poured over horses. I'm glad he's not here to do that to Clementine. Antibiotics do a quicker job, don't they?' She reached out and stroked the sleeping baby.

Toni bent over her beloved and felt her forehead. Then she frowned. 'You know, I once heard an apocryphal story about old Burkitt. I think it was a warden in the Mara told us. Something about keeping someone alive with a bicycle pump? Ridiculous!'

'Oh that! It's perfectly true. Early days, must have been in the thirties. Yes, that was Stanley Polhill. He came out from England to work for Powys Cobb up at Mau Narok. Cobb was thought to be a bit daft by everyone else. Perhaps because he tried to farm on a grand scale that most others couldn't afford. He imported some huge combine harvesters and they didn't have engine guards. Polhill was in charge of them and one day his jacket got caught in the machinery. One lung and some ribs were torn out and he was slashed open to the groin. Somehow, someone got him the thirty miles down a rough track to Nakuru hospital and Burkitt was there. Actually, Burkitt had trained in surgery though he had to do everything else as well. Polhill's surviving lung had collapsed, so before he started sewing him up, Burkitt fitted a football valve to a bicycle pump and made two African men, in shifts, pump air into the lung while Burkitt stitched. Polhill survived, though he was nearly a year in hospital.'

'Strewth! You're not joking?' Mark's eyebrows were halfway up his forehead.

Frances giggled. 'Not at all. I guess a book could be written about old Burkitt. He was quite a tartar and everyone dreaded him, but he did the job with whatever he had to hand. And it wasn't much in those days.'

Jeremy was laughing. 'Remember to call me, Mark, if you get to mix with all the animals you hope to. And be careful where you drink the waters of the Nile, especially if you go up to Murchison!'

The golden glow of late afternoon had burned away and a green dusk was seeping through the trees. Gabriel rose and tapped her watch. 'I must be getting back to the smalls.' She held out her hand to Toni and gently touched the sleeping Clementine. 'Thank you for a grand afternoon. Please let us know how she does?'

'Will do.' Toni looked hopefully at Jeremy.

Perpetua rose. 'I see Daudi's gone out to the back with Jerome. Good night, doctor. Mark, you're off duty now.'

'There's still some good food there, you boys.' It was out before she could stop it and Frances blushed for herself. For heaven's sake, when did one stop regarding all young men as one's hungry sons? 'Remember Jerome's pride. Toni, thank you. It's been splendid. Goodnight all.'

They walked out into the quiet garden, perfumed with

gardenia, brunfelsia and ginger blossoms, and paused to watch hawk moths darting under moonflowers. When they emerged on the lake shore, sacred ibis were winging in to roost on the silver branches of dead trees and beside the glinting water a pair of blacksmith plovers ran tinkling to one another. Gabriel forged impatiently ahead into the papyrus, but Frances and Perpetua dawdled, savouring the breeze off the lake. They ambled to the wooden bridge where Frances insisted on watching the last glints of light over wide water. Perpetua sighed. 'Sometimes I envy your East African childhood, Frances. My Cambridge youth seems rather tame in comparison. Don't you sometimes miss it all? That free life?' Frances picked a gloriosa lily and turned its wavering, flame-shaped petals. 'I do and I don't. After loss, one has to find new ways of belonging. I've never regretted entering the order. I have a home and very good friends.' She handed the lily to Perpetua whose spectacles flashed in touched surprise.

'And we have plenty to keep us busy, don't we?'

'No doubt of that.' Perpetua's left cheek twitched.

'And, thinking it over, don't we live with as much passion and excitement as all the "free ones"?'

Perpetua, reminded of late events, nodded and turned into the path uphill, holding the flame lily to her chest, while Frances followed, watching with amusement her thin, agile ankles in ungainly sandals and wishing she could capture the strength of those dedicated feet on paper, or, better still, in a terracotta statue of some wiry saint. She would attempt it … someday.

'Oh Frances, come on!' Gabriel was in the driver's seat, tapping the combi door.

'Just a minute. I've got two *kikapus* but I think we need a box for the chickens.' She burrowed among discarded cartons at the back of the garage and emerged with a sizeable specimen. She stowed the box and *kikapus*, filched from Consolata's pantry, on back seats and climbed in. Damp morning air cooled the sweat on her forehead as they rumbled under spreading flamboyants. Further down the hill, Gabriel slowed as they approached the chestnut rumps of cattle. Wide, pale horns clacked as the herd was jostled forward by boys with sticks. A flurry of goats trippled down the bank followed by laughing children and a woman with a baby on her back and a *kikapu* of pawpaws and oranges on her head.

'Leeft! Leeft!' Arms flapped and expectant eyes swivelled. Gabriel stopped. 'I can take you in but I can't bring you back.'

'Is alright, is okay.'

'Climb in.'

By the time four children and the loaded mother had ensconced themselves, the cattle and goats had reached the level ground below and were being whacked off the road. Gabriel hooted and the herders raised their sticks in salute as they rumbled past. When the little red road joined the road into Kampala they dodged between loaded bicycles and *boda-bodas* and finally pushed their way into the throng of taxis and top-heavy trucks streaming towards Kampala market. Gabriel roared and hooted into the market square, spotted a corner between stalls and parked. Her *mutata* disgorged its occupants who disappeared into the throng that milled in a square awash with chewed sugar cane, orange peel and peanut shells. The two nuns took their *kikapus* and, avoiding cheap jewellery, cameras, watches and radios of dubious origin, headed for the stalls of fabric sellers.

'Ah!' Frances peered over neatly-folded *basuti* lengths and pounced. 'What do you think of this for Namugasi?'

Gabriel scrutinized the blue and mauve floral. 'Isn't it a bit wishy-washy? Something brighter?'

'She's a very dignified old woman. I wonder ...' Frances dumped her basket and riffled with both hands through rows of folded colour. 'No ... no, not quite. Ah, what about this!' She extracted a length of violet with gold patterning and let it spill open. 'This is celebratory but also quite regal, don't you think?'

'That's the one!'

Frances paid for it, folded and wrapped the fabric in brown paper and stowed it in her *kikapu*. She was about to finger the other brilliant designs her pupils would have to emulate when Gabriel locked her arm in hers and steered her firmly towards the entrance of the food market.

They merged with the human river flowing up the steps into the old covered market, quickly fishing small change from pockets to bestow on cheerful ragged lepers who thrust out eroded hands. It took a few moments for their eyes to adjust to the dim hall where long concrete plinths formed rocks of stillness between the human tides that washed them while the din of speech and shuffle echoed in the rafters above.

They dodged decapitation by bundles of sugar cane and branches of *matoke* swung shoulder-high and made their way to where women had piled neat pyramids of aubergines, tomatoes, plastic-shiny peppers, chillies, beans, cassava tubers, magenta sweet potatoes, peanuts cocooned in their shells, oranges, pawpaws and peach mangoes oozing resin. Gabriel pounced on a pile of custard apples, paid for them and handed them carefully into her basket. 'Guavas.' She hovered 'I love them but they smell of cat's pee in the car. I'll wait to have them stewed. Ah, grenadillas!' She bought a dozen and then tore herself away to follow Frances to the end of the hall where the chicken sellers sat.

The dim crooning of fowls, tied by the feet and lying in ruffled heaps, always pierced her heart. She never smiled at the chicken women. They squatted behind baskets of eggs and bowls of water into which each egg was dipped before sale, as proof of its integrity. Those that bobbed to the surface were laid aside with extreme caution. All the while the chickens croaked and flapped despairingly.

'How much – those ones?' Frances peered uncertainly at heaving feathers beside a huge woman in green and scarlet.

'Two thousand, *nyabu*.'

'Show me.'

Two in each hand, she grabbed scaled legs and hung the hens upside down, shaking them.

'What do you think, Gabriel?'

'They're very scrawny.'

'Young, perhaps? Isn't it best to get pullets rather than old ones who might give up laying soon?'

'What about those, over there?' Gabriel pointed at a pile prodded invitingly by a wizened crone with glinting eyes.

'Mine, *nyabu*? Very good, much better. Nice and fat. Look very fat. She wrenched a fowl from a pile and, with one hand round its neck and the other gripping its feet, demonstrated a dubious girth.

'We need chickens who will lay lots of eggs, not for eating.' Frances wiped the sweat pouring down her cheeks. 'Will these lay eggs?'

'Look, *nyabu*-Seestah.' The crone fumbled the basket beside her 'Lots of eggs.'

The huge chicken seller in green and scarlet snorted contemptuously and turned her head away. Undeterred, the crone toppled three eggs into her water bowl. One bobbed but two sank, 'Very good eggs, these ones.'

'Oh dear.' Frances wiped her forehead. 'What does one believe?'

Gabriel's eyes wandered to other feathered heaps. 'I don't think we're going to do much better.'

'I want to give Namugasi nice chickens, not old *shenzies* who'll never lay.'

Gabriel summoned her force. 'If these *enkukus* don't lay eggs we shall bring them back and you will have to give us back the money. We want strong, egg-laying *enkukus*.'

Crafty wrinkles unpleated and the old face became a tragic mask, '*Nyabu*-Seestah, you are eating me.'

'Then we shall go to another one.'

The crone sighed. 'This one and this one.' She extracted two brown-speckled masses. 'This one and this one, they will lay eggs.'

The two fowls were laid over the brown paper in Frances's *kikapu*. They moved on and probed other bundles of scaly legs and feathers until, at last, five hens lay crooning a sad song in the depths of the basket. Gabriel piled sugar cane for her children to the brim of her *kikapu* and they began to head back towards the door. 'Wait!' Gabriel spotted neat piles of brown and milky white. 'Fried termites – wouldn't she like some?'

'Ooh yes!'

Gabriel scooped up several handfuls and dropped them into a newspaper cone held by the vendor. 'Shall we get some for ourselves? I can't resist them.'

'You'll have to.' Frances was firm. 'You've had enough gut trouble. Namugasi's resistant to the local bugs but you're not. If you're dead set on them, ask Paulo to bring you some next time he *pigas*.' Gabriel sighed and followed Frances out of the entrance into head-smacking sunlight. They heaved their baskets into the car and Frances tenderly transferred the chickens to the box on the back seat and pulled down the flaps. 'I do hope they're not *shenzies*. I asked Consolata if we couldn't give her two of our Rhode Islands but she said no.'

She climbed in and slammed the door before a crowd of roving urchins could bombard them with trinkets. 'Would you take us to Ssemogerere's? I must talk to him.'

Gabriel hooted through the crowds and brought them at last, with a lurch, to the door of The Real Things. The musty darkness was welcome and Mr Ssemogerere greeted them with charming affability. 'Ah, Sister Frances, Sister Gabriel, to what do I owe this pleasure?' All unpleasant memories, all embarrassment were waved into a distant past. 'What can I do for my ladies?'

'Mr Ssemogerere, I wanted to thank you for helping us retrieve the Madonna. Did the American make you pay him back in full?'

'He ate me, Sister. He ate me. That is business.' His hands assumed almost the position of the crucified. 'That is business. But that Terence Motongo, it is another story.' His eyes slid to a woeful mask across the shop.

'How will you get him to pay?'

'I have not decided … yet. But he must understand he cannot cheat me.'

'Mr Ssemogerere, I'm worried. This young thief has begun to pay bride price for one of our pupils, Dolosi Sebange. She is a nice girl from a good family. I think it would be awful if she married Terence Motongo. Is there nothing we can do about it? Could you, perhaps — well, could you somehow show him up — his true character, I mean?'

'Expose him? Make it impossible for him to be accepted into a respectable family? Yes … yes. That, it could be done.' A pleasurable gleam dawned in his eyes.

Frances nodded. 'But not yet. Not in such a way that Dolosi is humiliated. All the girls have heard she's going to be married. And she begins O-level exams soon. If anything upset her, she might do badly. She deserves to pass well, you see?'

Mr Ssemogerere absently tapped a little drum on the table, 'Ye-e-es ... it can be arranged. I think so. Leave it to me. Two birds with one stone, as you say, Sister Frances. Two birds with one stone.'

'But please don't do anything until after the seventh of December when school breaks up.'

'Very well, Sister. I give you my word on it. The family will be extricated from this undesirable connection and I will be repaid in full.'

'Thank you Mr Ssemogerere. I'm sorry it turned out this way. But, you understand, I could not allow Benedicta's Madonna to go. And I'm sorry if I was a little rude?'

'You had the right, Sister Frances, you had the right. Trust me. This matter shall be rectified.' All smiles, Mr Ssemogerere accompanied them to the door and waved them into the sunlight.

'We-e-ell.' Gabriel was steering out of the main road into the Kubiri turn-off. 'I wonder what he's got up his sleeve.'

'As long as it's after the seventh of December it'll do,' said Frances. They jolted over a deep rut where rain from uphill had tunnelled under the murramed surface and from the box on the back seat issued a pained skrawking. 'Those poor, wretched things.' Gabriel glanced at the box on the back seat,

'I hate the way they bind their legs so tight. Can't you loosen them just a little?'

'Gabriel! Five chickens loose in the combi? Our local fowls are olympic athletes. They won't sit sweetly clucking on the back seat. Anyway there's nothing to cut with.'

'But can't you loosen the twine, and keep the lid over them?'

'Hmph — I doubt it.'

'Oh Fran!' Gabriel's bosom heaved and her pansy-brown eyes flared reproachfully.

'Oh, alright. Just one, if I can untie it. If there's pandemonium, on your own head be it.' She bent round to the back seat and wrestled half-heartedly with twine and scaly feet. Suddenly something gave, claws scraped her wrist and with a swift squirm a chicken sprang from the box. It leaped at a window, was foiled, leaped again, and again met glass. With a maniacal cackle it launched itself at the front windscreen. Yellow legs scrabbled at the dashboard, wings slashed the dangling rosary, breast feathers fluttered in a valiant dash for freedom. Gabriel raised her left arm to parry the demented bird and the combi swerved to the left bank. Then it lurched back into the road again and the chicken hurtled into Gabriel's lap.

'Wah!' Talons grappled her thighs, the car skidded right and then swung back. Frances stared primly ahead. The chicken scrambled up Gabriel's arm onto her shoulder and finally onto her head. Its claws dug through her wimple into her scalp and its head and tail seesawed vigorously for balance. The combi swerved into the left bank and stalled.

'Begorrah! Birdbrain!' Gabriel swiped at it and the chicken hurtled into Frances's lap where it was caught and clamped down. Gabriel brushed chicken shit off her sleeve. 'You win.' She pulled a hankie from her pocket and wiped sweat and breast feathers from her face. 'Dear Lard, I could do with me tea!'

She turned the key in ignition, revved thunderously and they roared up the little red road, circled The Welcoming Mother and parked in the deep shade of the mango tree beside the garage, while the chicken crooned murderously in Frances' lap.

Gabriel sprang down, retrieved twine from the chicken box and tied the strong, kicking legs. Then she returned the hen to the box and pushed the flaps down. 'Well, that's what I call a good day at the market. Let's have that cuppa before going down to Namugasi.'

After her first emotion at Ignatia's retrieval, Perpetua had maintained a chilly distance from Namugasi's involvement. Yet her sense of justice had agreed that gifts were appropriate and she had provided funds. She was closeted this morning with weaker pupils and refused to accompany them to Namugasi's home. But she had given Frances an envelope which contained a letter of thanks.

Namugasi and her kin were sitting in the shaded courtyard of their homestead, shelling peanuts. Chairs were brought for Frances and Gabriel and, while daughters and granddaughters listened, Namugasi was thanked for her part in the rescue of Ignatia. Frances handed her Perpetua's letter but Namugasi hung her head coyly. 'You read for me, Sister, so that I can hear it, so we can hear it all together.'

Frances read in Luganda the dignified thanks of Sister Perpetua for the role Namugasi had played in saving a star pupil who would bring credit to the school, to her community and her country. Namugasi rocked herself, uttering soft cries of pleasure and her kinswomen smiled on her with pride. Then the gifts were presented; first the lady's fingers, then the chickens, examined only as far as was polite, the cone of nut-sweet termites was handed round and finally Frances took the *basuti* length from its brown paper. The look in Namugasi's eyes told them it was the right choice. I shall insist on painting her in it, she mused. That violet and the echo of purple on her skin where the sun slants onto it. Come the blessed holidays, I shall come and sit in Namugasi's timeless world of courteous presence. Tea was served on a sparkling table cloth. Their cups brimmed over.

***

A brood of quiet nuns was roosting under the trees in the quadrangle, their soft clucking blending with the murmur of the fountain. Twirling a yellow coreopsis in her fingers, Frances strolled slowly towards them. Singing and dislocated dance rhythms floated from the school hall where Agnes, Gabriel and Claire were putting the girls through their paces for the end-of-year concert. But Theresa was sewing, Felicitas's needles were clicking and Sister Helena was reading to her waifs. Four pairs of eyes watched solemnly as she turned the pages. Mattea sat a little apart, yawning over a sheet of paper. Frances took the other end of her bench, fished coloured papers out of her *kikapu* and began to make patterns in gold and silver on Christmas cards. Presently she sent a sidelong glance over Mattea's paper. Lines were growing slowly. 'A new poem?'

Mattea nodded, 'Funny, I always liked to work alone. But now,' she whispered, 'there's something about being near Helena, you know.'

Frances looked over at the tiny, round nun. Yes, there was something, some sort of flow – comfort, or tranquillity, or reassurance? Words couldn't define it. But the children felt it. Each new orphan sought it in bereavement. The latest orphan's head could barely be seen under Helena's grey wing and a soft, weathered hand curled round a small shoulder. In their first flood of grief, hers was the name they cried. Helena was the one who sat beside them with a nightlight in the hours of desolation. She never seemed to hurry, never raised her voice yet her class was always calm. Wherever she was, peace reigned. Insignificant to look at, ugly even with her broad nose, wide mouth and green-mouldered spectacle frames that continually slipped down her nose. And yet somehow indescribably beautiful, as her voice was. She and Mattea shared a love of poetry. Frances recalled how they used to sit in a corner of the verandah and read each other's poems aloud, which, Mattea insisted, was the only fair way to assess what one had written. But Sister Helena's time for poetry was past. *Slim* was swinging a scythe through the mothers of Uganda, through aunts and sisters who could take their place and the number of children who had no one to go home to was growing. They were Helena's children now. Presently a bell announced tea. Helena read slowly to the end of the book, closed it and tucked it under her arm. She rose and headed towards the dining room, a child holding each hand and two grasping her habit.

***

During the Saturday evening film in the hall, which Frances watched in order to watch the children watching, Consolata swept in and bent over her shoulder. 'Sister Frances, there is a telephone call for you.'

'Any idea who it is?' Frances rose and followed her towards the house.

'A man. I do not know him.' Consolata was curt with disapproval.

'Good evening, this is Sister Frances.'

'Ah, Sister Frances, good evening, good evening.' She saw a fat starfish gripping the other receiver. 'It is James Mujaju here. You remember our little talk, Sister?'

'Of course, Mr Mujaju.'

'I have been wondering, Sister, if you wish to reconsider my offer?'

'Oh, Mr Mujaju! No, I haven't changed my mind.'

'I have been thinking that not only a combi and a generator but a new slide projector might speak for me?'

'Oh, Mr Mujaju, you are too kind. But we cannot possibly part with the Madonna. I'm sorry but that must be my final word.'

'Ah, Sister Frances. I am sorry. But, if you wish to reconsider at any time, my offer will stand. Anything you wish, Sister, anything you care to mention. Let me know.'

'Thank you Mr Mujaju. Good night.' She put down the receiver. 'Puffadder,' she muttered. 'I doubt if I'm wrong. I'd better check the chapel doors.'

7. Friends in Low Places

The first day of the all-important O- and A-level exams had dawned. Frances hurried into the gardens with a basket and secateurs and stared over the lake. At six o'clock she had peered from the upper verandah and seen clouds brooding to the horizon. Today of all days! When they needed sunlight on petals, highlights of gold on the blue vase! She glared from the misted shoreline into dull grey wool till, in the far distance, a faint blue rent began to widen. Her heart gave a little skip. Possibly, by the time chapel was over the sun would be shining? She crossed herself and marched to a bed of day-lilies, selected golden blooms and green spears. She was tugging at peach mangoes under dark leaves when a lion's roar startled her.

'Sister! Si-i-ster Frances!' Daudi was lunging over the lawn towards her with Fesito hobbling in his wake.

'Daudi, what is it?'

'Again!' His massive neck swelled, his voice was a husky whisper. 'Again, Sister Frances! At seven o'clock I unlock the chapel but I don't go in. Fesito goes in now – she is not there!'

'But ...'

'Again she is taken!'

'Seestah, is true.' Fesito's face was wrinkled in a knot of outrage. 'I open the door. I go in and always I look first at Holy Mother. She is gone!'

'Come!' Daudi commanded. 'You will see.'

Frances followed them, trotting to match Daudi's enraged strides with Fesito stumbling beside her. Daudi flung open the chapel door and gestured to the empty recess.

'But how?'

'I do not know. The keys I keep always with me, on this ring.' He hefted a fistful of keys out of his pocket, 'See, one – two, they are here, the padlock keys. No one has used these ones.'

'And the others?'

'They are as usual. The two that hang in the sisters' house are there.'

'And the night watchmen saw nothing?'

'They saw a light in the bushes beyond the netball pitches. They go there but they find nobody.'

Frances sighed vehemently. 'Really, Daudi, I wonder if they're any use at all. They fall for the same trick every time. Now we've got four they should always send two in the opposite direction from noise and lights.'

'I am thinking the same.' Daudi clasped his hands. 'Next time, I am telling them, next time they fail I sack them!'

Frances glanced at her watch. Chapel would begin in ten minutes and she must arrange the flowers and set out paper and pencils. 'Daudi, better say nothing just now. But, if you have time, perhaps you could look for any signs?'

'I shall do it.' Daudi strode away and Fesito turned to her.

'I am sorry, Seestah.' He tapped his heart. 'I am sorry.' Then he lifted his broom from against the wall and trailed down the steps. She heard the soft sighs of his sweeping as he edged slowly round the chapel.

'Well,' she stood and took up her basket. 'There's no time to think about it now.' She looked once more at the empty space. Today of all days! The start of exams when nothing must upset the girls' equilibrium! The offerings today to the Mother of God would be lavish. Flowers, ribbons, snippets of embroidery, sweets, biscuits – each one an earnest supplication to the Mother of God to watch over them. She turned and hurried to the art room. She filled the blue vase with water, arranged lilies to face sideways and three quarters to the front and then placed gold-and-pink mangoes in front of the vase to echo the gold of the flowers. She walked to the back of the classroom and surveyed the arrangement from several angles. She laid sheets of thick paper, a pencil, sharpener and rubber on each desk. Dimly she was aware of a bell and footsteps on pathways. She locked the classroom door and went to the chapel.

She glanced only once at the piles of offerings to an absent Mother of God and looked at no one except Mother Julienne whose penetrating eyes were ranging over the rows of girls. Agnes raised her hands, the school rustled to its feet and launched into the first hymn. The nuns' voices soared bravely and the hesitant and staring children followed them, gaining force and volume as they gathered assurance from Sister Frances's clear and confident face. By the time Mother rose to give the final blessing, unease at the absence of Our Lady had subsided. The all-important examination blessing proceeded. Then Mother gave a little smile, as if communing secretly with the gap at the back of the chapel. She took a deep breath and crossed herself carefully. 'Children, remember that the Mother of God watches over you today. Our little Mother of the Chapel has been removed for a while. But Our Mother in Heaven will help each one of you to do your best today!' Agnes's hands fell upon the piano keys and thundered out the stirring march that sent scholars trooping to the fray with lifted hearts.

Frances waited till her girls were seated, darting glances of nervous apprehension at the still life on the table. 'Ah,' she touched the lilies, now fully open to the sun streaming through the eastern windows. 'What a perfect day for our first exam, girls! Nothing is nicer to paint than petals in sunlight. Remember, everyone, keep your eyes only on the still life and your own paper. Any work that is copied will be disqualified. Not that any of you would do that, but it has to be said before each exam. Raise your hands if you need anything. I shall bring the paints and brushes when you are ready. Just do as well as you have been doing, and all will be well.' As the first tremulous lines were sketched she stopped in her pacing at the back of the room and crossed herself. 'Mother,' she said silently, 'thank you for, for improvising. But where is she? Who's taken her this time, just before exams?' Her hands clenched. 'Obviously a thief who neither knows nor cares what she means to our children.'

When it was over and the girls had departed she scrutinized the paintings, mentally bestowing assessments, and came to the conclusion that her pupils had acquitted themselves well and at least three merited distinctions.

Veronique, thanks to her father's loan of well-trained guards, had resumed attendance and had excelled. She carefully laid the paintings on the table at the back of the room to dry. At a knock on the door she looked up.

Daudi entered and in a conspiratorial whisper reported that he had found the tracks of car tyres in the road downhill. The tracks turned into the *shamba* of the Matufuna's homestead. Was it not possible that from there the thieves had made their way up the hill to the school?

'What sort of car tracks?'

'The tyres are very broad, they are new, expensive. It could be a Mercedes, Sister.'

'Thank you, Daudi.' A visiting *mafutanyingi*. The puffadder?

After tea-break, on the way back to class, she smiled at the quad routine, the entire school subdued to silence by Perpetua's stern vigilance over an A-level science exam in progress. Theodora, a forbidding presence, glared at the streams of girls passing between classrooms, lest any child forget herself.

The afternoon exams passed uneventfully and Frances surveyed a crop of work that pleased her. Certainly no failures here and four had performed better than usual. After supper she knocked on Mother Julienne's door.

'Entrez! Ah, Frances. How has it gone today?'

'Well, Mother. Better than I'd hoped.'

'You are happy with the work?'

'They've all done themselves justice. There should be some distinctions too.'

'C'est bon.'

'Mother, thank you for covering up the Madonna's disappearance.'

'Mais, que faire? They were dismayed. At such a time, ma fille, at such a time, to steal Our Lady! It dismays me to think that someone had access to the chapel keys. Daudi is beside himself. Have you any idea at all?'

Frances told her of Mr Mujaju's repeated offers.

'If I were a man and not a nun I would say a certain word.' Mother Julienne murmured. 'But, voilà, I am not and I am, so I shall not say it. Yourself, do you think it possible that this Mujaju is behind it?'

'It would not surprise me.'

'A *mafutanyingi*. Almost, I feel like putting Sergeant Kakonge onto him and have done. He would be shot in several places while questioned, I am sure. But that would mean having to deal with Sergeant Kakonge too,' she sighed. 'Alors, à la prière!'

'Your prayer, ma mère, is efficacious in these matters,' Frances winked and then yawned.

'It is all I have,' said Mother simply. 'Now, you're tired. Take an early night. I will let you know if anything comes to me.'

But for days nothing came to Mother. Frances, when not invigilating exams, found herself often sitting in the chapel staring at the empty recess. Strangely, touchingly, the offerings still appeared daily for the Madonna in absentia. But what would happen if she were not there on St Cecilia's Day? One of the happiest days of the year when, exams just over, the school and all the valley people gathered for her joyful process through the grounds? Every year for the last seven years the Madonna had presided over this day. Unthinkable that she should not be there! The theft could not have been more cruelly timed. At the thought of James Mujaju her fists clenched again.

***

The routine of exams continued until Friday afternoon. Daudi replaced the padlocks on the chapel doors and the keys were secreted in inaccessible drawers.

She was sitting at the refectory table on Friday night poring over a woodcut design for cards to be sold for AIDS orphans while Perpetua beside her toted up the exam marks of her first year A-level pupils.

'Good heavens.' Perpetua rubbed her forehead. 'Almost full marks! Who'd have thought it?'

'Who?'

'Nasuna.'

'Oh, the quiet one who lost a year?'

'Mm. Very solid, but not brilliant like Ignatia. I've asked her whether she'd like to teach. She's always lagged behind Ignatia and I didn't want to suggest medicine, because of the pressure. But with marks like this, she could do anything she liked. Well, well.' A small smile was tugging Perpetua's left cheek. 'Well, well.'

Frances shuffled her drawings into a neat pile. She was glad for Nasuna, shy and self-effacing, always looking down with a smile that was half a frown whereas Ignatia shone with regal self-confidence. One of life's surprises.

Suddenly Felicitas was at her shoulder, 'Mother,' she whispered. Frances rose and went to her.

'Frances.' Mother's smile was a little rueful. 'I think Someone is teasing me. It seems that we are to embroil ourselves in what you call "the low life".'

'Mother?'

'All that has been vouchsafed me is "set a thief to catch a thief!" Nothing more. What do you make of it?'

Frances sat down and began to laugh, '"Set a thief to catch a thief!" But which one? Buganda's full of thieves. It's a national pastime.'

'Not a pastime, ma fille, a passion. A profession. Dr Anderson came to look me over yesterday. No, no, all is well. Only

159

the checking of blood pressure and such things. But he was remembering the days when every time one went to the Odeon Cinema in Kampala you had to remove the starter motor of your car because if you did not, it was stolen during the film and there would be rows of cars all making the same noise – the noise of a car that will not take.'

'So,' Frances was frowning, 'now I have to go and find some thief or other in order for him to steal the Madonna back from Mr Mujaju, if it is Mr Mujaju who's stolen her?'

'So it would seem.'

Frances shook her head, 'But I don't know any thieves – unless I don't know that I know them,' she added.

'A possibility, certainement,' Mother nodded.

'Oh Mother!'

'Go and sleep on it. The morning is wiser than the evening, as the Russians say. Tomorrow is Saturday. You may do as you think fit.' After breakfast Frances passed Felicitas in the quad and stopped her. 'Would you tell Mother I've gone down to talk to Jerome. She'll know why.'

'Alright, enjoy yourself.'

I hope I do, thought Frances, walking through dew-drenched grass downhill. I hope he'll know someone a bit more sophisticated than Thomasi's lads. Someone who's up to all the tricks.

Then, as she went, the innocence of the morning lifted her into its lightness. A milky softness shimmered in the air over the valley and the lake. Two hornbills honked at her approach and flew before her, flap-flap-glide, into an mvuli tree to gorge on dangling brown fruit. A kite's mewing drew her eyes up to where it circled, lazy-alert, balancing on the breeze and from over the lake floated the sad, gulping calls of fish eagles. The valley scintillated with the calls of children and goat bells. She crossed the bridge and swung left into the orange dust of the road that led to Toni's place, stopping to watch a wydah flaunt his trailing tail out of the elephant grass. She walked slowly, sniffing the scent of dew dissolving in sunshine.

Suddenly a movement caught her eye. Above the elephant grass to the left of the road, an upside-down chair was moving slowly towards her. It wove a little to the right, swung left again and then came hovering on in stately progress. It was singing,

'What a frie-e-e-nd we have in Je-e-e-sus!' in a gently swooping baritone. Frances darted across the road. The chair rounded a bend. 'Are you weak and heavy laden, Burdened with a lo-o-ad of care?' It hovered beyond lantana bushes and finally revealed itself, poised above a pile of *matoke* and dangling chickens. Underneath it, pedalling with slow and steady thrusts, was an elderly man. He looked up as he approached.

'Seestah Francees! *Wasusiotiano!*'

Her heart somersaulted. Motavu! She'd completely forgotten him. It had been five years. 'Motavu! *Wasusiotiano!*'

'*Bulungi, nyabu*-Seestah!' Motavu braked, dropped his feet into the dust and turned to steady the load behind him with one hand. 'You are well? And Seestah Perpetua and Seestah Agnes, they are well?'

'They are well, thank you, Motavu.'

'And the Holy Mother? She is well?'

'She is very well. And your wife, Motavu, and the children?'

'My wife is getting old, like me, *nyabu*. But the children are well. They have given us five grandchildren. All everybody is well.'

'It is good, Motavu.' Dear Lord, she thought, surely there is no thief more indebted to us than Motavu? And, after all, he was once a true professional. She took a deep breath and laid her hand on the handle bar of the aged bike. 'Motavu, we are in good health, but we have a trouble. A heavy trouble.'

'A trouble at the school?'

'A big trouble. Very big.'

'Then I can help you?'

'I think perhaps you could, Motavu.'

A deep-wrinkled smile lit the long, mobile face and Motavu fixed his eyes on hers. 'Then you must tell me the trouble, Seestah.'

'It is this, Motavu …' She told him of Mr Mujaju's insistent wish to acquire the Madonna in exchange for various goods, of her refusal and the Madonna's subsequent disappearance.

Motavu's face grew long with gravitas. 'Eeh-eh! It is wicked.' He spat in the dust and contemplated the patch of saliva. Then his eyes narrowed and he looked thoughtfully into the distance.

'Do you know anything about Mr Mujaju?' she prompted hopefully.

Motavu took a red handkerchief out of his pocket, wiped his forehead, pocketed the handkerchief and shook his head ruefully. 'Seestah, I have left those ways, since you helped me. But my brother's son, Samweri, he drives a taxi in town. Is one of Mujaju's taxis. He has many, many, many. I am going to my brother's place now. He will help us. Samweri will help us.'

'Motavu, nobody must know about it. Nobody. Only you and Samweri.'

A knowing smile, 'I understand it, Seestah. Nobody will know.'

'*Webali*, Motavu, *webali nyo, nyo, nyo!*'

'Do not worry, Seestah. Do not be heavy. If Mujaju has not taken the Holy Mother, then we shall find the one who has taken her. I know those who – '

'Yes, Motavu, yes.'

'She will come back to you. You are my friends!' Motavu swung up the right pedal with horny toes while Frances steadied the *matoke* and chair, then he pushed down with a wheezing groan and the bicycle lurched forward. '*Weraba*, Seestah Francees!'

'*Weraba*, Motavu!'

She contemplated the singing chair till it disappeared round a bend in the road. A friend in Jesus, indeed! She turned back to the bridge and paused, remembering. Her first meeting with Motavu was not easily forgotten. They'd been walking back one afternoon, she, Agnes and Perpetua, from St Paul's, two miles along the road through the valleys. They had been to visit the Brothers – Agnes to discuss with Brother Joseph-Marie the performance of a new mass to be sung at Rubaga Cathedral in which the choirs of St Paul's and St Mary's would combine, Perpetua to wheedle from Brother Simon some copies of pages in a new physics textbook that St Paul's had afforded but which St Mary's could not. She herself had gone to Brother Sebastien's workshop to beg a small chunk of *majarati* for a carving that Benedicta had made drawings for. They had come away well pleased and were ambling gently back to Kubiri when they'd heard a strangled scream from the bush above the road.

'Good grief, someone's in trouble!' Perpetua had leaped up the bank and charged into thick bush with Frances on her heels and Agnes panting behind them. They'd burrowed through lantana and coffee bushes and then suddenly into an open space below a group of huts. A man was lying face down on the ground, his ankles tied with rope and his wrists tightly strung above his head. Six men stood over him, lashing him with *kibokos* and long staves. Over his back, buttocks and thighs were scarlet stripes of raw flesh.

'Stop that!' Perpetua had flung forward, grabbed an arm with her left hand and with her right hand wrenched loose a whip and flung it away. 'Stop at once!'

Before her towering glare the men had dropped their arms and stepped back.

'Why are you doing this?'

'He is a thief, Sister. Look!'

A bicycle lay flung on the grass nearby. Next to it lay a shabby leather bag, disembowelled of two small radios, smart shoes, a wrist watch and several wallets. 'All these he has stolen from our place. It is not the first time. Now we are finishing him.'

The avenging angel in spectacles was unmoved. 'You are Christian people. You cannot do this.'

The men had shrugged and edged a little nearer. Perpetua had knelt down beside the victim and laid her hand on his arm. 'What is his name?'

'It is Motavu.'

'Motavu, Motavu, can you hear me?'

A small sigh fluttered from bruised lips and Perpetua bent to his ear. 'Motavu, do you repent of this theft?'

Motavu managed a weak croak before lapsing unconscious and Perpetua stood up and loomed. 'He repents. He will give back everything. Take it. Take it all and go!'

Only one man had stood his ground and glared at her resentfully, clenching the whip in his hand. Perpetua returned the stare with quelling authority until he turned and followed the others who were picking up their strewn possessions. With a last defiant glare at Perpetua the sixth man had picked up Motavu's bicycle and followed the others past the huts uphill. Perpetua had watched their backs until they were out of sight and then turned at Agnes's trembling sobs. She was standing at the man's feet, her hands over her mouth, the tears spilling down them, 'He will die, he will die! The sores will rot. He will die!'

'Nonsense. We must get him to Mengo – quick! Frances, would you go and bring Daudi and Paulo with a stretcher. We'll stay here so none of them come back to finish him off.' She had glowered into the bush that was now quiet as the grave. Frances had run all the way to the school. It was almost dusk by the time she, Daudi and Paulo had returned with the stretcher. Perpetua was still holding her vigil at Motavu's head and Agnes still weeping at his feet.

'He's out for the count – mercifully,' said Perpetua, 'but there's blood coming from his mouth.'

'That is the sticks.' Daudi had bent over him. 'With the *kibokos* they take off the skin but it is the sticks that break the ribs to kill them.'

Motavu had screamed a high, wavering scream as they lifted him gently, face down, onto the stretcher. Daudi and Paulo had led the sorry procession up the hill, Perpetua striding very upright behind the stretcher while Agnes had followed, sighing the deep, quavering sighs with which the women of Africa vent horror and grief. Frances had felt glad of them, she who after years at boarding school seldom allowed herself to cry. The ooze of blood from his wounds and mouth and the thin child's wails had continued all of that stumbling hurry up the hill till they had loaded him into the combi and Daudi and Perpetua had driven to Mengo.

Motavu had spent many weeks lying face down in a hospital bed till his broken ribs and lacerations had healed and Agnes had visited him regularly with small, pocketed comforts from Consolata's domestic science classes. Then, one day, an old car had driven up to the school and Motavu had climbed out, somewhat bent to one side, but beaming with restored health. He had brought, in a wire cage, five beautiful hens, their progeny still the best layers in Consolata's run, and three sleek brown goats which had joined Daudi's flock in his *shamba*. For a year afterwards, he would arrive now and then with gifts of bananas, eggs, peanuts or pawpaws which were deposited reverently at the kitchen door. She had even glimpsed him a couple of times standing shyly at the back of the Sunday congregation. She turned and hastened up the hill to convey to Mother a thief's affectionate remembrance.

Sunday afternoon brought a storm rumbling over the lake and just as it was passing away north-west and the sun was throwing long, late rays over a dripping world, Mark and a fair young man with a red face, appeared in the refectory doorway. They were very dirty and very wet but wore the air of two schoolboys who'd scored a winning goal.

'We've done it!' Mark beamed at the nuns, while his friend hovered in the doorway, peering a little apprehensively at the assembled sisters with cups of tea in their laps. 'Come in, Greg,' Mark beckoned. 'They don't bite. This is my friend Gregory Turner who's doing time at the Fisheries Department.'

Gregory grinned sheepishly and entered, glancing at his feet in slopping sandals. Frances rose to replenish the teapot and cut into chocolate cake.

'Well,' Perpetua put down her cup, 'what have you done?'

'Hallo, Gregory, welcome. Join us in some tea.' Frances was pouring two cups. 'There's masses of cake left.'

'We've hit back at Makubenge's. I decided to take up Toni's offer. She took us over to Bulebele, to Thomasi's place, and we met the gang. The boys bolted at first, thinking we'd come to make trouble about Ignatia, but Jerome and Toni rounded them up and convinced them that we actually wanted to help. She speaks the lingo and I didn't get much of it, but Jerome gave me the gist. We all agreed they had every right to protect their own waters. We could outwit Makubenge but it must be legal and blowing up boats is not legal. Would they cooperate if I brought my friend who knew about fish etc etc.? In the end they agreed. Next weekend I brought Greg and we hatched a plan. Greg got permission to do a project with tilapia fry at the far end of Bulebele – you know where the river comes out through the swamp into that little estuary. Perfect spot to monitor. Then Toni said what about getting Fisheries' permission to cordon off the whole area from Thomasi's place to the little island and then over to the shore beyond the estuary. We got it. We got some buoys from Fisheries, which Toni stumped up for. To do them credit, Fisheries are aware of the threat that joints like Makubenge's pose for the small fishing industry. They were pretty sympathetic. So, this morning, at about five am we were there and ready.' He glanced at Gregory who nodded over a mouthful of cake, his eyes very blue above a peeling nose.

'Well, we set out with Thomasi's lads in four *kaseses* loaded with the buoys. We planted buoys, some of them linked by ropes, all the way from Wachanga to the little island half way to Bulebele and then across to that patch of forest beyond the estuary. Every buoy had a notice saying: "Fisheries Dept. Keep Out".'

'And you wallowed around in the black bog.' Gabriel nodded. 'Do you stink!'

'Well, yes. All in the cause of science.'

'Mrs Thompson seemed pretty chuffed,' Gregory added.

'Made us drink a glass of beer to celebrate.'

'Better have some more cake then.' Frances hovered with the plate.

'Ah! That,' Mother Julienne favoured them with her arched

smile, 'is what I call a happy ending to Ignatia's startling adventure.'

Gabriel winked slyly at Mark. 'Now d'you get the point of Mother's little blue boat?'

For another week examinations proceeded with exemplary decorum and no one incurred Theodora's wrath for unseemly behaviour in the quadrangle. Frances frequently hovered on the path down to the bridge, as if by peering into the valley she could divine activity on behalf of the missing Mother of God. But Motavu never came.

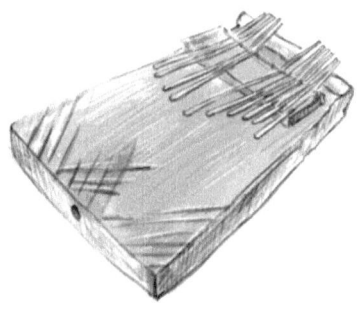

8. Singing the Saint

The high tide of examinations was ebbing. Little swirls of activity in corners were swelling into a flood as St Cecilia's Day approached. In the shade of mango trees Gabriel and a sweating, pink-faced Claire were conjuring a pageant while Theresa pinned up a slipping tunic over the shoulders of St Cecilia herself, a tall eleven-year-old, who gazed with steadfast eyes at her imminent martyrdom. In the chapel, *amadindas* were rattling under a mournful chorus of Agnes's devising. Behind a garden wall, arthritic fingers were weaving the base of a heavenly wreath.

Only Frances felt the sweat of anxiety seep into everything she touched. True, the little old figure of the harp-playing saint would sit on the bier the men would carry into the gardens. But always the Madonna had stood tall behind her, blessed reminder of the

Mother of God who had surely welcomed that saint into bliss. There were only three days left and still Motavu had brought no news. How could they possibly carry a half-empty bier to the hundreds of faithful from the hills and valleys around who gathered to celebrate the presence of The Mother among them, and the endurance of a saint whose suffering spoke to their own? The only thing she could think of was to make a larger St Cecilia. After supper she went to the art room, turned on the lights and dragged an oblong of clay wrapped in plastic from under the back table. She heaved it onto the modelling plate, laid out her tools, filled a bowl with water and addressed herself to the heavy earth.

In each spare moment the next day she toiled at the figure of St Cecilia, her face, an African face, lifted skywards with an open singing mouth. She was at it in the late afternoon when there was a knock on the door. It was Fesito. 'Seestah, it is Motavu here.' He slipped tactfully away and Frances ushered Motavu into the room and closed the door. 'Motavu, *wasusiotiano*. You have come, you have found her?'

'I have found her, Seestah. It is not that Mujaju. It is somebody else.' Motavu described how he had visited Samweri. Samweri had inveigled himself into the favour of the housemaid in Mujaju's large house on Tank Hill. He had found no evidence of the theft there.

Motavu himself had gone visiting relatives and friends along the valleys, picking up news. Gossip had led him to a *shamba* on the edge of the forest, Masenge way, where queues of sick people were converging on a fig tree. There was a man under that fig tree, taking money from the people before allowing them to enter a place of grass below his homestead. All, all they went to a shelter of thatch on poles, Motavu peaked his hands. Under the thatch, it was The Mother. He asked a woman standing to one side, what are they doing here? They are paying to come and touch and stay with The Mother to get healed of the *Slim* and the other things that come from too much sex. Also, she was good for the eyes that had yellow pus and the headaches and for the stiff fingers, the coughing and the diarrhoea. That man had a big bag of money, Motavu nodded.

Frances sat down suddenly, 'I see.'

'I have done well, Seestah?'

'You have done very well, Motavu.'

'What to do, Seestah?'

For a long moment she could say nothing. Motavu shifted his feet. 'I can get men, my friends, to take her from that place. We shall bring her back from that thief.'

Frances frowned and rubbed her forehead. Such was the desperation for healing that Motavu might be met with anger and violence. The man who was taking rich pickings would surely not let go of a gold mine without a struggle. 'Motavu, I don't know. There could be trouble with that man. First, I want to see it myself. Wait for me here. I shall come back soon.'

She hurried to her bedroom and changed into the black slacks and dark shirt she had worn for Ignatia's rescue. She found her old green cotton hat, went quietly downstairs and knocked on Mother's door, swiftly apprised her of Motavu's message and asked permission to go with him to the thief's *shamba*.

Mother gripped the arms of her chair, 'Promise me, you take no risks and do not make yourself known.'

'I won't drive there. We'll walk and stay out of sight behind the trees. Motavu said the *shamba* is by the forest.'

'Don't you think Daudi should go with you?'

Frances pondered and then shook her head. 'He's too visible. Somebody's sure to know him and our cover would be blown. I just want to go quietly with Motavu.' Mother said no more, gave a curt nod and closed her eyes as Frances left.

Frances went back to the art room. She asked Motavu to take off his *kanzu*. Underneath he wore an old green shirt and khaki shorts. 'The white is too easily seen,' she said, 'I am wearing dark clothes. Nobody must see us, Motavu. Nobody, you understand. They could be angry if they think we come to take away The Mother.'

The old thief's eyes lit with comprehension, 'Nobody will see us, Seestah. Nobody, nobody, nobody.'

They left the classroom, hurried over the lawns to the mango trees and headed down into the valley. At the bottom of the hill Motavu turned right, into the road winding south. There were few people on the road but Frances pulled her hat low over her forehead and looked no one in the eyes. Still she felt nervous. The sisters of Kubiri were well known in the homesteads here. A group of women was approaching, Namugasi's eldest daughter and her two children among them.

'Motavu!' she hissed, 'I know these people. They must not see me!' She ducked behind lantana bushes under a loquat tree. Motavu followed her and they watched friends pass unwitting.

'Motavu.' Frances's nerves were getting the better of her. 'I don't like going on the road. Is there another way?'

Motavu scratched his head. 'Seestah, I must make water. Stay here, I shall return.'

Frances resolutely faced the road while a powerful stream of urine hit the earth behind her. When Motavu came back he was smiling. 'Seestah, all the small paths here, I know them. We shall go this way.' He pointed with his chin up a path, winding into a coffee grove. 'Come, Seestah, I go before you.' She followed him through coffee bushes, then into long grass, through thickets and more lantana, then through banana groves and patches of forest. Paths like red snakes slithered in all directions but Motavu showed no hesitation in selecting a path that wound between banana groves and patches of forest. At last they descended into a tongue of forest licking a steep hillside. Motavu halted as the bleating of goats rose from somewhere below. He stepped aside into the trees and parted the leaves of a shrub. 'It is there. See?'

In a clearing below the forest was a homestead where banana trees and cassava crowded the huts. Below them stretched a bowl of grass where women, children and a few men were sitting round a scanty peak of palm leaves on poles.

'It is there they have The Mother,' Motavu whispered.

Frances nodded and then peered at a large fig tree beyond the grass. A man was standing before a dam of people who passed in ones and twos to join the crowd round the shrine.

'Motavu, I want to go closer, to see better.' They inched their way downhill to where the forest trees thinned, sat down on a twisting root, and peered through a curtain of lime-green creeper.

A man of about thirty, leaning on a staff, was making his way to the shrine. As he drew closer, she saw sores on his body, the running cancerous sores that were among the last symptoms of *Slim*. He paused a long moment before the shrine, took from his pocket something that glinted in the sunlight. Frances leaned forward and saw him place a watch at the feet of the statue. Then he limped to an open place behind a group of sitting women and, slowly and painfully, subsided onto the coarse grass. His eyes never left the figure in the shrine. A boy holding a stick with a blind man gripping its other end led him towards the shrine and the man fumbled out his hand till it touched and held a fold of the Madonna's robe. Then the boy tugged the end of the stick and pulled the man over the grass to an empty spot. The man's lips moved incessantly. Two young women followed him, very thin but still with the saucy, hip-waggling gait of bus-depot girls, successors of the original truck-stop women who had first spread *Slim* across the country. Hand-in-hand, they approached the shrine, dipped their knees in respect, laid a couple of gaudy trinkets at The Mother's feet and picked their way over legs to sit and stare into her serene face.

Suddenly Frances sucked in her breath and bowed her head. A nightmare face was approaching. A thin child with a vast swollen mouth, a pink cancerous gape, a fungal growth from which teeth protruded at crazy angles, was being led towards them by a woman who was covering her mouth with her hand while tears oozed down her face. A quiver of shock ran through the crowd, some stared and others turned away their faces. Frances forced herself to look again at a Burkitt's lymphoma. Motavu was shaking his head. 'Eh, it is too bad, this one! Too bad. Where is God today, Seestah? Where is God now?'

'God will take him very soon, Motavu. This disease moves quickly. It will not be long.'

People shuffled aside to make a place for the boy and his mother who subsided between them, turned her son to face the Mother of God and held his limp body on her lap.

Now a gaunt but beautiful woman, supported by a teenage daughter, a thin child with grey mucus trailing from his nose clutching her dress, picked her way slowly towards the shrine. When she stood before the Madonna she made the sign of the cross. Her thin body folded itself to the ground, her children sat beside her and they stared up at The Mother.

Frances whispered to Motavu, 'Has anyone been healed here?'

'They say one woman. She came holding her belly. Now the pain is gone.'

'Hmm. Anybody else? The ones with Slim?'

'Nobody is telling of that.'

Frances raised her eyes to the Madonna, lit by sunlight piercing the scanty palm leaves. The Madonna's left arm cradled the child that looked up into her face, her right hand cupped his feet. Her head was tilted a little to the left, her full sad mouth was tender and her eyes ... her eyes looked over the head of her child and beyond him. They looked into the eyes of the living and dying around her. Frances's mind went back to the day they had brought her to life. The moment when she had pointed to where the awl must pierce the waiting iris, the moment when, pierced, the eyes see. They had held their breath as she had given the awl to Benedicta whose hand had trembled slightly as she made the final life-giving thrust. Then the blind eyes had seen. As they now saw the mute and expectant suffering before them.

What did the assembled crowd see? Who were they seeing, these unwelcome women who hid their disease in dark huts? An omnipotent Mother of God, a merciful dispenser of healing? Or the unmarried girl with a swollen belly, whose motherhood within eight days was to be haunted by the prophecy of grief to come? She longed to ask them. Motavu shifted uneasily and glanced up into the forest, 'Seestah, it is time to go. Soon the boys will bring the cattle down this way.'

She sighed and stood up, 'Yes, we will go.'

'You have seen, Seestah. You have seen it now.'

What had she seen? As they tramped back along the twisting path she found distaste battling with a strange feeling that while paying for the unlikely they were somehow being granted something else. She wandered absent-mindedly behind Motavu, trying to fathom what it might be.

***

'Well?' Mother Julienne cocked her head like an eager bird.

'She's where Motavu said she is. The sick pay to come and touch her and then they just sit and look at her. Apparently only a woman with belly ache has been healed.'

'I see. And many are coming?'

Frances nodded.

'So someone is getting rich. Like so many in our past who peddled tufts of hair, bits of bone, wood and nails or gathered the faithful to contemplate statues with relics embedded in them. Statues that wept and bled. So, what is to be done?'

Frances was silent and stared at the floor. Presently she sighed, 'Motavu has offered to recover her, with the help of friends.'

'I think we should accept his offer. His friends are sure to have certain skills.'

Frances nodded but stared on at the floor.

'You are not overjoyed at the thought?'

'We must get her back, of course.'

'But?'

'It's just, she seems to give them something. There may be no healing but there's a sort of – I can only call it comfort. Her presence, the way she looks at them.'

'That I can understand. That is the inspiration of Benedicta. But it is not to be paid for. Not with the money of those who have so little and suffer so much. Motavu is right. Let him arrange it.'

Next morning a son of Paulo's delivered a note to Mr Motavu

Kimirenge. That night, after Daudi had locked the padlocks on the chapel doors, Frances sneaked out and unlocked them. The following morning the Madonna resided again at the back of the chapel. As Mother commented later in private, it paid to have friends in low places.

***

The day of St. Cecelia's commemoration dawned fine. The school converged on the chapel where Helena lifted the small ones to garland Our Lady with frangipani and hibiscus. *Amadindas*, *mbiras* and two small drums thrummed like rain. Mother Julienne, carrying a crown of Madonna lilies, processed slowly towards the altar behind Père Sulpice and Frère Joseph-Marie. Then Mother turned to face the school, her eyes sparkling, her smile slowly embracing each soul before her. 'My children, today we remember a saint who died for her faith. She died by heat and steam. Today we also remember the young men of Buganda martyred by fire at Namugongo by Kabaka Mwanga in 1886. When the Emperor Nero set alight Christians to be human torches for his feasting, little did he know how brightly those torches would burn across the world. They have been lit here in Africa, never to go out. Gloria tibi, Domine. Gloria in excelsis Deo!'

'Gloria in excelsis Deo!' the choir echoed and St Cecilia's mass proceeded in Luganda mingling with Latin and English and culminating in Agnes's pulsating anthem.

Then silence fell. Mother rose and went to the top of the chancel steps. She raised her eyebrows and a small, ferociously scowling emperor was launched from the back of the chapel to ascend the steps below her. Swirling her cloak, she summoned her guards to bring the recalcitrant saint. St Cecilia was hustled to the august feet where she knelt and listened with bowed head to the accusations brought against her. The emperor stamped and demanded revocation and when the saint lifted her head and refused it, the emperor pronounced the death sentence with the flourish of a sword that nearly whacked both Mother and saint into oblivion. Cecilia rose, not a whit disconcerted, and was dragged away by guards to the left chapel door to be steamed to death. *Amadindas* pounded, drums rolled, tears slid down the small cheeks of a stricken congregation. Suddenly Mother's face lit at an apparition at the chapel's right door and the saint, now clothed in white and glittering raiment, walked up the carpeted aisle. The emperor, head hanging, moved aside and St Cecilia stood before Mother. A small angel crept to her side with the wreath of Madonna lilies and Mother raised it high and settled it in Cecilia's dark hair. In a melody all her own, Agnes led her heavenly choir in a burst of rejoicing.

Suddenly men's voices soared rich and strong from the back of the chapel. Daudi, Paulo, Wiriamu and Fesito entered with the bier. It was of shining mahogany, cunningly designed by Daudi, with a well in the centre into which the base of the statue fitted, to hold it firm as it was borne aloft. Daudi and Wiriamu lifted the flower-entangled Mother from her shelf, placed her reverently in the well, took the statue of St Cecilia from the recess and placed her on the bier in front of The Mother.

Paulo settled a large, rolled blanket on Fesito's right shoulder. Then, sweat beading their faces, the four men lifted the arms of the bier to their shoulders. St Cecilia, with Mother at her shoulder, processed gracefully down the aisle behind the bier, followed by the priests. Men, women and children from miles around, thronging the paths in anticipation, parted with cries and murmurs to let them pass.

Accompanied by the ululations of mothers, grandmothers and

aunts they paced round the school quadrangle while Père Sulpice and Frère Joseph-Marie sent holy water sparkling over the grass. Then, followed by a flock of starling children, the Madonna made her way down the wide steps. Frances, standing to one side, watched the men circle her. Daudi, holding the front right arm of the bier, proudly erect, his eyes on the next steps ahead, Paulo, next in seniority to his left, Wiriamu, awed and sweating, supporting the right back arm and Fesito, humblest of all, the left arm. But Fesito's face was alight with the radiance of a young man in love. Stooped and wrinkled, the blanket on his right shoulder barely raising him to the height of the others, his claw hands, the injured feet of a wagtail, gripped the wooden bar with trembling effort but his smile lit the world and spread into smiles on the faces of the children. Nothing, Frances thought, could be more beautiful than those three-fingered wagtail claws.

Now they processed over the lawns towards three shady mahoganies where a wide semi-circle of trestle tables had been arranged. The central table was draped with a rich cinnamon bark-cloth dazzling with embroidered flowers. Here they lowered The Mother and the saint to rest. A bright crowd flowed in towards them, including the repentant emperor and guards. The saint walked through them all, head high lest her crown should slip, closely followed by attendant angels and staring children.

Consolata and Annunciata came sailing into sight with a procession of their own, bearing trays of sandwiches, fruit and cake and large jugs of orangeade. Graciously smiling seniors and prefects walked among nuns and guests with laden platters while Claire, Gabriel and Helena made sure that the very young ate sandwiches before cake. Then, from the chapel, Daudi and Paulo brought *amadindas* and a small band gathered at the feet of Our Lady, with St Cecilia on a chair below her, eating cake. The sisters

179

sat ranged in chairs behind the tables but Helena prowled with a basket of sweets which she tossed in sparkling benediction to fall into the upstretched palms of the innocent as well as emperor and guards, included now in the Lord's general forgiveness.

Presently Gabriel put down her glass and took her chair to the feet of Our Lady and St Cecilia. She reached for a guitar under the table, tuned it and strummed a sequence of chords.

'Come on, Cecilia girl, your turn to dance now!' She drew the saint from her chair and twirled her while Cecilia clutched her lily-crown.

> 'Cecilia was a brave, brave gal –
> sing, sing, sing along with me!
> They told her to renounce her Lord –
> sing, sing, sing along with me!
> But she said: "No, I never shall!" –
> sing, sing, sing along with me!
> Try me by fire, try me by sword!" –
> sing, sing, sing along with me!'

Gabriel nodded at Agnes who took up the improvised tune on an *amadinda*, and the crowd began to take note. Gradually, cake was wiped from lips and glasses relinquished.

> 'They shut her in until she died –
> sing, sing, sing along with me!
> But still she sang, she sang, she sang –
> sing, sing, sing along with me!
> With Jesus there, right by her side –
> sing, sing, sing along with me!
> He took her up where the trumpets rang –
> sing, sing, sing along with me!'

Two more *amadinda* players snatched up their mallets and the second guitarist began to strum.

> 'And now in heaven she sings and plays –
> sing, sing, sing along with me!
> And angels dance wherever she goes –
> sing, sing, sing along with me!
> 'She makes music all her days –
> sing, sing, sing along with me!
> Dance, dance, you twinkle-toes –
> sing, sing, sing along with me!'

By this time the *mbira*-players and drummers had found the rhythm and the crowd was beginning to sway from foot to foot. Helena had thrown aside her empty sweet basket and, flapping her arms, became a round grey hen gathering a hopping circle of chicks.

> 'Music, music, music, music.
> We make music in her name.
> Music, music, music, music.
> Dancing, singing all our days.

When the last verse had been sung several times someone shouted, 'Again, again!' 'Lard luv yer, I've forgotten how it began!' 'Cecilia was a brave, brave gal!' the saint prompted. 'Why, so it was. All together now! Cecilia was a brave, brave gal, sing, sing, sing along with me!'

The saint's acknowledgement was sung again and yet again while the crowd shuffled, swayed and sang. Mother Julienne, sitting back and watching the precarious jigging of the saint's crown, was nodding in time and Felicitas, smiling and nodding beside her, knitted in accelerating tempo. Frances noticed that even Perpetua, standing aloof with her hands behind her back, was tapping her long toes in time. 'One has to hand it to the Irish, when it comes to something like this, they've, er, got it, you know. She comes up with a new one every year.'

Frances peered across the lawns to where people and yet more people were emerging from under the mango trees at the border of the grounds. She recognized Anglicans and Pentecostals in the crowd. 'They can't resist the *amadindas*,' Mattea murmured. Frances caught sight of a gold and violet *basuti* wafting through the throng. Namugasi was here with her youngest grandchildren in tow and so was Motavu with his wife, children and grandchildren.

She found herself caught up in the music and began to jig and sway with the children round the band. Presently Namugasi sidled in beside her, her old face radiant, and they danced shoulder to shoulder, catching one another's eyes in a joyful secret, clapping each other's hands as they swayed apart and together again. The Namugasi beside her seemed young again, as spritely as when she first got to know her, when she had related the myths of old Buganda, stories of the heaven-country of King Gulu, creator and sustainer, who gave his daughter, the beautiful Nambi, to Kintu, a son of earth with his one cow, coming alone out of the barren north to this heaven-country of fertile hills and valleys.

Gabriel's ode to St Cecilia gave way to choruses and Frances's knees began to ache. She sat back in the shade and marvelled at the spontaneous movement of a people whose hearts found bodily expression so natural. Only The Mother was still in the swaying throng. Her face, above the garlands of red and white, gazed with quiet compassion over the heads of rejoicers and, beyond them, at the sick and despairing who had come to sit beside her and had now lost her. King Gulu had been generous to one who had come from the parched and barren places, where so many found themselves now. Frances hung her head. Yes, it had been wrong of her thief to make them pay for miraculous cures but it was not that that she had given them. They had found something else, surely. What was it the wise Abbé of St Denis had said, he of the blue windows? Something to the effect that earthly images of beauty drew the mind to the Creator of all images, all form, all being. The mothering divinity, humble, accessible, cradling in her arms the misery of the world. Wasn't that what she'd been to them? A simple reminder that, beyond all pain and grieving, were arms that gathered? She hung her head and felt like a thief herself.

She looked up at a call from Gabriel. With vigorous sweeps of her arms she was gathering the juniors. Still singing, she Pied-Pipered a trail of tired children to the boarding house. Shadows had grown long over the emerald lawns. Her four bearers had gathered round the Madonna and her saint and lifted them onto the bier. The crowd parted for them as they made their way back to the chapel. Then, still singing, the congregation drifted away over the lawns, sated shadows into the gathering dusk, leaving only the crickets to sustain the music of the heaven-country.

***

Frances rose and went to the chapel. When her bearers had restored The Mother to her niche, she lifted the wilted flowers from her shoulders, but left St Cecilia to preside beside her for a week. Agnes bustled in to supervise the return of *amadindas* and finally Gabriel trod slowly up the steps with a guitar and two *mbiras*.

'Well, Frances, she's had a good day. Got her back just in the nick, didn't we?'

Frances nodded.

'How, I wonder? D'you know?'

'I know who, but not how.'

'Hmm. Frances …' The tired brown eyes turned solemn.

'Don't you think it's time you nailed her to her perch? I'm superstitious, it's the Irish blood. I can't help being scared of the number three. What if …?'

'Mother would never agree.'

'But twice in one term, after seven years peace. It's crazy! One expects the combi and hi-fi to get stolen, but this! Thank heavens tomorrow's Saturday. I'm flaked.' She was gone and Frances turned off the chapel lamps, locked the padlocks on the doors and told herself firmly that the number three had no significance whatever in the greater scheme of things.

Next morning, after tuck-shop duty, with Mother's permission, she hurried over to visit Motavu. At the little duka in the valley she purchased a tin of condensed milk and a few cigars by way of thanks. She found him sitting in his courtyard mending a punctured bicycle tube. He accepted the cigars and condensed milk with an appreciative twinkle. He was pleased that Holy Mother was once more in her place. Everyone, everyone was so happy yesterday.

'How did you do it, Motavu?'

With a quick glance over his shoulder, Motavu obliged her with an account. He kept his voice low but as he got into the swing of his narrative, Frances saw him, Motavu, with a few well-chosen friends, pay a call on the Madonna's new owner, to gossip over the wonders about to occur in his homestead. They took with them some welcome beer and a bottle of whisky liberally laced with *waragi*, which has an inevitable effect on those who imbibe it. When Mr Muwonge and his older sons had slumped snoring in their chairs, Motavu had directed the silent lifting of the Holy Mother to a car parked down the road and his nephew Samweri, taxi driver to Mr Mujaju, had brought her home to the chapel. 'I tell them, it is to be very careful,' Motavu added. 'Nothing is to be broken, nothing, nothing.'

'She is perfectly well, Motavu. There is no harm done. We thank you very much. It is a big thing you have done for us.'

'You saved me.' Motavu screwed up his eyes and gave her a stare.

Frances laughed. 'Jesus saved you.'

'You and Seestah Perpetua and Seestah Agnes and Jesus,' he corrected. 'But I am looking at the padlocks on the doors of the church.' He shook his head. 'Those padlocks are no good.'

'But they're big, strong padlocks. Daudi bought them and we keep the keys hidden away. No thief could find them.'

Motavu shook his head again, helped himself to a cigar, extracted a box of matches from his pocket and lit it. As the first smoke curled from his lips he said pityingly, 'Seestah Frances, for that padlock they don't need keys. They only need this thing.' He took up a piece of wire lying beside the lame bicycle, tweaked it deftly into a series of angles and held it up.

'You push this in the lock, you do like this, like this,' he twisted it from side to side, 'and the lock is open. I threw it away, that tool of Satan, when I came to the Ba-Apostoliki.'

'Of course! A lock picker!'

'A key is no good, Seestah. Also a padlock is no good – only one is difficult for them.' He pointed to a door in a hut across the yard. A massive steel padlock hung from a powerful door bar. 'That one! Eh! It takes too long. It makes too much noise. That one, Seestah, it is the one you must put on the doors of the church to keep The Mother inside. It is the only way against this tool of Satan.'

Frances went over to the padlock and noted its name and size.

'Motavu, thank you.'

'You will tell the Holy Mother about that padlock?'

'I will.' Frances checked herself. 'I will tell Daudi.'

'That is good.'

She was smiling as she walked home, warmed by the cunning and tact of the good old thief. Yet, as she walked past the chapel, surrounded now by cricket song and the gentle tinkling of frogs, she felt that she herself was a thief and a less than generous one.

9. Again!

O nly eight more days, only eight more days!' Four O-level girls, arms round waists, were parading the quadrangle, followed by a chanting crowd. Frances, working in the art room through the morning tea break, smiled as she bent over tables covered in lino-and woodcut-prints. Still so much to do! Today her classes would embellish the prints. Slim, agile brushes would glide in flecks of brilliant colour between the black lines. Bursts of music erupted from the hall where school-leavers, swallow-free after exams, were preparing for their party. Shrieks of saucy laughter from middle-schoolers followed sweating protégées of Consolata's bearing party fare in covered dishes from the domestic science rooms to the main kitchens. Altogether, and deplored by Perpetua and Theodora, discipline was unravelling.

When the last card-embellishers had trooped with coloured fingers from her classroom, Frances bent over the holy family.

Each year they grew again in clay under her hands, finding life and shapes of their own, a little but not too different, from past years. Always first the holy family, oxen, sheep and camels. Then she let herself go. Elephant, giraffe, zebra, rhino and buck crept in, one by one, to stare at their Creator incarnate in humble fragility. And each year, after Christmas had been celebrated and the children had gone, they would travel with Gabriel to her camp. What could she add this year? Wasn't there potential in a gnu … comic potential? She could pull down the long nose, squiffen the cranky horns, exaggerate the ruff…. She straightened her aching back and leaned against the wall, 'Tired work is no good. After lunch maybe ...' The next class would be in soon. She wished she'd had that cup of tea at break. She wiped her face with a paint-flecked handkerchief, filled a mug at the sink and drank as if her life depended on it.

***

Next morning, as she stepped out of the refectory door, Fesito was standing in the pathway. 'Seestah, come!' He laid a trembling hand on her arm. 'Come, Seestah, quickly!' He hobbled ahead of her to the chapel and up the steps. 'Look!' He swept a despairing arm at the recess in the back wall. It was empty. 'She is gone! Again they take her. I am calling you, Seestah, not Daudi. Always he is angry and shouting.' Fesito flinched.

She stood beside him and stared. 'It is good you called me.' She flopped sideways into the back pew and looked at the vacant niche. Again! Gabriel's third time. She felt an impulse to giggle and stifled it. Fesito would be affronted. 'Fesito, have you seen anybody, heard anybody?'

'No, Seestah. Nobody. If I see somebody I tell you!'

188

Only a week before the final, crowning service of the year! Christmas Mass without the Madonna with her tall candle before the altar! Never in seven years had that happened. What was she going to do? She glanced at her watch. 'Fesito, thank you. I shall tell Daudi later, but not now. Morning prayer is soon.'

Fesito lingered. He made a small tentative gesture towards her with his wagtail claw and sidled out. It was his honoured task to stand and watch the hands of the clock in the quadrangle till the precise minute when he must ring the chapel bell. She sat a moment longer. Could it be a joke, this time? The middle-schoolers were quite out of hand, spoiling for a prank. She heard quick feet on the chapel steps. Gabriel hurried in, guitar in hand. 'Hi Fran. I left my strings in the choir and I've got to fit one quick.' As she turned she saw the empty recess, 'Ach no, Frances! So … it had to be three times!'

'Irish witch! You made it happen by thinking it.'

Gabriel plumped down on a pew, her eyes fixed on the blank wall. 'Only a week till Christmas Mass – Mother of God!' The chapel bell began to toll and Gabriel darted to the choir stalls, retrieved a paper packet, extracted a string and hastily began attaching it.

As the school assembled for morning prayers, the disappearance of Our Lady was noticed without consternation. She appeared and disappeared, it seemed, in accordance with the Divine and Inscrutable Will. Only one small girl tugged at Frances's habit in the quadrangle afterwards. 'Sister Frances, has Máma Méri gone to be polished for Christmas?' And Frances bent over her with a finger to her mouth, 'Ssh! It's a secret!'

At morning tea-break she found Daudi in his workshop and alerted him to the theft. He slammed down a hammer and expanded like a toad threatened by a snake. 'Sister, I shall speak with those men now!' Rumbling like an enraged bull, he stormed out and strode to the row of rooms where the night watchmen were sleeping in innocence. Frances followed him. Summoned by shouts and bangs on their doors, four owl-eyed men emerged and were interrogated. No, they had heard nothing at the chapel. Had they walked the perimeters of the school all night? All night, all night they had walked. Only at one o'clock they had gathered for tea and bread behind the garage. That one, Solomon from Mr Kaburungu, he had the radio with music and they had listened while they ate. It was lonely, a man must eat, a man must have a little rest, the night work, it made a man very tired, very hungry.

As Daudi glared at Solomon, Frances felt compunction, 'I, er, Daudi, I forgot to tell you ... those padlocks on the chapel are not completely proof against lock pickers. Motavu has a better brand but I forgot to tell you. You know how quiet and quick these thieves are. It's my fault in a way.'

Daudi deflated and shook his head. 'Sister Frances, you have too much work. It is these men who should be walking all night. They must answer. I shall speak to Mother.'

The loud trilling of the bell announced the end of tea break and Frances started, 'I've a class, I must go.'

'Leave it to me, Sister. I am going to fix this thing.'

Frances hurried through the quad to her class room. It was partly her fault. If she'd seen to the new padlocks this would never have happened. Now the Christmas mass would be a disappointment. Our Lady, with her great candle, surrounded by small gifts made for the children in Gabriel's camp, was the crowning glory of the Christmas mass. Few things dragged on her heart quite so much as disappointment in small faces.

The weekend passed in a daze of work. So many hundreds of cards to fold and stack in boxes to sell for funds. Mattea, as always, helped out. She came in with a thermos and mugs on a tray, found a small space uncluttered by cards and poured tea. She sat down opposite Frances and held out a mug. 'Frazzled Fran.' She gave a down-turned smile. 'Take a break. No good killing yourself.'

Frances quaffed gratefully. Mattea's dark-fringed grey eyes regarded her steadily. Cat's eyes, Frances had always thought them, absorbing much but revealing little. Sea-grey and sometimes, mysteriously, as cold as slate. Even Perpetua, with her almost masculine incuriosity, had once called Mattea "A bit of a closed book." How well they all knew each now after years together. But after seven years in her company Frances felt she knew Mattea as little as when she had first come from Nairobi and before that, Ireland. No, that was not quite right. She knew her inspirational capacities as teacher, her strange, often sarcastic, aloofness, her love of storms. But she knew nothing *about* her in the way that, essentially for women, the past explains the present. Only that she had a highly-rated Masters in English from Dublin. Her past was indeed a closed book.

'More tea?' Mattea reached for the flask.

'Please. Didn't realize how much I wanted it.'

The mugs were refilled and Frances added two spoons of sugar while Mattea grimaced. 'For energy,' Frances sighed.

Mattea sipped and glanced at Frances's sweating face. 'Who on earth has stolen the Virgin this time? Could it be somebody who came up with the valley crowd on St Cecilia's Day and decided to take a chance?'

'You mean after what happened with the science exhibition.' Frances rubbed an aching forehead. 'But the folks who come for St Cecilia's Day are our own Catholics. None of them would do it.'

Mattea put away her mug and began folding cards, slipping them under the flaps of envelopes and laying them in piles to fill ten boxes of cards for AIDS funding and ten for leprosy missions. 'This business of the school belonging to the local community is all very well, but ...'

Frances nodded and began sorting the cards into piles of superior and less good for pricing.

Mattea's eyes softened suddenly. 'It'll be miserable not to have her for Christmas Mass. It's always a highlight – the Mother and Child with the huge candle and those presents for camp children piled around her.'

'Mother's idea was to confer a sort of blessing on the children's generosity to those less fortunate. I remember her saying we must make mothers of them, not just to their own, but to all. They're proud of the presents. The bigger the pile the closer they watch her face.'

'If we don't get her back in time, or at all, what are you going to do?' Mattea's elegant fingers stopped folding, slotting and piling.

'I suppose I could make a really big crib scene to fill the space. I've made the holy family already and I haven't time to redo them. But I could make some large elephant, another rhino ...' Frances looked over at the figures under the window. Mattea swung round and a dimple suddenly dug her cheek. 'I like your crazy gnu. You should do another.'

'It's too late to bake them, but with thick acrylic paint they'd be colourful enough.'

They rose and began to pack the cards into boxes. Frances's hands were numb and stiff but Mattea shuffled, sorted and boxed like lightning. Frances, forewarned, glanced at her. 'Hey, you're snaffling the best for leprosy again.'

Mattea's grey eyes twinkled. 'Well, the leprosy patients are more deserving. They don't bring it on themselves as at least half the AIDS patients do.'

'Not the children!' Frances countered in a years'-old tug-of-war.

Mattea continued to pack ruthlessly. Frances quickly swiped a pile of high-class woodcuts exquisitely coloured by Veronique lying perilously close to Mattea's fingers. It always ended in this race between them. Presently Frances relented, 'You're right, though. Leprosy's a dreadful thing. Absolute and terrifying physical mutilation. And the rejection, even by their closest family. They must suffer dreadfully.'

'They do ... and they don't.' Mattea's hands fell still and she was looking out of the window. She suddenly became remote again. Then she shook herself. 'Well, we seem to have finished this lot. How many more?'

'About two hundred and fifty – I think,' Frances surveyed a spread of still unfolded sheets on the back tables.

'Tomorrow?'

'It would be nice if we could get them off in time. The ones for Ssemogerere I can do later.'

'Are they selling well there?'

'Yes. It seems the tourists like them.'

'I'll take the boxes for Makerere, Mulago, Rubaga and Namirembe over on Monday. Give you a break to create more gnus.'

'You're a brick, thank you.'

On Sunday, after chapel, they packed cards again, conscious of Mother's half-resigned disapproval. After lunch Frances slept for three hours and Mother smiled on her again. On Monday morning it was her turn to do the chapel flowers and she went into the garden early. In defiance she placed a vase of red and orange-speckled yellow cannas in the Madonna's niche and then sat to look at them. The colour of courage. The courage of tough flowers that persisted, come rain, drought or neglect. Flowers that had continued to bloom, untended, through years of dereliction. Yes, courage that she didn't feel would emblazon the niche of the Absent Mother. But the empty space before the altar at the Christmas Mass. Emptiness crying to be filled. Perhaps those wisest and most protective of matriarchs, an elephant or two?

She glanced at her watch. There were half an hour before Morning Prayer and the chapel was blessedly quiet. The only sound that broke the silence was Fesito's sweeping between the choir stalls. A soft cool wind was blowing up from the lake, rolling the clouds towards them and bringing the scent of water. She sniffed happily, leaned over the back of the pew and contemplated the movements of branches against a sky luminous as an oyster shell. The sigh of Fesito's sweeping was as gentle as the wind. She turned and watched the twist and twirl he gave the long grass broom. His wizened stumps and fingers had created an intricate art of broom-handle management and he smiled a small, concentrated smile as he shuffled slowly between stalls and aisle, lifting, twisting, swooping to sweep and lifting again. The wind rustled the trees outside, dislodged a folded scrap of paper under a pew and tumbled it down the aisle towards the chancel steps. Dust swirled up at Fesito's feet and he subdued it with a twirling thrust. Then he bent and very carefully lifted the piece of paper wedged in the angle of the first step. He turned it over and straightened up, his face solemn. Fesito could not read but he had an awe of the written word. He looked over at Frances and came shuffling crab-wise down the aisle, holding the folded square in his right hand.

'Seestah, it is reading.'

She took it. '*Webali*, Fesito.' He walked back to the choir stalls and continued to sweep. She held the note a moment without bothering to look at it. Little notes between girls were often dropped under pews. Then, idly, she glanced at the much-folded scrap of school-book paper, slightly muddy. It was uncharacteristically grubby and folded with more care than the usual note. She opened it and held it up. In childish but very neat script that testified to considerable effort were written the words 'do not wury I boro it is kironde'. She sat up and read it again. 'do not wury I boro ... it is kironde'. Boro – borrow what? Who *was* Kironde? It was a boy's name.

'Do not wury I boro' Could 'borrow' *possibly* refer to the Madonna? Or was she going crazy with obsession? Was there a Kironde among the school staff? She did a quick résumé of the sub-gardeners, of Daudi's, Paulo's and Wiriamu's families. No Kironde. Who was Kironde and why on earth had he 'borrowed' the Madonna? *If* he had? The swishing of the broom had stopped. She looked up into Fesito's enquiring visage.

'Seestah, who is writing?'

'Someone called Kironde. Do you know anyone of that name?'

Fesito shook his head. Then he scratched it and looked out of the door. She knew he would conjure a Kironde out of nowhere if it would please her.

'Fesito, thank you. This is important. I shall take it to Mother Julienne.'

Comforted by this appeal to the source of all knowledge, Fesito returned to the conquest of broom over dust and Frances left the chapel.

'Touching, is it not?' Mother smiled at the grimy sheet in her hand. 'I wonder who Kironde is. Well,' she laid her head back against her chair and regarded the crucifix on the wall.

'Prayer and waiting, as usual, ma fille. I wonder,' the glance of a naughty girl slid towards Frances, 'I wonder what will come to us this time?'

'Let me know, Mother. I'll be waiting. But even if something comes, there's no time to go and hunt her down. And, since it's so unlikely we'll have her back for the last mass, I must get on and finish some large crib animals. I can't bear the thought of that gap.'

But the day dragged on without word from Mother and Frances threw herself into creative labour. By late afternoon, the menagerie of adoration included two buffalo, another gnu, a family of elephant with two babies that waved enquiring trunks and two reverent baboons. Her hands were cramping, her head throbbed and her neck and back burned villainously. She groped to the tap, drank three aspirin, washed the clay from her hands, locked the classroom door and made her way to the nuns' house.

Late in the evening, after another two hours' work, as she was half way up the stairs to her room, Felicitas hurried out of Mother's sitting room, beaming conspiratorially. 'Frances, Mother's had a word.' Frances turned and came sagging downstairs. She found Mother sitting up in bed.

'Frances something has come to me but I cannot believe it. It came in the same way as the others, but perhaps this time I've got it wrong. It is too strange.'

'What is it?'

'I saw one of those … those what do you call them? The scaly animals with the long tail? They eat only ants.'

'A pangolin?'

'Oui, that's the name.' Mother clicked her fingers. 'It was hanging by the tail from a woman's hand. Croyez-vous?'

'Mother!'

'I know – it is absurd! I'm a little tired, ma fille. Perhaps it is the old brain playing a trick.' She looked shame-faced.

'No! Don't you see? It's too absurd to be wrong. It's not something you could have dreamed up. Wait! If it was hanging by the tail from a woman's hand, it must be a tree pangolin. They're rare. I've only seen one. The hand! What was it like?'

Mother put her head on one side and pursed her lips. 'A woman's for sure, wrinkled, very mottled …'

'Like Toni's?'

Mother nodded, 'Yes, like Toni's.'

'But Toni hasn't got a tree pangolin.'

'When did you last see her?'

'Oh, weeks ago.'

'Well, as we know, ma fille, anything can happen in a few weeks.'

'Have I permission?'

'As soon as you wish.'

'Tomorrow morning I must finish the crib animals but I'll go as soon as I'm done.'

'Bien. And Frances, do not be angry with this Kironde. He endears himself to me. The writing, it cost him much effort.'

'Oh, Mother! I am cross. I'm very cross and very tired. But I'll try not to be cross with Kironde. Bonne nuit, ma mère.'

'Bonne nuit, ma fille.'

***

The valley was screaming with cicadas. Heat clotted the long grasses, oozed like treacle along the road. To breathe was to inhale warm water. It was a relief to stand a moment on the sand and let the slight lake-breeze cool the rivers running under her wimple into her neck. She turned and entered the leaf-shadowed gloom of Toni's garden. As she came round a corner, the scent of a cigar wafted to her and she followed it. Toni was sitting in a chair under moonflower bushes, reading and dangling a foot which Clementine, lying on her back, was clutching with hands and feet. 'Frances! Just in time for tea. Jero-home!'

'*Mamsab?*'

'Bring two cups please – Sister Frances is here.'

'It is coming.'

Jerome issued from the kitchen balancing a tray in one hand and a small folding table in the other. 'Greetings, Sister Frances. All is well?'

'Very well, thank you, Jerome. And with you?'

'All is well. And with the school?'

'All is well. Except …'

'What is this except?' Jerome deftly unfolded the table next to Toni.

'The statue of the Virgin and Child has gone again. It's the third time.'

Jerome's eyes rolled heavenwards. 'Eh! These people. These pagans have no respect!'

'We would like to have her back for the Christmas Mass.'

'God must help you, Sister, God must help you now.'

'He must indeed – if he wants us to have her back. Perhaps he doesn't?'

'She belongs to St Mary's, Sister. It is a heavy sin to steal her.' He brought the table a precise six inches closer to Toni's right hand and neatly deposited the tray. Clementine sat up at the clink of china and the smell of freshly baked biscuits. Jerome vented a long 'Eeeeh!' of disapproval and strode back to the kitchen shaking his head.

'Clementine has developed a weakness for Jerome's coconut biscuits.' Toni stretched over to a piled plate. Clementine's long lips pouted forward. 'There, my love, don't gobble it and choke.'

Toni lifted the teapot and poured. 'Damn this theft business! Isn't it time you welded, or whatever you do, that statue firmly in place, Frances?'

'Mother doesn't like the idea. The whole point is to share her with the wider congregation. They set great store by her, just as the girls do.'

'One of these days she might take off and never come back.'

Clementine tapped Toni's knee for a second biscuit. 'Tea first.' Toni poured a liberal mug of milk, laced with tea and two spoons of sugar. 'That's my girl. Nicely does it. She's taking well to a cup,' she nodded in motherly pride, 'but she still demands a bottle morning, noon and night.' Clementine slurped noisily, holding the mug with both hands till it was poised upside down over her face and the last sugary drops had trickled out. Then she tossed the mug onto the grass and pouted her lips towards the biscuits again, giving soft hoots, her eyes those of a destitute starveling. Another biscuit was granted and she sucked at it, meditatively surveying Frances.

'She's looking grand, Toni. She's put on weight.'

'Right as rain, thanks to the good Doc. I like that young man.'

'He's not so young, is he?' Frances remembered the grey strands in his beard and something about the rather deep-set grey eyes.

'To me anything under sixty's young. Two days after our Ignatia party, Clementine's temperature soared again. She had a fit in the middle of night and I phoned Jeremy. He came right away and gave her a different antibiotic. It's worked, thank God. Her arm's healed perfectly. Jeremy's a good egg, poor fellow.'

'Why "poor fellow"?'

'Doc Anderson came yesterday to do my usual check and give me a tetanus booster. I confessed to him that I had suborned

Jeremy to treat Clementine and he said, "Good show, that should lighten him up a bit." When I asked why he needed lightening up he said that he had lost his wife, a teacher, to encephalitis in Papua New Guinea. He'd rushed her to Port Moresby hospital but the doctors there couldn't pull her through. He'd had to bring her in along terrible roads from a remote area. He'd done all he could for her, but it hadn't been enough. Anderson said he blamed himself somehow, though he couldn't see what more he could have done. Anderson says doctors always blame themselves for what happens to family, reckons it's a good thing Jeremy's in charge of Clementine.'

'Good for him and for Clementine,' Frances murmured and understood the indefinable something she had sensed in Jeremy.

Toni glanced at her watch. 'Goodness the time – Muwanga! Muwa-a-anga!'

'*Nyabu?*' Muwanga came trotting from the animal pens beyond the kitchen.

'Muwanga, it's time for the olugave's supper. Bring her please?'

'I am coming, *nyabu*.'

Frances helped herself to a third biscuit, crisp as a macaroon, and accepted another cup of tea. Muwanga appeared some minutes later, carrying a *kikapu* which he put down at Toni's feet.

'How is she?'

'She is eating, *nyabu*.'

'Good. We're giving her mince and egg but unless they get enough ants they die on you.'

'Ants, Toni?' Frances's hand suddenly wobbled and tea slopped into her saucer. She craned forward. 'What have you got there?'

'Arboreal pangolin. Some boys brought her in two days ago. They found her in a snare in the forest down Wachanga way. Her hind leg's injured,' she bent over the basket and lifted a young pangolin onto her lap. 'Ever seen one of these before, Frances?'

'Only once. Jim had one, years ago.' She stretched over and slid her hand over honey-coloured scales. Lustrous brown eyes regarded her without apprehension and a pink-brown nose rose and sniffed the warm scents of the afternoon. Toni inspected the injured leg liberally painted with gentian violet.

'No sepsis yet. I hope we don't have to call the good doctor for you, my dear. I take her into the forest every day after tea for ants. You can come with us if you like – no Clementine. Leave pangolin alone – no. N – o!' She prized Clementine's fingers from a scale. 'She keeps trying to pick her scales off and pangolin doesn't like it. She's had enough persecution. There, have a biscuit instead.'

Clementine, her eyes beady with jealousy, sat back and eyed the intruder. Toni turned the creature very gently on her back and stroked the pink stomach under cream-coloured fur. 'You like that don't you, my honey. Oh, yes, that's nice. No Clementine!'

Foiled, Clementine swivelled her eyes to the biscuit plate again. She rose from her bottom, lurched on bandy legs towards the table and Frances quickly handed her a biscuit.

'How like one's children they are!'

'You can say that again! Clementine, if I let you go on like this your stomach will be dragging on the ground before you're two. I'd better eat the last myself.' She tossed the biscuit into her mouth, crunched noisily and drained her cup. 'Right, now it's time for the evening ramble. Ants in the forest. Coming, Frances?'

'Indeed I am.' She rose with a fluttering heart and dusted biscuit crumbs from her habit.

Toni called to Muwanga who came over with a banana to entice Clementine into his arms. '*Webali*, Muwanga. Take her on her walk round the front garden. No carrying, remember. It's for exercise.' Muwanga made off with Clementine and Toni got to her feet. 'She makes the ant walk impossible, interferes with Pangolin every three minutes.' She draped the pangolin's tail over her right hand. The fleshy mushroom-pink pad under the tip of the tail gripped her palm and the pangolin, supported by powerful tail muscles, lifted her body into a horizontal pose. Her forefeet with their long, curved claws waved expectantly as they crossed the garden to the forest path. 'This is the only creature I've ever known to habituate so easily.' Toni picked her way through undergrowth to a termite mound with a freshly-repaired patch on its side. The pangolin reached out and scratched into the soft mud. As the ant runnels were exposed, her long, glistening tongue probed their depths and emerged iced with fat termites.

They wandered deeper into the forest, tacking from mound to mound until Toni stopped and peered into a group of trees on her left. 'Ah, there it is! These are the ones she's mad about.' She made her way to a low branch with a strange papery efflorescence dangling from its elbow, like a papiloma on an old man's arm. 'Tree ants.' Toni lifted her arm and the pangolin rose and dug her claws into the nest. A storm of ants rustled from dark crevices, their heart-shaped abdomens raised and glinting metallic blue. The long tongue slithered and caressed the seething swarm and Toni and Frances ducked as ants dropped on their heads. Frances's wimple deflected those that fell on her but they snagged, winking in Toni's hair and she batted them off, grinning. 'Lucky the little beggars don't bite – not much anyway!' The pangolin calmly scraped ants from the fur round her eyes with a fore claw and dined with relish. At the next tree-ants' nest Frances stood back and watched, darting in now and then to flick her handkerchief over Toni's head and shoulders.

She stiffened. Beyond the pangolin's wheezing sniffs she heard something … alien. She moved away, back to the path and listened. 'Tock-tock … tock-tock … tock-tock-tock!' The sound of wood on wood. Perhaps one of Toni's people was cutting wood for the stove. What else could it be? And yet … the pangolin. She quietly slipped along the path between trunks and buttresses. The leaf mould, chocolate and yellow, was damp and her feet made no sound. Once, the tocking stopped and she waited, not daring to move. Then it began again, closer. Suddenly, a little way ahead, the forest canopy opened. Afternoon sun poured into a glade as Frances ducked behind a tree.

In the middle of the glade, bathed in green-gold light, stood the Madonna. Her serene gaze was fixed on a boy, sitting about ten feet from her. He was staring into her face. His thin legs, half-crooked, merged to where he grasped a rough chunk of wood between his foot soles. In his left hand he held a beaten-out screwdriver and, in his right, a square of wood, a rough mallet. As she watched, he drew his eyes from the Madonna to the lump of wood between his feet, looked up once more at the Madonna and, in a series of deft blows, struck a curving line from the top of the wood down to what was becoming a shoulder. Again he stared with wide, alert eyes and tapped rapidly. He paused, shook his head, tapped the battered screwdriver again and once again, looking continually from the statue to his work.

Suddenly Toni came tramping along the path. 'Frances! Where are you?' The boy jumped as if shot, dropped his tools and scrambled to his feet. Frances came out from behind the tree and walked into the glade with Toni panting at her heels, batting ants off her shirt. The boy faced them, a startled buck poised to flee.

'*Wasusiotiano*, my friend.' Frances stepped forward. 'You are making a statue? May I see it?'

The boy's adam's apple rose in his throat but he uttered no sound. She bent and picked up the crude chisel and mallet. 'You need better tools than these, my child. Is your name Kironde?'

'It is Kironde, *nyabu.*' It was a raw whisper and he stepped back as Toni advanced, her eyes sparkling with indignation.

'Kironde, I found your letter. Thank you for telling me. Do you want very much to make a statue like this one?' Frances laid her hand on the Madonna's head.

Kironde shuffled his feet, 'Yes, *nyabu.* I want it.'

'Little blighter! How the hell did he lug her down here? Kironde,' Toni launched into fluent Luganda, 'how did you bring it down here?'

Kironde made a vague gesture towards the valley. 'Big boys, my friends, from our church. We have no Máma there, by our church. The big boys, they know another one, the somebody who can fix the lock. They bring the Máma here, they tell me, make the Máma Méri for our church, like this one. They are from our church, *nyabu.* Good people,' he croaked. '*Nyabu,* we only borrow, just a little.'

Toni, dangling the pangolin in her right hand, put her left hand on her hip. 'Do you not know the difference between borrowing and stealing? If you borrow you ask first, you ask permission. Then, if permission is given, you take a thing. What you have done is not borrowing. It is stealing. It has caused much searching, much heaviness to this sister.'

Kironde looked down, cracking his knuckles apprehensively. Frances laid her hand on his shoulder and felt him flinch.

'Kironde, you say you want to make a Mother like this one for your church?'

'Our church is very small, *nyabu.* No Máma Méri, no Jésu Christu. We see the Máma Méri of St Mary's church. They tell me I must make one for our church. They see my carvings, my grandfather he taught me, I make the small things there at our place. They wish for the Máma Méri at our place.'

'When did you see our Máma Méri?'

'That time the *amadindas* are calling, when they are dancing for Máma Méri in the garden.'

'I see. Kironde, where do you live?'

'Over there,' Kironde's chin jutted towards the fisher villages.

'I've never seen you.' Toni glared at him. 'Are you telling the truth?'

'It is one month only I am here, *nyabu*. My father died last year. My mother she dies now. I come here to the people of my father's brother. Our church is very small.'

Frances remembered suddenly a tiny mud and thatch church on a hilltop a few miles beyond Masenge. The brothers visited it once a month. 'Kironde, it is good that you make a Mother for your church. Shall I help you?'

'Frances, for heaven's sake!'

'Toni,' she kept her voice low, 'the child's got something. The way he's managed that line from the head down the shoulder, the position of the child, the angle of the head – it's rough, but he's grasped it. You can't teach just anyone to see that. Good carvers are very rare in Buganda, not like the Congo. Kironde, you want me to help you to do it nicely?'

A brief smile wrenched open his wooden face. 'Yes, *nyabu*. I want it.'

'Good, good! How old are you?'

'Twelve years, *nyabu*.'

'Do you go to school?'

'Not now, nyabu. No money. I work, I clean the fish, I clean the boats.'

'Would you like to go to a school where they teach this work, this carving?'

'Yes, nyabu.' His eyes clung to her hungrily but then he shrugged and scuffed the chips of wood at his feet.

'You shall come with me to St Paul's School. Brother Sebastien will teach you.'

'But, *nyabu*, the money?'

'I will arrange it.'

'Frances, don't be daft!' Toni hissed.

Frances laid a hand on her arm. 'Can I borrow your car to get the Madonna back to the school right away?'

'Of course, if it'll start.'

'Could Jerome and Muwanga carry her to the car for me?'

'I'll go and call them.' Toni hurried off down the path with the pangolin dangling replete at her side.

Frances turned to the boy whose eyes still lingered over Our Lady. This child, she thought, this orphaned child who cleaned fish and boats at his uncle's place, had talent and more, a passion to create beauty, to transcend the blows that fate had dealt him.

'Kironde,' she said, 'are you happy at your uncle's place?' He looked at her in surprise, '*Nyabu*, is okay.'

She supposed it must be. It was, after all, tradition among his people to send a son at a certain age to live with a father's brother who would discipline him better than a father. But his mother was gone now too. No wonder these orphans longed for the lost mother. 'Kironde, the wife of your uncle, she is kind to you?' So many women felt overburdened these days with orphaned family members and the people who fished along the shore earned very little, too little to welcome an extra hungry mouth.

Kironde looked away into the trees and murmured. 'The sister, she likes me.'

At least there was someone. 'Kironde, do you have a brother, a sister of your own?'

He shook his head. 'My small brother died. It is only me here.'

She felt the prick of tears behind her eyelids. A child of rare talent in a strange place, too poor to further his gifts. She couldn't just leave him to his fate.

'Kironde, come to St Mary's school tomorrow afternoon. Three o'clock, you understand? Do not be late. My time is very little now. Three o'clock. I shall take you to see Brother Sebastien at the school where they teach carving. He will help you, teach you. You understand me?'

'I will come.'

'Now I must take the Mother back to the chapel because we need her. You will make a Mother like this one.'

'*Nyabu*, I will come.' At the sound of men's voices along the path, Kironde's face turned to wood again.

'Go now,' she said. 'Take your wood and your tools and I will see you tomorrow. Three o'clock. Don't be late, Kironde!' By the time Jerome and Muwanga strode into the clearing, Kironde was gone, only the wood chips scattered on the forest floor testifying to his guilty passion. The two men carried the Madonna along the forest path and laid her carefully on the back seat of Toni's car while Frances slipped into the driver's seat. The car started after the seventh attempt.

'You must come in and have a drink when you return the car. I don't need it tomorrow,' Toni waved at her over Clementine's embrace, 'and tell me what happens next. Little blighter. Hope you're not mistaken in him. Borrowing, my foot!'

Frances waved, the car lurched into the rutted drive and with a sudden spurt of joy she cried, 'I'll be back for – a lemonade with a drop of sherry, if you won't tell!'

At three o'clock the following afternoon, Frances washed the clay from her hands, locked the classroom and hurried out. There was no sign of Kironde in the quad, or in the school driveway. She circled the nun's house and peered into the trees beyond Mother's garden. Perhaps, after all, he'd been afraid to come. Then she saw a slender figure under the furthest mango tree from the chapel and hurried over to him. He stood, shifting his feet apprehensively, hugging his wood and tools.

'*Wasusiotiano, nyabu* Seestah. I am here.'

Frances glanced guiltily round the perimeter of the school grounds. The stalking figure of Theodora was visible at the corner of the netball pitches. She was heading towards them. 'I see you, my child. Come with me quickly!'

She hustled the forbidden male to Toni's car under the mango tree by the garage, settled Kironde in the front seat and slammed the door. After several false starts, the engine ignited. She hurried down the drive and turned left downhill, into a winding track, the back road to St Paul's Dominican School. Kironde sat very stiff and straight, clutching his mallet and screwdriver and said not a word. Frances suddenly found herself humming that ridiculous tune of Gabriel's to St Cecilia.

Frère Raphael, young and athletic, met her on the wide front steps of St Paul's and hurried off to find Frère Sebastien. He came slowly out of the entrance hall, yawning and rubbing his wiry grey thatch. 'Ma soeur, what brings you today?' In French Frances explained Kironde's 'borrowing'.

'Alors! Un petit voleur, hein? Well, let me see, let me see.' She extracted Kironde from the car and pointed to the statue on the floor. 'He's done that with only these.' She held up the beaten-out screwdriver and chunk of wood. 'You know Benedicta's Madonna, Frère. Now, look how he's caught the angle of the shoulder and the exact position of the child's head. He saw it for himself. Don't tell me this boy is without talent?' Brother Sebastien's sharp grey eyes ran over the figure, then he shot a glance at her from under shaggy brows. Then he looked at Kironde who looked shamefaced at the ground. 'Not bad, ma soeur. But what do you want me to do about it, eh?' Frère Sebastien put his head on one side and gave a French shrug of his heavy shoulders. 'What is it you have in mind?'

'Well, I wondered, I hoped that perhaps … well, he's twelve years old, you see. He's obviously had a little schooling. Do you think perhaps St. Paul's could …?'

'Take him on? We would only take him at a very low grade. Voilà, that is not without difficulty. And the fees – what family has he?'

'He's lost both parents,' Frances pleaded. Again the shrug. 'So have many!'

'He's recently come to live with an uncle in a fishing village. There's no money. He's gutting fish and doing odd jobs on the boats. With a talent like this!'

Frère Sebastien scratched a stubbly chin and looked at the statue again. He took it out of the car and turned it in calloused hands. 'Yes … yes, it is not so bad, but ...' He scrutinised the carving from all angles and rounded on her. 'Ma soeur, the world is full of orphans who need schooling.'

'But not full of artists who will repay a little tuition with more than money,' she whispered. 'If you would take him on, I could … well, surely we could find the fees from somewhere?' Frances crossed herself mentally.

Frère Sebastien tucked the lump of wood under his arm.

'Come.' He jerked his head at the boy.

Frances and Kironde followed Frère Sebastien into a school quadrangle larger and more imposing than St Mary's and then down steps into a path between long lawns, to a building set among trees at the end of the sway-back hill. Frère Sebastien dug deep into a pocket, rustled up a bunch of keys and opened the door into a capacious hall. Immediately the perfume of wood and wood oils enveloped them. They followed him through the workshop where half-made furniture reposed on workbenches and Kironde's eyes widened at neat rows of woodwork tools ranged in slotted shelves along the walls, each graded meticulously according to use and size. Frère Sebastien threw open a door at the end of the hall into a room where a terrible angel with raised wings and windswept drapery gazed from remote eyes.

'Ah, mon frère! Qu'il est féroce!'

'Certainement.'

She turned to Kironde. 'This is the work of Frère Sebastien.'

The boy's eyes were glazed with awe. He put out his hand to touch a swirl of drapery. Then he looked down at the chisels on the table and touched each one, glancing up to measure its gauge against the strokes in the wood. 'This,' his hand trembled over a wide-curved blade, wickedly sharp, and then he ran a finger over a long hollow in the angel's robe, 'this makes this one?'

Frère Sebastien ducked his head and grunted. He jabbed at the dark centre of a wing-feather. 'Which one did I use here?'

The boy searched from one blade to the next. 'It is this one?'

The old man nodded, lifted the chisel and fitted it to the groove in the wood.

'And this one?' Suddenly the boy found his tongue. He touched a long flake of feather on a lower wing. 'How do you make this one?'

Frère Sebastien shot a look under his eyebrow-hedges at Frances and lifted two chisels. 'With this and this, this one going this way and that one angled to it, to make the fine hairs of the feather.'

Kironde was nodding, his face transformed, just as the wood had been transformed by passion. His eyes were alive and Frances found tears suddenly stinging her own.

Frère Sebastien turned from the angel and his big, calloused hand slapped the rough statue Kironde had laid on the table. 'Now, show me what you would do with this one – here.' He handed the boy a chisel and pointed to the half-articulated flow of the Virgin's mantle between the head and right shoulder. He picked up a smooth-handled mallet and put it in Kironde's right hand. Frances held her breath. Kironde stared at the beautifully honed chisel as if it were some vision. Then he looked carefully at the drapery so meagrely delineated on his block, then he looked long and carefully at the drapery of the angel. Frère Sebastien shot a challenging glance at Frances who looked away from him and focussed on the slightly trembling point of the chisel. Kironde took a breath, lifted chisel and mallet and started a stroke from the head down the virgin's right side. At the first tap of the mallet he looked up startled. Under the razor-sharp chisel the wood melted as it never had under his screwdriver. Frances held her breath. Kironde hesitated a second and then continued the stroke, creating a fine and gentle curve that did no violence to the hidden shoulder and ended in a sweep near the elbow. Frances breathed again. 'Well?' She raised her eyebrows and out-stared Frère Sebastien.

'Eh bien,' he growled. 'He is a natural. I could take him on – and see.'

Frances suppressed an impulse to fling her arms round Frère Sebastien, a gesture he would not appreciate. Instead she said sedately, 'I thought you would see his promise, Brother. Thank you. I shall take him back now. When should he come?'

Sebastien rubbed his chin and looked at the boy. Kironde's eyes were feverishly tracing the contours of the angel. 'We close the workshop for the December vacation, of course. But I shall be working on the angel in the weeks to come. If he would like to come and watch, he may.'

'Do you want to do that, Kironde?'

'Yes, *nyabu*. I want it.'

'It's a long way from his home, mon Frère. Would there be room for him to sleep here somewhere? I'm sure he'd be happy to do chores, to help you in the workshop, pay his way a little?'

'I could make a plan,' he grunted. 'I could make a plan, yes.' Again an equivocating shrug. 'Always I am forced to make a plan for you, hein!' He shot her a malevolent glance and Frances beamed at him.

As they retraced their steps through the long room Frances ran her hand over a beautifully polished table with ten chairs round it. 'Lovely piece of wood. Where did you get it?'

'Budongo. It's a suite for the Minister of Health's residence. We pay our way. We have others on order. And non, ma soeur, as always you linger, you run your hands over my wood. Flattery, I know it. I have absolutely no wood to spare for you.' He stood in the doorway, glowering down the long room and Frances, the incessant and ever-hopeful recipient of Frère Sebastien's leavings, nodded submissively. 'Eh bien,' he closed the door and turned the key in the lock. 'You are a troublesome and plotting woman, Soeur Françoise, as I have said before. But sometimes – occasionally – you are right. And me, it will be nice to have one pupil who has the passion to carve, to create. Furniture, good furniture, yes, it is a worthy craft and our boys will make furniture of the best and earn a good living. But only one in ten thousand has the passion to create an image that is beautiful and the stubborn will to carry it through. We will be d'accord.'

When they reached the car, Frère Sebastien leaned one hand against it and extended a great paw towards Kironde, 'Now give me that execrable tool.' He pointed to the screwdriver.

Kironde looked at the screwdriver and then into the inscrutable grey eyes and then at the huge hand. Slowly, with a small sigh, as if it hurt, he relinquished it. The hand closed and the other hand was laid flat before him. 'And the other.' Kironde let go of his makeshift mallet. 'No more rubbish like this again, you hear?'

'Yessir,' Kironde whispered.

'On Monday you return, hein? You come here on Monday and find me in the workshop. Understand?'

'Yessir.' Kironde's eyes slid once to the battered metal shaft protruding from Sebastien's paw. Then he clasped his own empty hands together and cracked his knuckles.

'Do not do that!' His mentor growled. 'Your hands are your best tools. Do not weaken them, understand?'

'Yessir.' With a brief imploring glance at Frances who smiled and nodded at him.

'Well.' Frère Sebastien hitched up the grimy rope round his broad middle and made for the steps at the entrance to St Paul's. 'Monday!' He shook his finger at Kironde, 'You hear?'

'Yessir.'

Then, as an afterthought, he threw over his shoulder, 'I have ordered wood for the middle of January, Soeur Françoise. There may be the odd piece of *majarati* too small, too ill-shaped for furniture, hein? But for red mahogany ...' He rubbed his thumb over his forefinger. 'For the mahogany you pay!'

'Merci, mon frère.' Frances batted her eyelashes, such as they were, smiled sweetly, bundled Kironde into the car and slid into the driver's seat. After only three tries, the car shuddered to life and they swung round the drive as Frère Sebastien's formidable bulk disappeared into the shadowed arch of the doorway. *Cunning old bear,* Frances smiled to herself. *He's got the carving and the tools. There's no way Kironde will duck out of this, no matter how scared he is. And after using that chisel … and the angel …*

Kironde was silent and gazed intently ahead, seeing nothing. After a while, as they swooped up a hillside and then slowed down behind a herd of speckled goats, She asked, 'What are you thinking, Kironde?'

'Seestah, I am seeing the angel.'

'It is a fine angel, is it not? A fierce, strong warrior.'

'Very strong.' Kironde swallowed with emotion. 'It has much power, very much power.' He tapped his heart with a closed fist. 'It is burning me.'

'Brother Sebastien – you must call him that – can teach you everything about wood.'

'He has power, Sister. Too much power. Sometimes I think he is angry with me?'

'No, that's just his way. He only gets angry when boys are lazy and spoil their wood with stupidity. Do not be afraid of him, Kironde.'

The goats dispersed and they crested the hill, swerved round the end of it and down into the narrow forest track to Toni's back garden.

'Sister, I will make an angel one day?'

'It will take time, Kironde. You will make small things first. But one day you will make an angel. Do not forget Monday or Brother Sebastien will be angry. He hates it when people are late.'

Kironde's huge eyes held hers for a long moment. Then he looked steadfastly ahead and she knew he did not see the forest trees or the garden or Toni coming over the lawn with her child in her arms, but an angel with wings and windy drapery as wide as the sky.

She slammed the car door. 'Toni, Brother Sebastien will take him on! I'll have that lemonade now!'

***

She woke suddenly and sat up. A distant cock was crowing and she looked at the luminous dial of her bedside clock. Twenty to five. With awful clarity she saw the fragile, threadbare Kironde among the sleek pupils of St Paul's. *What had she done?* The élite went there, top pupils from reputable primary schools, boys from wealthy Kampala families and the highly placed of other counties. After meeting Kironde for only ten minutes, she had bludgeoned Frère Sebastien into taking him on, ignoring his misgivings. Worse still, she had committed herself – and St Mary's – to finding his fees. Even worse, she had done it without consulting Mother. She sank her face in her hands. Crazy, impulsive fool ... would she ever learn to consider, to weigh things before ... 'Headless chicken, Mother, headless chicken!' Her sons had been right.

She took a deep breath, swung her legs out of bed, wrapped her dressing gown round her and went out on the balcony. One cock crow echoed another in the valley below, mocking ... mocking a chicken that spied a tempting morsel and pounced on it, only to have it stick in its throat. It would cost thousands of shillings to keep Kironde at St Paul's. That spelling of his – he'd be the dunce in a class of boys years younger. Could he have the dedication to bear up under that? Hundreds of thousands of shillings, when they struggled to subsidise worthy pupils at St Mary's!

She walked the length of the balcony and back. What made her do it? What made her rush in where any angel with sense would have stopped to consider? Rushing in with promises because of a look in his eyes, a look of aching love. The look Benedicta had had. And one or two others, only one or two in all the years of teaching. She walked the length of the balcony again, gripped the wall and sighed. It was what it always had been, she supposed. As a very small child she had been entranced out of herself into something she saw, into the ecstasy of form, colour, and the light ... A light that shone through things, 'homelight' she'd called it, though she didn't know what she meant by it. It dimmed as she grew older, though she had never forgotten it. She'd often felt a stranger among others, stopping to stare at things they only glanced at and passed by, feeling excited love thudding under her ribs. And then the compulsion to recreate, that set her drawing, drawing, painting to capture the radiance ... and the bitter frustration as it eluded her. Something that had glowed as she painted it, became a faded leaf the next day. It was a lonely thing. Friends and classmates had either mocked or over-admired which had counted for nothing, because she knew when her work lived ... or did not live.

When she saw that love in another's eyes, she found a friend. Benedicta and now Kironde. Mattea, too, sat in abstraction as she saw and heard nothing but the words of a poem rising. Agnes entered a world of sounds no one else could hear. Yes, she had friends here. But was she being a friend to Kironde? Would he, could he manage the leap from nothing to the expectations of St. Paul's?

When a faint light revealed quarter past five on her watch, she hurried into her room and dressed. At five-thirty she knocked on the door of Mother's sitting room. Mother rose at five and enjoyed an hour of silence before the day descended on her shoulders.

At a startled 'Entrez!' Frances took a deep breath and went in.

10. Mother Julienne's Confession

It was two days before the end of term. All staff were in the staff room for morning tea, suffering from terminal fatigue. Even Gabriel and Mark slouched listless in their chairs and the only sound was the clink of cups on saucers. Suddenly Theodora put down her cup and stood up, facing Mother Julienne from a height. 'Mother, it has happened three times now, the theft of the Virgin and Child. It is not right. It must be fixed. It must be fixed to the wall with iron. We cannot allow it to continue like this. It is inviting disrespect and sin.'

Mother glanced at Frances and Frances felt a sudden flood of relief. She had not yet dared broach the subject, had been putting it off till term was over. She knew Sebastien had made some cunning plan with the statue of St Paul and she'd wondered. Theodora fixed her hypermetropic eyes on her. She sat up straight and said, 'I think you have a point, Theodora. We don't want it to happen again.'

Theodora turned to Mother. 'You see. Sister Frances agrees with me. You refuse to have the fence around the school. Our statue will be taken again by thieves. It is not right.'

Mother glanced round the tired faces in the staff room.

'You are all aware of my reasons for having kept the chapel open at all times to our wider congregation. But it has been a very trying term for Sister Frances. If everybody is in agreement, I shall leave the decision to her and abide by her wishes.'

Nods and murmurs affirmed Mother's pronouncement. They were all aware that, since her rejected appeal for a fence, Theodora stalked the boundary in every spare moment in stern reproval of Mother's laxity. But she could not stalk it all night long, and the watchmen had been outwitted every time. The bell rang for lessons and as they filed out of the staff room Mattea slid next to Frances and whispered, 'Wouldn't be such a bad idea, would it?' Gabriel brushed against her and said, 'Nail her to her perch, Frances.' Frances felt limp with relief and decided to phone the bear that afternoon. Enough was enough. For the first time she felt unforced charity towards Sister Theodora.

On the last day of term, Frances entered the chapel carrying The Holy Family in a box. She was followed by Nambi with reverent African fauna and Grace with the unruly elephants. They walked into a sacred gloom created by Theresa and Annunciata who were hanging black curtains in the windows. All traces of last night's enactment of the Holy Nativity had been swept away by Fesito. While the school-leavers had partied in the hall, the rest of the school had witnessed the sacred birth, the arrival of shepherds and wise men, Herod's rage and the flight into Egypt. Paulo's tiny granddaughter had behaved with placid decorum throughout. Only fragments of glitter from angels' wings twinkled where Fesito's broom had not quite reached.

218

Frances led her girls to the chancel where they laid the ingredients of the crib scene. 'Thank you, girls. You can run along now.' Grace and Nambi, savouring the miracle of darkness, dawdled down the aisle, stifling giggles behind their hands as they passed the looming backside of Annunciata, perilously determined, on a stepladder. Then, to Frances's relief, they were gone and no glimmer of light-hearted mockery could spoil the companionable rituals of Theresa and Annunciata who was heavy and painstaking. Theresa, standing under the last window, held up a black curtain glittering with satin stars to Annunciata. Annunciata, breathing hard in concentration, attached the rounded curtain to the arched window frame. Theresa stood back. 'It is not perfectly straight at the bottom.'

Annunciata peered at an insolent crack of light and made adjustments. Theresa nodded. 'It is right now. It is perfect.'

Creaking, Annunciata descended the stepladder and stood beside Theresa to survey their handiwork. Then Annunciata, who was Candles, solemnly trod the aisle cradling a long wooden box. She bowed before the altar, laid the box on the floor, lifted a long white candle and fitted it into the candlestick on the left of the altar. She lifted another and fitted it into the right candlestick, each time bowing and retracing her steps backwards to the box. She clasped a heavy white candle to her bosom and inserted it in the carved ebony holder beside the Virgin and Child who stood in front of the altar, a little to the right. Again she bowed and retreated to the box. She drew out and installed the last great candle behind The Holy Family, genuflected and crossed herself.

Frances rose from a choir stall. The moment had come for delicate consideration. Annunciata, with a grunt, knelt on the old blue chancel carpet while Frances pulled the boxes over to her. One by one, Annunciata lifted out The Family. She raised each figure, examined it from all sides, breathing soft sighs of congratulation, and placed it in a time-honoured position. Theresa, a sprightly shadow behind them, danced to and fro in the aisle, her head to one side, murmuring, 'Joseph is too close to the Virgin. From this side she hides him too much,' or 'Now the children will not see the legs of the camel. Place it to the right, Annunciata, no, no, more so, more so. Yes, now I think, eh …' She dodged into the fourth pew from which small heads would crane eagerly. 'I think now it is perfect.' Annunciata, breathing with the concentration of a child absorbed, arranged and rearranged until the demanding shadow exclaimed, 'Eeeh, my sister! You have done it. It is good.' And Annunciata's gap-toothed smile wrinkled her cheeks. 'Frances, the animals are so happy this year. Happy like never before.' At this point the largest gnu, top heavy, fell on his snout. When righted he did it again and Frances steadied him with dabs of prestik under his hind hooves to ensure dignified behaviour during the mass.

'But the elephants?' Annunciata peered into the last box, 'Where is room?'

'They must give joy to the Saviour!' Before Annunciata could heave to her feet, Theresa skipped over to the elephant box, extracted the three matriarchs and two trunk-waving infants and stationed them round The Holy Mother. Annunciata, finally on her feet, ambled over and made several minute adjustments. Then they stood back and together pronounced it perfect.

They bowed once more to the altar, Annunciata retrieved the candle box and they turned and trod silently to the chapel door. As they went out, Fesito, whose head had been visible several times at the door, crept in reverently to remove the stepladder. Frances sat down in a choir stall. Every sheet of music had been set in place by Agnes and each candle sconce had a wisp of green tinsel round its base. At the back, in the empty recess, stood a huge vase of

Madonna lilies and blue agapanthus. Mattea, who was Christmas Flowers, had pillaged Mother's garden to good effect. Poinsettias and branches of deodar and cypress arched above the vase. In the chapel reigned a cold, northern night but through an open door the unrepentant African sunlight streamed in to proclaim the paradox of African Christmas. Over the lake purple-cream cumulus were massing. It was perfect. To us, she thought, in the cold, dark north he came as the light. To the people of Africa, surely, he comes in the rain, which is life. She became aware of movement outside the chapel. Girls with baskets of gifts had gathered and Helena was leading them in to place the gifts round the Virgin. She picked up the crib boxes and went into the vestry. There was just time to wash her hands before mass.

Agnes lifted her hands from the piano. A hush fell over the candlelit congregation. Then, from the quadrangle outside, rose the sweet voices of children singing 'Once in Royal David's City'. The voices drew nearer, to the light crunch of feet on gravel. Père Sulpice, bald head gleaming, stood in the doorway, a gentle smile pushing apart his beard, with Frère Joseph-Marie and Mother Julienne at his heels. The congregation rustled to its feet. The priests and Mother processed slowly up the aisle followed by the choir, robed in white, carrying candles. Agnes, hands still dramatically poised, watched her choristers file into the stalls. Then, with head-wagging vigour, she brought down her hands and the congregation broke into the second verse to the rare accompaniment of male voices. Children's eyes wandered from hymn sheets to the great candles, to the crib and the pile of gifts for Gabriel's children that spilled round the Virgin's hem. Mother, wisely conspicuous, widened her eyes in delight at the heaps of purple, red, pink and yellow wrappings and beamed at her smallest daughters with an approbation that created squirms of ecstasy.

As the carols and readings followed in the age-old ritual, so too, in a ritual almost as old, the nuns looked thoughtfully at pupils leaving their tutelage. Perpetua's spectacles glinted as she surveyed Ignatia, Kiza, Kiwala, Serafina and Namkya but Frances noted also a proprietary gleam when she glanced at Nasuna. Thank heavens there was someone to take Ignatia's place. What would Perpetua do without her 'pupil of promise' to bestow her formidable dedication on?

Frances looked at Veronique beside her distinguished parents. Veronique, a little heavy-eyed after last night's party, her languid manner betraying a sharp and perceptive mind, was sure to pass with distinction. She was sure of a career in fabric design and fashion. She was forever doodling exotic clothing on voluptuous figures. And Nampa and Kamya, Kaminda and Kika would surely find niches in an economy where there was hope for these gifted children.

She began noting details to report to Benedicta who would be desolate in the coming months. At least she'd have two weeks over Christmas with Mary Soames in Oxford. They'd been at school together and Mary, with ebullient children and grandchildren under her roof at Christmas, with her kitchen Swahili and memories of Kenya, would give her warmth. 'Dear Benedicta, the Virgin is once again restored. You'll never believe who took her the third time …'

Her eyes wandered to small faces in the front pews. Those who could not yet read were picking up phrases from the choir but their eyes, their eyes returned to the candles, the tall altar candles, the candle beside the Mother, polished to a high gloss by Fesito, and then to the crib candle, a golden star over The Holy Family. Christmas was candles in the eyes of children, of small boys past and the three small boys and a little granddaughter coming to her soon. She would make them a crib with a pangolin in attendance, its forefeet raised in adoration.

The congregation was rising. The service had slipped by. Mother had pronounced the final blessing over those who were leaving and those who would assemble next year and her diminutive form was progressing slowly towards the chapel door, into the radiant light of midday. She was followed by the choir chanting in Luganda, 'Hallelueeah, Christ is come to us! Hallelueeeah!'

A surge of parents and starling girls was flowing down to the drive to bid farewell to tearful nuns with handshakes, hugs and promises of letters. The boarders were scuttling away to lunch and then to disembowel lockers and pack trunks.

On Saturday morning Daudi's sons, Paulo's sons and hangers on and Wiriamu, bumbling but willing, lugged boxes, trunks and ancient cardboard suitcases from the boarding house to cars and *mutatas* in the driveway. Daudi was filling the back of the combi with suitcases while Claire wedged herself in with four new orphans bound for foster homes. Helena sat in front with a bulging *kikapu* on her knees and Frances and Gabriel, looking on, made bets as to how much of its weight consisted of sweets and how much of gifts for foster families. 'Sister Canderel,' muttered Gabriel. 'They need all the sweeteners they can get, poor mites.'

'The one redeeming factor in this misery is that the African extended family is so much more generous than ours,' Frances murmured. 'The obligation to adopt and succour is taken for granted.'

'They're so small and desolate, going off, aren't they?' Gabriel's generous bosom heaved and she stooped to comfort Salva. 'I hope she's picked them right — the families, I mean.'

'She's certainly taken time and trouble over it. The Rubaga

welfare grants will be the real Canderel.'

Gabriel tore her eyes from the combi. 'Will you be here this Christmas?'

'Yes. Ted and his family are coming up from Naivasha and Jim and his from the Park. They've friends in Kampala to stay with. When are you leaving for the camp?'

'Father Joseph can get me a lift to Gulu on the fourteenth and he's coming to Kampala on the fifth of Jan. We can have a lot of fun in three weeks.'

'Does the Lord's Army take Christmas off?'

Gabriel shrugged, 'We carry on regardless. It's important to have good times.'

'Could it possibly get worse before it gets better, do you think? All the talk about more talks with the LRA doesn't seem to be going anywhere.'

'I just don't think anymore.'

'Think of yourself a bit and don't get enteritis again – or dysentery. One time too many and the damage can be permanent.'

'Ach, sure there'll be a medic or two.'

'You watch the water all the same.'

'Lunch time!' Felicitas waved a half-knitted yellow jersey from the refectory door. Salva pricked her ears and lolloped after them.

***

Mr Ssemogerere was sitting at his littered table with a coffee pot beside him and a mug in his hands. 'Ah, Sisters! Sister Frances, Sister Gabriel. Welcome, welcome! You are well, all is well? I am taking a break. Business is getting hot now. You will have some coffee?' He rose and pulled out two chairs.

'Wonderful!' Frances sat and made a small space for a mug

amidst papers and delicate *ketitis*. Mr Ssemogerere shouldered his way into a precarious passage between hanging *kitenges* into the tiny back kitchen. Gabriel stared wistfully at the *kitenges*. 'Ach, Fran! Sometimes I get bored with what we wear. Why can't we ever drape ourselves in a *kitenge*?'

'Well,' Frances considered the brilliant blues, greens and reds with their *maradadi* patterns. 'Regulations aren't very specific about nighties, are they? Just, maybe not red? No harm, perhaps, in a chaste blue?'

Mr Ssemogerere returned with mugs, poured coffee and milk, extended a startling pink and orange sugar bowl that proclaimed 'What is life without sweetness?' and a generous wooden spoon. 'Ladies, Sisters, this is a pleasure! Help yourselves. What is life without sweetness? It is true, very true. I see you bring two boxes.' He swivelled to contemplate his brimming shelves. 'I think there,' he jabbed a finger at a space near the shop front between grass-fire-baked pots. 'There they will show to advantage. Yes, you have the AIDS notice. After Christmas they will be coming. The Germans and the Dutch they are very generous to AIDS. They contribute with great generosity. All the cards will be sold by February.'

Frances bit her lip at the evil twinkle in Gabriel's eye. 'Mr Ssemogerere, this business of Terence Motongo and our pupil Dolosi – were you able to help us?'

Mr Ssemogerere put down his coffee and added another spoonful of sugar, 'I have arranged it,' he stirred his coffee, tasted it and stirred again. 'It is taken care of.'

'Well?' Gabriel leaned forward, 'Tell us…'

Mr Ssemogerere glanced at Frances, 'You want to know, Sister?'

'Er, yes, of course,' she stirred uneasily on her chair.

Mr Ssemogerere put down his coffee, 'I will tell you – in confidence, you understand?'

'Of course, Mr Ssemogerere, that is quite understood.'

His face wrinkled in malicious cunning. 'Two birds with one stone, I tell you, eh, Sister? Two birds with one stone. I promised. And I remember the date – not before the seventh of December. So, on the ninth of December, very early, I phone Terence Motongo. I tell him to go now, now this minute, to Busoga. I hear they are making sets of drums there, the traditional way, very nicely with the twisted thongs, old-style, not like the new rubbish. He must go to Kagulu, Buyende, Bugaya, Nawaikoke, that way, all those small villages. Sister Frances, the roads are very bad that way. I tell him he must get there before Kajubi's agent. I emphasize that. There is hot competition between Kajubi and myself. So, he leaves.' A pregnant pause ensued while Mr Ssemogerere savoured his coffee. 'Ignorant young man.' He shook his head mournfully. 'They have never made those drums over there. It is all research.' He tapped his head. 'All research. I am always telling them, do your research. That is the difference between a purveyor of African cultural artefacts and a thief.' He raised a minatory forefinger. 'On the twelfth he returns, late. He is tired and he has no drums. "Go home," I tell him. "Sometimes there is no luck. Maybe Kajubi's man was there long before. Go home and sleep. Come to me tomorrow." Well, I have not seen him since then.' He spread helpless hands.

'Why?' Gabriel persisted.

'Sister, they tell me he arrives at his house in Wandegeya. He finds the doors open. Inside is nothing. Nothing! Not even the kettle, not even a bar of soap. He is cleaned out.'

'You swiped the lot?' Gabriel beathed.

'Me? No, no, no, no! It is not me. I never go near his place.'

'So *they* stole all the stolen hi-fi's, radios, bicycles, fetishes etcetera, etcetera ...'

'Etcetera, etcetera!' Mr Ssemogerere echoed as his hands dropped gracefully to the table. 'I recoup, as you say, my loss. He has only that car. It will not go much longer. It is worth nothing.'

'By selling the stolen goods?'

'Me? I sell nothing but – I am satisfied.'

Frances met Gabriel's eyes for a second and then looked down and controlled the desire to smile. Wheels within wheels, each one with many tiny cogs. The brilliant 'social networking' of Africa.

Suddenly the light from the doorway darkened. Six tourists, speaking soft and cautious Dutch wandered into the dim passages between the spilling shelves. They had raw peeling noses and were dressed in identical multi-pocketed shorts and pastel shirts, socks under sandals, both male and female with indistinguishable haircuts and beige cotton hats.

'Ah!' Mr Ssemogerere rose. 'Welcome, ladies and gentlemen, come inside, take your time!' his arms widened to infinity. Then he turned quickly to the table. 'You are happy, Sister Frances? Your pupil is safe. She is safe, you will see. It is against custom for a man who has no wealth to marry. The parents of the bride – they must know. You are happy with me, Sister Frances? I put the cards well forward!'

Frances and Gabriel went down the steps of The Real Things into the warm water of Kampala's air. 'Well!' Gabriel settled behind the wheel. 'Well, well, well!'

'I must say I'm relieved. That young man would never have done for one of our girls. I suppose it takes one diamond to grind another. Now,' Frances glanced at the six remaining boxes of cards, 'only the hotels and then we're done.'

227

***

A frangipani-scented lassitude pervaded the long verandah of the senior nuns' house. Even the click of Felicitas's knitting needles was languid. Against the raucous squabbling of hornbills in the sausage tree, the desultory talk of the sisters was but the crooning of contented hens in a dust bath. Perpetua was yawning over a list of chemicals to be ordered from Nairobi, Frances was carefully wrapping the crib and its creatures in soft rags so they might travel safely with Gabriel to the camp. Annunciata, who was Crockery and Cutlery, was running her finger down a list. The finger stuck and she cleared her throat,

'It is still six teaspoons missing. Who has not given back?' Eyes rose and mouths fell open in an examination of conscience. Frances gave a guilty start. Something had winked at her in the recesses of the paint cupboard. She hurried down to the art room and returned with three spoons taken from saucers for doling out poster paint. 'Sorry, Annunciata.' After more consideration, Felicitas retrieved one and Gabriel two more from unspecified and guilty corners. Mattea packed the last cards for leprosy and wiped sweaty hands on a handkerchief. Gabriel, red in the face from tidying classroom cupboards, took up her guitar and began to strum a carol. Salva flopped down over her feet, a Salva, Frances noted, with gleaming ginger hair to the tip of her tail, cream fur over a bulging belly and delicate black markings round ears and eyes.

Mother Julienne and Theresa had been away for a week in the two mud guest-huts in Toni's garden in remote and well-tended peace. Perpetua and Mattea would be the next to go into the same care that Clementine, the pangolin and all creatures in need found in that garden.

Suddenly Gabriel, fingers still plucking, looked up. 'Say, Felicitas, didn't you go down to the Sebanges yesterday?'

'Yes ... two, three, four, five. Dolosi came up and asked for help with the treadle band. It was slipping and I showed Mr Sebange how to tighten it. I must say, she's got going quick. She's made some fetching dresses for local girls ... six, cast off, cast off.'

'And,' Gabriel's innocent stare did not waver, 'any other news? Wasn't she going to get married soon, or something?'

'Well.' Felicitas continued casting off. 'Well, the Sebanges were in a bit of a twitter. It seems the young man's disappeared. A party'd been planned and he never came and they heard nothing. Then, yesterday, no, the day before, the uncle came to take back the cows. He said his nephew had had a misfortune and could not consider marriage now. Mr Sebange was very concerned.'

'And Dolosi?'

'Well, to be honest, she seemed rather chirpy. I was a bit taken aback. While we were having tea a nice crowd arrived, two of her friends with boyfriends and this lad Titus from St Paul's. They were all going to the disco.'

'That's more like,' Gabriel bent over the guitar. 'She's well out of it.'

'I say all's well that ends well.' Felicitas laid the orphan's jersey over her knees. 'She's a nice gal. All she needs is a decent, steady boyfriend. Better than these older men they go for, really.'

The next day Daudi brought Theresa and Mother Julienne back. Frances took Mother's small bag, helped her up the steps and along to her room. When Mother had sunk into her chair, Frances unpacked her bag and hung up her spare habit. She glanced over her shoulder. 'You're looking rather spry, ma mère. Did you have a good rest?'

'It was heavenly, Frances. I was utterly spoiled. Jerome could open a restaurant in France any day. He has the delicate touch – his cheese soufflés, those mango and banana mousses!'

'I've been over to see Kironde.' Frances sat down. 'With Sebastien's help his Madonna should be ready for his little church by Christmas. He's getting over his awe of the bear but he still jumps when he growls. Sebastien is letting him sleep on a mattress in a corner at the back of the workrooms. He keeps him very busy with chores.'

'Under the old bear he will grow. I still remember Pius Lumago and the work he did. That St Paul of his is remarkable. Now, why this frown?'

'The fees?'

'Hmm ... I have spoken to Father Bonaventure. By taking Kironde to Sebastien you circumvented all the rules of admission and ...'

'I know.' Frances hung her head. 'I went completely mad.'

'Alors, I told it to Bonaventure as you explained it to me. Well, you know, he is a big man. I felt obliged to spell out Kironde's note: "do not wury I boro." He is apprised of the boy's near illiteracy. He will not fit into any class of his own age. It will remain to be seen where they will place him and whether he will tolerate being with boys of eight or nine. However, it seems Frère Sebastien has affirmed the child's talent. St Paul's is prepared to give him a year's trial. If he does not show academic improvement by then ...'

'He's out?' Mother nodded.

'And the fees? How can we find the fees?'

'For the orphaned and indigent St Paul's do as we do. Even so, it will be many thousands.'

Frances dropped her face in her hands. Then she sat up again. 'It's only fair I should be responsible for fundraising. Is there anyone we could apply to for sponsorship?'

'I have drawn up a list. Together we can approach them and put Kironde's case. But only when he has produced some pieces of quality.'

Frances nodded. 'That'll only be possible after the first term.'

'Naturally. So, we shall put our minds to raising the fees for the first term. I shall consult with Felicitas and Frère Roman about instalments. Frère Roman might be accommodating. Perhaps a concert during the first term will help?'

'It seems I've embroiled the school in a lot of work.' Frances sighed. 'I'm so sorry.'

'Sorry to give a talented boy the opportunity to grow into a sculptor with the best tuition we have? That is nonsense.'

'I think he's got it in him. But what if it doesn't come off?'

'Then we shall think of something else. He will not be cast off, if that is what worries you. Whether he makes the grade at St Paul's or not, we shall see to it that he becomes literate and numerate and continues training in his craft.'

'Thank you, Mother.' Frances breathed out in relief but her hands kept twisting in her lap. 'I may have been an interfering idiot again. I confess I couldn't leave that business of the Muwonge theft alone. I couldn't help wishing those sick folks had a Madonna for comfort. When we took our statue over to St Paul's for the bear to fix her base ...'

'How will he do it?'

'It's quite clever. They fixed St Paul by putting a metal rim round the base of the statue. That fits into a cast cement base – he's instructed Daudi how to make that and attach it to the recess in the chapel – and there's another metal rim in the base with a sort of spring thing that matches a niche in the rim round the statue.

It has to be turned in a special way before ...'

Mother raised her hand. 'Enough. I have no mechanical aptitude. If it works for St Paul's it will work for us. What was it you were saying about a Madonna for the sick?'

'Well, when I was in Sebastien's storeroom I noticed an old Madonna stashed away in a corner, behind a lot of wood. One of the traditional red, blue and white ones and rather battered. The folds of her mantle are chipped and her hands and nose. But she has a gentle face ... not prim, like some of them. I asked Sebastien if they still wanted her and he said heaven forbid. I asked if I could take her and he wanted to know why I wanted the shabby old thing. I just said I knew someone who would appreciate her. He gave his usual shrug and heaved her out and into the car for me. Daudi has stowed her in the art room and I'll patch her up, repaint and give her a darker skin.'

'So now you have "lifted" somebody else's saint. You are learning. Where will she go?'

'Well, there's a patch of open grass between Motavu's *shamba* and the Busiwes', just downhill from him. His goats graze there. There are two nice shade trees and he's happy to make a little shrine for her. It's good of him. The Ba-Apostoliki aren't into images as we are, but I think he understands. He says he will let it be known that those who wish to pray may come and no one will have to pay a cent. Who knows if anyone will come? At least they'll have the chance to, well ...'

'Feel the presence of comfort?' Mother nodded slowly, 'Surely at this time something is better than nothing. It is worth trying. While I have been resting you have been busy.'

'I'm exhausted but it's been a relief.'

'It has been a trying term for you, n'est-ce pas?'

'Nerve racking. And for you, Mother, with Ignatia's

kidnapping.'

'Or should we call it "borrowing", as Kironde did?' Mother gave a sly chuckle.

'I don't think I could bear another "borrowing" of the Madonna. I have to confess to weak nerves, Mother. I've never been so glad of the end of a term. I'm hasty, over-involved, not detached enough, too easily frazzled and fretted. I wonder if I shall ever achieve your calm about things.' Frances laid her head back in her chair, sighed and looked out of the window into the still trees of Mother's garden, trailing creepers of scented flowers. She needed to spend an entire day in that garden with only the sound of Teresa's fountain in her ears.

Then she looked again at Mother Julienne. A slow smile was spreading over her face. 'Alors, if we are into confessions, I also must make mine.'

'Shall I call Père Sulpice, Mother?'

'Absolutely not. It is to you I shall make it. And … '

'Well?'

'You are to grant me absolution before I confess.'

'Mother?' Frances drew herself up, clasped her hands in her lap and regarded her delinquent with patient severity. 'I am saddened by this fall from grace. Confess, my daughter.'

'Well, I have fallen in love. With that pangolin.'

'That is understandable, ma fille. To fall in love is natural. But such passions must be controlled and offered up to the divine will.'

'You grant me absolution?'

'I grant it. Confess further.'

'She is so gentle and unassuming. To meet a creature that is completely unafraid of you is rare. It has given me intense pleasure. Now, St Francis preached to the birds, did he not?'

'He is an example to us all, my daughter.'

'Bien! Well, yesterday morning we were conversing, she and I, sitting in the sun outside my hut and I uttered my appreciation of how she has led Kironde to Frère Sebastien. She has brought a gift to future generations. She has been an instrument of grace. And, before I had thought it out carefully, I found I was taking water from the birdbath. I dropped three drops on her nose – it is true she sneezed, but only once. I signed her with the cross and blessed her in the name of the Trinity, most especially in nomine Spiritus Sancti. Then I baptised her. There, you have it.'

Frances looked severely at Mother Julienne. 'Would Père Sulpice call that a debasement of the sacrament?'

'I fear he might. Particularly as it was done by a woman. Imagine! But you have absolved me, hein?'

'On one condition.'

'And that is?'

'You tell me the name you have given her.'

'I baptised her Visio Beata. You approve?'

'I approve and I absolve you, ma fille. Visio Beata is entirely appropriate.'

'Thank you!'

Glossary

Excellence of the Best!

*_Slim:_ the Ugandan term for AIDS, owing to the fact that victims become very thin.

*_basuti_: also known as a 'gomezi', the traditional dress of Baganda women: a square-necked bodice with puffed sleeves and about three metres of fabric wound round the body and tied at the waist with a broad sash. Originally women wore a length of bark cloth round the waist or under the arms. Edwardian missionaries introduced the addition of a blouse on top, for the sake of modesty. In traditional culture it was acceptable to expose the breasts but not the knees.

*_kanzu_: a simple long dress worn by men, introduced by the Arabs in the early 19th century.

*_makeka_: matting woven from palm fronds, often with green and magenta strands.

*_shamba_: Swahili for homestead and farm.

*_mabati_: Swahili for corrugated iron.

*_webali_: Luganda for 'thank you.'

*_majarati_: African olive wood.

*_kirikiti_: _Erythrina lysistemon_, the lucky-bean tree with scarlet flowers and red seeds.

*_Sengawe:_ aunt, father's sister.

*_Wabenzi_: the people with Mercedes-Benzes.

The Real Things

*_Mushenzi:_ the Swahili word 'shenzi' denotes anything shabby, second-rate or worn-out, as well as mongrel dogs.

*_wasusiotiano_: Luganda for 'Good day, how are you?'

*_bulungi_: Luganda for 'I am well.'

weraba: Luganda for 'Goodbye.'

ketitis: delicate baskets of varying shapes, woven from fine grasses by young girls.

boda-boda, or poda-poda: a small scooter.

mutata: a local taxi, often old and overfilled.

matoke: large green plantains, the staple food of Buganda. They are stripped of skin, wrapped in banana leaves and steamed. The texture is dense, the flavour is similar to potato and it is eaten with sauces and relishes. Matoke is transported on branches over a metre long.

Find a Little Blue Boat

kasese (or sese): Luganda for sharp-prowed canoe.

hodi: Swahili for 'Hallo, may I come in?'

karibu: Swahili for 'Come in.'

shauri: Swahili for business, affair, legal wrangle.

memsab mzée: the old lady/madam.

msabu, mamsabu: short for memsahib, ma'am.

kikapu: Swahili for a flat-bottomed basket with handles and pliable sides of woven palm fronds.

magendo: a broad term for financial dealings that arose during times of turmoil in Uganda. When the currency went into chaos people took to an exchange of goods instead of money. This led to loss of import/export controls and tariffs. Because currency was not used, many financial deals never appeared 'in the books', income was unknown and therefore untaxable. Magendo became a humorous term for shady/ untraceable deals.

ngege: *Tilapia esculenta*, a now rare cichlid mostly wiped out by the introduction into Lake Victoria Nyanza by other tilapias and Nile Perch.

enjugus: Luganda for peanuts.

rungu: Swahili for wooden staff.
kipandi: Swahili for letter, note or official paper.

Home and Dry
Shauri ya Mungu: Swahili for 'It is God's affair'.
nyabu: Luganda for madam.
pigas: Swahili for to tap or hit. When rain is due, termite mounds are tapped with sticks to imitate the sound of falling rain. This draws the winged termites to the surface and as they flutter into the air they are caught and eaten on the spot or fried or roasted. They have a milky, nutty flavour.
UPDF: Uganda People's Defence Force Uganda's current army.

Friends in Low Places
mafutanyingi: Swahili: literally 'one of much fat' i.e. rich.
webali nyo, nyo, nyo: thank you very, very much.
kiboko: Swahili for a long, hide whip, usually hippo hide.

Singing the Saint
mbira: a thumb piano.
waragi: Luganda: an extremely potent spirit distilled from grain and other ingredients.

Mother Julienne's Confession
kitenge: Swahili: bright, printed cloths from the Kenyan coast.
maradadi: Swahili: bright, pretty, colourful.

Maps

The counties of Uganda, before independence,
as delineated by the British colonial government.

The areas of Buganda surrounding Kampala

Historical Overview of Uganda

Some insights into Uganda for those who would like to know more.

For years, whenever I mentioned Uganda, people tended to say 'Idi Amin'. Yes, Amin's reign of terror was Uganda's nadir, but Uganda's rich and colourful history is so much more than that. And its people deserve to be better known for their warmth and resilience.

We lived in Buganda, on a hill between Kampala and Lake Victoria Nyanza. Buganda is richly green, a series of flat-topped hills receding into the distance and a shining lake open to the sky, reflecting the huge clouds that float above it. Its lacustrine rainfall, up to 80 inches a year, enables two annual harvests. Glossy groves of indigenous robusta coffee, plantain and banana groves, cassava, sorghum, peanuts, pawpaws and guavas surround one, between papyrus swamps and the dark froth of forest.

When, during Obote's early 'culling' of Makerere academics, my father left the Makerere medical school and came to Wits in South Africa, we remained in touch with friends and colleagues in Uganda who had managed to stay on. For many years we received letters detailing events there. Years of heartbreak followed, spiked with stories of courage and dedication that stood out as bright lights in a dark place.

When, owing to age and leaving for safer climes, our friends no longer wrote, I traced events in Uganda through the internet and occasional newspapers brought by East African friends.

The tragedy of Uganda began with Europe's 'Scramble for Africa' when Central Africa was carved into pieces that bore almost no relationship to ethnic divisions. In Uganda, a Protectorate, Nilo-Hamitic peoples from Northern Africa were gathered into an artificial state with Bantu peoples from Western Africa. Their utterly different languages and cultures had to be welded into a British imperial mould of central government. From the very beginning this created tensions between ethnic areas that had nothing in common and had traditionally raided and made war on each other. When the Protectorate of Uganda gained independence in 1962, long-simmering ethnic tensions, damped down during Pax Britannica, broke out again and raged for twenty-four years. A country that was flourishing was broken down into brutal chaos. Let me take you to back to the early days, to give some explanation of how this was possible.

In 1874, when Stanley reached Uganda and was admitted to Kabaka (King) Mutesa's court in Mengo, now Kampala, he was impressed by the area's abundant fertility and the civic sophistication of the Kingdom of Buganda, on the northern fringe of Lake Victoria Nyanza. Inspired by Livingstone, Stanley was eager to discuss the slave trade with Mutesa.

Since the 1840s an Arab slavers' route from the East African coast passed through Buganda to the Congo, bringing guns and cotton fabric, in exchange for slaves and ivory. Mutesa exacted taxes from the slavers and eagerly bought guns in exchange for slaves and ivory. He was also intrigued by the Arabs' ability to communicate in writing and he established Arab slavers at his royal enclosure to teach reading and writing. They also instructed Mutesa in the Muslim faith, together with many of his court. They introduced homosexual practices there that later gave rise to the early martyrdoms of those courtiers of Mwanga's (Mutesa's successor) who, as Christians, refused these practices. These young men had their arms hacked off and were slowly spit-roasted.

Stanley persuaded Mutesa to allow missionaries to enter Uganda. Since the abolition of slavery in Britain, British consciences had been pricked. While Colonel Gordon set out to fight slavers in the

Egyptian Empire, embracing large areas to the north of Uganda, Stanley attempted to pioneer the anti-slavery cause further south. In 1878, Alexander Mackay, the most courageous and persevering early missionary in Uganda, reached Kabaka Mutesa's court.

Mackay was a professional engineer of great ability. Stanley had advised that it was not enough to teach God's word but to cure diseases and turn one's hand to all practical tasks. Mackay built a printing press and proceeded to translate and print the gospel of St Luke and The Sermon on the Mount in Luganda. He installed a forge, a wood-work shop with a lathe and made a pump that spouted water 20 feet into the air. He talked about the gospel to the young men and boys who gathered daily to watch his activities, and taught them to read. 'Readers' became the name of all who would be converted. It was Mackay's practical abilities that drew the people of the Kabaka's huge royal enclosure to him. He had a way with young people. 'His eyes twinkled with kindness,' as one of Uganda's most famous Christian converts, Apolo Kivebulaya, later said of him.

However, as a Scottish Calvinist, he was dismayed when, in 1879, three White Fathers arrived at Mengo. Under the leadership of Père Lourdel, they had been sent by Cardinal Lavigerie to Uganda. Mackay had a profound mistrust of the Roman Catholic faith, 'that foul leaven which is hypocrisy'. It was not long before Kabaka Mutesa was aware of, and confused by, this enmity between two branches of the Christian faith and played the one against the other, to his own advantage. Later, followers of both Protestants and Catholics fought one another savagely. Mutesa also flirted again with the Muslim faith leading, in time to come, to savage outbreaks of fighting between followers of the two religions.

Mutesa was a highly intelligent man and an astute diplomat. At first he let Mackay believe that he was invited to Buganda to 'teach his people the knowledge of God'. Later Mutesa informed Mackay that he had been invited to teach them 'how to make powder and guns.' Mutesa's prime minister insisted that the white men, the Bazungu, were there to bring them 'guns innumerable as grass.'

When Mackay learned this, he wished to return to England but the Kabaka refused to let him go. He remained for several years as a virtual prisoner in the royal compound. His disillusionment with Mutesa increased when the king, afflicted by a 'loathsome disease', possibly a form of leprosy, ordered the sacrifice of about 2 000 of his people as propitiation to the gods for his illness.

Mackay had to listen to the drums of the executioners and the cries of men speared or roasted alive. He described Mutesa as possessing: 'All the faculties of lying, low cunning, hatred, pride and conceit, jealousy, cruelty … combined with extreme vanity. All is self, self, self. Uganda exists for him alone.' He knew then that all his attempts to convert Mutesa had been in vain. Mutesa died in 1884 and his 20-year-old son Mwanga succeeded him.

Mwanga was not as intelligent as Mutesa. He was unstable, smoked hashish and, in spite of having many wives, indulged freely in homosexual practices. He had Bishop Hannington murdered when he approached Uganda via Busoga, owing to an old prophecy that white men approaching from the East would 'eat up the country.' Père Lourdel, more tactful than Mackay, was closer to Mwanga at this time, and warned Mackay of further trouble coming to the missionaries.

Hard and dangerous times followed under Mwanga for all Christians and both Protestant and Catholic converts were brutally murdered. All this time, often in secrecy and at midnight, Mackay and his fellow missionaries, Robert Ashe and Philip O'Flaherty, continued preaching the gospel to their converts who refused to give up their faith and continued to 'read' with them. They carried on translating and printing St Matthew's Gospel, teaching and praying with the converts, many of whom were to die willingly for their faith.

Robert Ashe wrote, at this time: 'My overmastering feeling was that I would go and shake off the dust from my feet. "Not so," said Mackay, "there is work for you to do." So we set to work printing prayers and hymns and reading sheets... there was scarcely time for grief.'

'Our people venture,' wrote Mackay, 'a few of them, to come to me every evening, after dark. Those... marked out for execution, and particularly sought after, dare only come about midnight. I give them a little instruction and comfort, and we pray together. Several of them I cannot refuse to help materially, as they are reduced to beggary, and are in want.'

Lies and rumours against the missions were spread at this time by Mwanga's prime minister, an ardent Muslim, as well as the Arab slavers who hated the Christian missions that threatened their livelihoods. Wanting to scotch these lies, Mackay asked permission to leave Uganda until this trouble had blown over. However, only Ashe was given permission to leave, in 1886, and Mackay was kept well-guarded in the Kabaka's enclosure.

In 1887, the news of Stanley's Relief Expedition, approaching from the Congo to rescue Emin Pasha, Gordon's second in command, reached Buganda. Mwanga grew afraid of European intervention and released Mackay, insisting that Rev. E.C. Gordon, take his place. Before he left, Mackay 'summoned the church council and made provision for the relief of Christians in distress. Every copy of St Matthew in Luganda was bought up. Mackay left Buganda on 21 July 1887, and E.C. Gordon arrived with the returning boat. The church leaders, still in hiding, came by stealth and helped Gordon take over the work. 'Readers' continued to come. In April 1888 the Rev. R.H. Walker joined Gordon.'

Such was the history of the early Christian missions in Uganda.

Other courageous missionaries followed and, after fighting between Christians, between Muslims and Christians had calmed, both Catholic and Protestant missions continued their work, founding schools and hospitals across Uganda.

Buganda, on the slave route from the coast to the Congo, was the hub of commercial and political activity in Uganda. The Baganda, settled agriculturalists with a strong central government, focused in the Kabaka's court, were a well-organised and sophisticated people. Long straight roads, unknown elsewhere in central Africa, radiated from Mengo into the countryside. The roads were built and maintained by conscripted peasant labour, as well as slaves captured in war. Along these roads a continual traffic of commerce in foodstuffs and other commodities passed, including the tributes that all the surrounding chiefdoms paid to the Kabaka. Buganda was the natural starting point for all foreign and colonial incursions into Uganda and continued to take pride of place in all developments. Kampala was established as the capital of the country and subsequently its surrounding areas became the power house of the Protectorate.

Thanks to the policy of Lord Lugard, active in Uganda before he went to Nigeria, the concept of indirect rule prevailed. Under the central, colonial government, power and administration were delegated to the Kings of Buganda, Bunyoro, Toro and Ankole. These beautiful areas of wide plains, lakes and rolling hills were not so affected by the years of turbulence between 1965 and 1985. The northern areas of Uganda (or counties, as they were then called) were in charge of various chiefs of higher and lower status among their own people.

The northern areas were less fertile and densely populated than Buganda and less civically organised. As agricultural developments were introduced by the British, such as cotton planting on a large scale across Uganda, the more fertile areas were favoured. Labour began to stream into Buganda from Lango and Teso, just north of Buganda. While the Baganda prospered and grew affluent, these labourers remained at a humbler level.

The first mission schools and hospitals were built in Buganda, again giving the Baganda an edge over their neighbours. When South Asians settled in Buganda they planted huge areas under sugar cane and built sugar refineries. They created cotton gins and coffee processing industries and influenced all aspects of commerce as well as endowing schools. The Baganda became affluent, better educated and able to hold higher positions in administration than their neighbours.

The colonial government, aware of the unequal development and the resentment it caused, attempted to balance the situation by enrolling soldiers from the northern areas, such as Lango and Acholi. This paved the way for the conflict to come.

Milton Obote, from Lango, Uganda's first Prime Minister, was educated at a Protestant Mission school in Lira and attended Makerere University, where he honed his considerable oratorical skills, without attaining a degree. He had wanted to study law but, as there was no law faculty at Makerere, he left to work in Kenya where he became involved in the national independence movement. He returned to Uganda in 1956 and eventually led the Uganda People's Congress in 1959. In the run-up towards independence elections, the Baganda and some other counties were in favour of a federal state, afraid of being ruled by northerners. Obote formed a coalition with the Buganda royalist party, Kabaka Yekka and the two parties controlled a parliamentary majority when Obote became Prime Minister at Independence in 1962. In 1963 Obote was designated Executive Prime Minister and the Kabaka, Mutesa II (or Freddie, as he was called) became Ceremonial President.

In 1964 the First Battalion of the Uganda Army mutinied at Jinja.

Obote sent his defence minister to Jinja to negotiate with the army. He was held hostage and agreed to significant pay increases and the rapid promotion of officers, including Idi Amin. Amin (whom my father inadvertently taught to box) was from the far north of Uganda, from the Nubian Kakwa tribe. His people were a far cry from the sophisticated Baganda and were loose groups of small individual chiefdoms, perpetually at war with each other. I've heard him described by a Ugandan as 'Not one of us, just a primitive Nubian'! This was the man who would oust Obote and bring eight years of terror to Uganda.

In 1965 Obote and Amin, now deputy commander of the Ugandan armed forces, were implicated in a gold-smuggling plot. When parliament demanded an investigation, Obote suspended the constitution and declared himself President. He declared a state of emergency and assumed unlimited power. Members of cabinet were arrested and Obote initiated an organised attack on Mutesa's palace and Freddie fled to England. His wife Damali, a friend of ours, was left to face the army. We were told she did this with dignity and survived unhurt. Obote instituted a new constitution and abolished the federal structure of the original constitution.

Naturally, he was unpopular in many quarters and in 1969 an attempt was made on his life. He banned all opposition parties and significant opponents were jailed without trial for life. The General Service Unit, led by his cousin, terrorised, harassed and tortured many. Obote now instigated 'A Move to the Left' and the government took over 60% shares in private corporations and banks. Widespread corruption prevailed, leading to food shortages and the persecution of Indian traders.

In January 1971, while Obote was on a visit to a Commonwealth conference in Singapore, Amin staged his military coup. Obote fled to Tanzania, a flight generally welcomed in Uganda. Amin's reign of chaos and terror is too well known to need comment here.

When Amin was ousted by Tanzanian forces and Ugandan exiles in 1979, an interim Presidential Commission governed Uganda until elections in 1980. Obote's Uganda Peoples' Congress won this election, but the opposition objected that the election had been rigged. The anger over this led to Yoweri Museveni's National Resistance Army (NRA) joining with other military groups to lead the National Resistance Movement (NRM).

In 1983, Obote's Uganda National Liberation Army (UNLA) launched Operation Bonanza against the NRA. This claimed hundreds of thousands of lives and caused great displacement of local peoples. The Luwero Triangle, north of Kampala, bore the brunt of vicious fighting.

In July 1985, Obote's army commanders Brazilio Olara-Okello and Tito Okello deposed Obote and ruled through a Military Council. They were finally brought down by Museveni's forces and, by 1986, Museveni was in control of Kampala.

Since then there has been a steady restoration and rebuilding of a beautiful country, torn by strife for over twenty years. Some of Uganda's Asians have returned and are again creating prosperity in the areas they left when banished by Amin. Improvements in roads and transport, health and the restoration of previously outstanding schools and universities, the creation of technical and vocational colleges, overseas investment in education and training have followed during the relative peace since the 1990s.

The only area of continued warfare has been the northern county of Acholi where the Lord's Resistance Army (LRA), boosted and abetted by the South Sudanese, continued to defy Museveni's military incursions and any attempts at a negotiated peace. Now that the LRA has decamped to the Eastern Congo where it continues to cause savage mayhem, Acholi and its people are slowly recovering and the rehabilitation of child-soldiers into the communities that they have scarred is its main concern.

My books are set in the first ten years of the 21st century, when the LRA was still tormenting the northern counties of Uganda. They were also years of restoration and renewed hope for Uganda. I wish to celebrate the resilience and determination of the many people who have been rebuilding with 'Dedication!' to create 'Excellence of the best!' – so many of them women.

The next in this series:

The Boy Under the Bed

Follow two brave sisters from St Mary's School to Acholi County in Northern Uganda. Acholi is terrorised by Joseph Kony's Lord's Resistance Army with its abducted child soldiers. Here many thousands of people have lived for years in Internally Displaced People's camps for safety. Sisters Frances and Gabriel go to bring books and encouragement to a struggling school in one of the camps. One night they encounter three boys, one seriously injured, who have fled the LRA and seek help. In a midnight rush, they drive the boys to Mengo hospital in Kampala where an amputation saves a young life. What to do with the boys when they are discharged presents a serious problem. But, in Buganda, anything is possible … with help from unexpected friends.

Sister Frances's protégé, the gifted orphan Kironde, disappears from St Paul's School. Where has he gone, and why?

What will happen when Sister Gabriel and Dr Pilkington are mutually attracted as they care for the three boys from the Lord's Resistance Army?

About the Author

Cicely van Straten lived her formative years in Uganda. She has published a number of books for South African children and youth. Her book, *Huberta's Journey*, earned a White Raven Award. She now lives in South Africa and writes for adult readers as well.